HOT
FLASH

Kathy
Carmichael

2/14/09

Jo Laurie –
I hope the story
makes you laugh!

Kathy C...

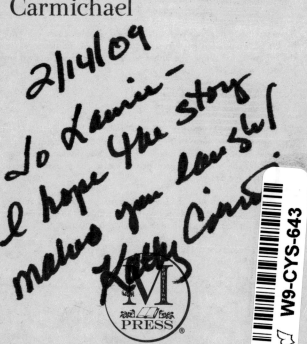

PRESS®

Medallion Press, Inc.
Printed in USA

DEDICATION:

This book is dedicated in loving memory to my
mother, Charlotte Daniels Lynch Nohr. May she
happily continue nagging me from the Great Beyond.

Published 2009 by Medallion Press, Inc.

The MEDALLION PRESS LOGO
is a registered trademark of Medallion Press, Inc.

Copyright © 2009 by Kathy Carmichael
Cover Illustration by James Tampa

Typeset in Adobe Garamond Pro
Printed in the United States of America

ISBN:9781934755037

10 9 8 7 6 5 4 3 2 1
First Edition

ACKNOWLEDGMENTS:

Hot Flash had a glamorous beginning. Authors Eve Gaddy, Kathy Garbera and I brainstormed my new idea over Cosmopolitans while seated at the Marriott Marquis s lobby bar in New York City. Thanks, ladies!

Special thanks to Michael Hague for his insight. I'm definitely one of his peeps! I'm indebted to Carrol Stringer, for her unwavering encouragement.

Alfie Thompson, Cheryl Mansfield, Joyce Soule and Danedri Thompson were instrumental in making the writing of this book so much fun. I especially appreciate the support from authors Kimberly Llewellyn, Tara Randal and Debby Mayne.

My gratitude goes out to Phyllis Cherry for her astute comments. And many thanks to Chef Kurt Michael Friese, Chef Jeff Benz, Chef Brad Stabinsky and the other friendly folks on the Professional Chefs Board at ChefTalk.com for their willingness to answer my questions. The brilliant book, Kitchen Confidential by Anthony Bourdain, gave me a true glimpse into the kitchen underbelly and provided inspiration. Please note that none of the kitchen staff in my books was modeled after any of these generous chefs! If any errors were made regarding kitchen operations, they were strictly my own.

Dear Happily Married Woman:

I saw your recent announcement in the newspaper celebrating many years of marriage.

Since my first marriage failed and I've been unsuccessful in my attempts to find a partner in life, I want to learn from the experts, women like you who've been married for years, about what makes a relationship work.

Would you mind, please, filling out the enclosed survey? I've included an SASE.

Many thanks,

Jill Morgan Storm

An Unhappily Single Woman

PROLOGUE

Birthdays are like a box of Tampax.

When the box is new, you thoughtlessly reach in and grab another but as the box empties you start worrying about running out before you're ready.

Not only was my Tampax supply getting low, but it was my fortieth flipping birthday, and did I mention I was bloated, too?

I stood in my bathroom, styling my hair and trying to get ready for a night out with the girls, when my phone rang. My stomach sank as I read the caller ID and saw it was from the hotel restaurant where I work as sous chef.

"Hello?"

"Jill, you've got to get down here, Right now." Big E, the pastry chef, blurted out.

I put down my blow-dryer. "What's wrong now?"

"Chef Radkin is what's wrong. He's always what's wrong."

"It's my birthday," I whined, but I knew my

protestations were useless. The five-star chef, while incredibly talented, was equally gifted at creating problems—especially when I wasn't at La Papillon to discourage him from drinking. For some reason, I was the designated problem fixer. "Can't you handle the disaster du jour?"

"You're the only one he'll listen to."

"I don't want to be late to my own birthday party. Can you put Radkin on the phone?"

"That's not possible. I'm sorry, Jill, but if you don't come, Juan will freeze to death. You don't want that on your conscience, do you?"

I hate it when he appeals to my inner guilt and makes me feel like I'm responsible for what happens there.

Within a short time, I entered the kitchen at La Papillon, only to observe Chef Radkin standing in front of the huge restaurant freezer, swinging a saucepan at one of the dishwashers who looked as if he was trying to open the freezer behind the mad chef.

As I stepped close, sure enough, I could just make out a very blue and probably frostbitten Juan through the tiny freezer window. Surely that wasn't an icicle dangling from his nose?

"So, Radkin," I said boldly, counting on his creepy crush on me to keep him from smashing my face in with the shiny pan and hoping that I was far enough out of reach for him to grope me. Did I mention that was one of his favorite pastimes?

"Jill!" He stopped midswing when he saw it was me. "Happy birthday!"

"I left my birthday petit fours in the freezer," I said as casually as I could, again hoping to preserve my facial features. "Mind letting me through?"

He looked a little mulish over the idea, and I made a mental note to not actually go into said freezer for fear I'd soon join Juan in his frozen hell. "Please?"

"Anything for you, Jilly," he said, turning and opening the freezer with a gallant flourish, fully intent on feeling me up if I took a step nearer.

However, he'd temporarily forgotten his captive. Juan spilled out and Big E quickly enfolded him in a few crisp white tablecloths while a cook rushed forward with a cup of coffee for the close-to-stiff man.

I turned to Radkin. "Thanks."

Unfortunately, I'd let my guard down and the chef took full advantage by grabbing my left breast. However, despite his smarmy smile, he must have gone heavy on the sauce celebrating my birthday because he slowly sank to the floor in an unconscious heap.

I'd need to bathe for a week to get the imprint of his hand off my mental body. "Clean up on aisle five."

After making sure he was safely stowed in his office and that Juan was okay and didn't plan to sue, I headed out, only a little late for meeting my friends for dinner and contemplating whether there was time for a quick shower first.

The Irish poet, Thomas Moore, said, "What though youth gave love and roses, Age still leaves us friends and wine." Updated for our current millennium, that means—hit forty and it's all over except for friends and good saki.

I hope he's wrong, but with fabulous friends and enough saki, who cares if he's right?

Celebrating my fortieth flipping birthday finally became tolerable thanks to the aforementioned combination. My dearest friends (we'd all met and bonded at "Baby Swimming" sixteen years earlier) met me at a fabulous Chinese restaurant on the strip and the remains of Moo Shu Pork, Sesame Chicken, and egg rolls congealed on the tabletop in front of us. From our booth, we had a view of some of Las Vegas's most famous casino hotels; and the fountain in front of the Bellagio twinkled with hundreds of lights and thousands of streams of water.

We were totally snockered—well, except for Susan, who was the designated driver. She couldn't drink anyway since she was mucho pregnant. We weren't liquored up enough to spend the evening in front of the porcelain god, but we were unsteady and relaxed. Very relaxed.

I'd reached that stage of relaxation where I was keeling over and Susan's shoulder was the only thing separating my chin from the tabletop.

Connie held up a saucer containing plastic-wrapped cookies. "Fortune time."

Thank God they didn't expect me to blow out candles. Good friends know that a cake set ablaze with a depressing number of candles is not a good thing. I grabbed a cookie. "I hope mine says *Congratulations. Your kid just won a college scholarship.*"

"Are you sure Stephen won't get a scholarship?"

I shook my head. The room spun like a dervish. I adore my son and know how wonderful he is, but not everyone appreciates him for the creative kid he is. He courageously walks to the beat of his own artistic drummer. "He went to his da—other mother's without sharing his report card with me. I hope he didn't flunk."

"That would give you another year to get college money together," suggested MaryEllen helpfully.

Like kids who flunk their junior year have admissions departments beating down their doors? "What colleges want kids who struggle with their academic classes?"

Getting college money for Stephen was my first priority. Somehow, I'd find a way to send him to whatever college would take him. Good mothers do that and, dammit, I am a good mother.

Stephen would never have to struggle to find a way to pay rent or buy food—or take care of *his* kid—like I once had to when his father left us. Stephen wouldn't have school loans so huge they rivaled the National Debt. That's an exaggeration, but as a percentage of income, it's not too far off the mark.

I'd been too proud to ask my folks for help. In retrospect, maybe I'd been wrong. The price of being indebted to my parents makes me cringe even now. My mom intrudes enough in my life without that.

As I tore the wrapping from my fortune cookie, I glanced at Susan. "Did your son, David, hear back on the music scholarship?"

"One of them. NU offered him a full, but he's holding out for Juilliard. I hate the idea of him being that far from home."

MaryEllen asked, "What about a school loan?"

Susan mentioned a Web site and told me to visit it. I grimaced. "Do you guys know how hard I had to work to pay off my school loans? It took forever on my salary as a cook. I don't want Stephen to have to do that."

"You're usually such an optimist, Jill. What's wrong?" Connie looked at me intently.

"The age thing is making me nuts."

"Deal with it." Susan patted her stomach. "You could be forty *and* pregnant."

"Good point. I keep reminding myself that getting older is way better than the alternative, but it's not working."

"Think of it as a chance to reexamine your life," Connie advised. "You need to consider your options for the future."

"What she needs is more sake." MaryEllen feathered her fingers in the air. "It'll bring back Jill's normal rosy glow."

"I'll drink to that," said Connie. "What's your fortune cookie say, Jill?"

Connie was the only one of us who didn't worry about tuition for her kid next year. Her daughter, Rachel, left home two years earlier to head for New York and fame as a fashion model. Now Rachel's lovely face is featured on the cover of magazines like *Cosmo* and *Seventeen*. Connie insisted Rachel get her GED, but she was dragging her feet about enrolling in college. Connie tried to act like it was no big deal, but I knew it bothered her.

"What does yours say?" MaryEllen asked Connie.

"*It is better to give than receive, but sometimes receiving is more enjoyable.*" Connie wiggled her eyebrows and everyone laughed.

"That's so you," said MaryEllen.

Susan read hers aloud. "*Take time to smell the roses but watch out for those thorns.*" She frowned. "Do you think thorns are a metaphor for labor pains?"

"If so, it was written by a man." Connie doesn't much like men these days, either. Ever since her divorce when Rachel was three, Connie's been looking for a man to solve all her problems. The problem is that the men in her life are the problem. She's drawn to bad boys, has a fierce need to redeem them, and in the end she's always left holding the bag in the form of credit card bills and late rent penalties when the men disappear.

Lately, however, she's sworn off men and I have a side bet with Susan over how long that'll last, because Connie really loves sex.

Connie, seated beside MaryEllen, leaned over to read her fortune. "Oh, that's a good one."

MaryEllen beamed. "It says, *Invest in manufacturing and manufacture goodness.*"

The three women looked at me. I hadn't opened mine yet, so I cracked my cookie and pulled out the thin white strip of paper. "*You will renew acquaintance with a dark-haired stranger.*"

What the hell was that supposed to mean? How do you renew acquaintance with someone you don't know? "I wanted a scholarship, dammit."

"Too bad it didn't work out with the Asshole Professor," consoled MaryEllen.

"Free tuition, down the drain." I sighed. It had been a perfect solution. If I'd married the Asshole Professor, Stephen would have gotten free tuition at NU as the son of an employee.

It took me a week after our breakup to realize I'd been "settling" when I considered marrying the Asshole Professor. But let me tell you, there's nothing wrong with settling when college tuition is part of the deal.

Connie pointed at my boobs with her chopstick. "At least you got something out of the bargain. I wish one of my ex-boyfriends had bought me bodacious cha-chas."

When the Asshole Professor offered me boobs, I figured, why not? I'd always been embarrassed by my lack of a figure, and having boobs would make me feel more . . . feminine. And they are awesome, even if I do say so myself. "I wonder if they're what gave him the idea of running off with his student? Once he saw the breasts of a twenty-year-old, maybe he had to discover what the rest of her looked like?"

Even worse, the Asshole Professor's new squeeze was closer in age to Stephen than to me. I sucked in my stomach. In the right light and with my stomach tucked in and if I didn't breathe, someone might conceivably think I was twenty or at least under thirty.

"Forget the professor. I have an idea that'll help me find Mr. Right—and hopefully he'll be in a position to pay Stephen's tuition." I pulled a list of questions from my pocket. "My parents' fiftieth wedding anniversary is coming up and Mom left me with a huge stack of newspaper '"Style"' sections about couples celebrating their anniversaries. Looking at all those photos of smiling married couples who seemed so happy made me want to know why their marriages lasted. I want to know if there's a recipe for marital success."

"So?"

"I'm going to ask them." I gulped, then unfolded the paper, smoothed it, and placed it faceup in the middle of the table, careful to avoid the soy sauce spill. "I'm tired of Mr. Wrongs. I need Stephen's tuition, and gaining a real relationship would be a bonus. I'm thinking these couples can point me in the right direction."

Susan grabbed it before the others got a look at it. "This is awesome!"

"What is it?" asked Connie.

"A survey for happily married couples. Why didn't any of us think of this before?" She passed the list to MaryEllen, who quickly scanned it, then handed it on to Connie.

"You're sending it to the couples in the newspaper?"

"That's the idea. I checked some of the names from the newspapers and most of them are listed in the phone book."

"It's a very good idea." Susan looked at me approvingly. MaryEllen looked at me encouragingly. Connie didn't look at me at all. She was mesmerized by my survey questions.

"You know," said MaryEllen, who by this point had lost her esses, "I think we can improve on the zurvey. There'z nothing on there about vibratorz."

"Vibrators! There's nothing on here about *sex*!" Connie looked at me as though I'd lost my mind.

"Give me the PDA I gave you," said Susan.

I remembered her giving me the PDA, but I a) wasn't sure how to use it and b) was fairly certain it was sitting with the pile of other birthday gifts I'd received from them at my apartment. I must have looked blank, because Susan added, "I stuck it in your purse."

It took me a second to find it and give it to her.

She opened the keyboard. "I'm going to retype your survey with our suggestions added to it. I really think you should do this. I'm dying to know what other married women think."

"Are you ready to type?" Connie asked Susan. "I've got suggestions out the ying-yang."

"Ready."

"In the section where they rate items of importance in a successful marriage, there has to be something about sex. Whether the husband or wife are great lovers, whether they both are, or whether they're both lousy. That kind of thing. Also frequency. Do they hump like bunnies?"

"Isn't that kind of personal?" I asked. "I mean, would they tell me that kind of thing?"

"I'm fairly certain I know how to handle it," said Susan, her fingers typing so fast I thought she might create some kind of minor cyclone.

MaryEllen spoke up. "You're mizzing one item that iz eztremely important."

"And it iz—I mean, is?"

"Doez the huzband azk for directionz when he'z lozt?"

"Does any man?"

"My huzband doez," said MaryEllen. "It'z one of hiz mozt a-mor-al traitz."

I think she meant admirable, but I'm not 100 percent certain. "Maybe we should add something about assembling bikes on Christmas Eve when the instructions are written in a foreign language?"

"Screw that," said Connie. "Just make sure that survey has plenty of questions about sex."

"Zex makez a lot of zenze." MaryEllen bobbed her head in agreement but couldn't seem to stop bobbing.

"Time to cut off the saki," said Susan, who cringed at each of MaryEllen's head bobs. "I don't want any of you getting sick in my car."

By the time we'd paid, Susan had a final draft of the survey, ready for me to send out.

MARRIAGE SATISFACTION SURVEY

1. How long have you been married? _____
    A) 25–35 years B) 36–45 years C) 46-plus years
    D) Can't remember
2. On a scale of 1 to 10, with 1 being sucky and 10 being awesome, how happy would you rank your marriage?
_____

3. Please rank the following on how important you believe they are in the success of your marriage (scale of 1 to 10, with 1 being not important and 10 being absolutely necessary):
    Being best friends _____
    Companionship _____
    Shared interests/hobbies _____
    Ability to make a budget and live within it _____
    Interests/hobbies outside the marriage _____
    Ability to follow or ask for instructions _____
    Commitment _____
    Sexual compatibility _____
    Sense of humor _____
    Honesty _____
    Fidelity _____
    Good at household or auto repairs _____
4. How often do you and your husband have relations on average: _____
    A) Hourly B) Daily C) Several times a week
    D) Weekly E) Can't remember

5. Are you happy with the frequency you have relations with your husband? Do you feel it makes a difference in your marriage?_____

_____

_____

_____

6. Is there any one thing you believe makes your marriage last?_____

_____

_____

_____

7. What other thing, or things, do you believe makes your marriage happy? _____

_____

_____

_____

8. Are there any character traits you think are important in selecting a spouse _____

_____

_____

_____

9. Does your husband:

    Fall asleep in front of the TV?_____

    Take you out to dinner or to the movies?_____

    If so, how often? _____

    Know how to assemble things?_____

    Give appropriate and well-thought-out gifts?_____

    Hold your hand when you walk?_____

    Help around the house?_____

    Help with the children?_____

10. What traits do you bring to your marriage that help make it work? _____

_____

_____

_____

Survey Comments: _____

_____

_____

_____

_____

_____

CHAPTER ONE

Dear Jill,

I don't usually respond to surveys, but your questions brought to mind how much I love my husband and how much I appreciate him. Thank you for the reminder.

We've been mostly happily married over thirty-six years. Of course there have been ups and downs, but we worked our way through them. As a salesman, he travels quite often and that's put him in the way of lots of temptation. Yet he hasn't once wavered in his love and devotion to me.

The best piece of advice I can give you is to be tolerant. No one is perfect, but if you let your fellow know you'll always be there for him, then he'll always be there for you.

All the best,

Mary Swift

A very wise woman once told me (okay, it was Susan, but she's really wise!) that all mothers make their daughters crazy. She said she began getting along with her mother after accepting that as a given and asking herself why her mom made her so nuts. I'm not sure she realized this beforehand, because her mother died five years ago.

Either way, for me the answer is simple. My mother makes me crazy because she *is* nuts.

I don't know about you, but whenever trouble looms, storm clouds gather, or Mom is within shouting distance, I head for the nearest bathroom, primarily because it has a lock and bringing guests in with you is frowned on.

It's a nice quiet little place—as long as no one knows where to find you. I flinched at the sound of determined knocking on the bathroom door, then stared at my self-portrait (drawn in lipstick) on the mirror.

I added a mustache.

The hotel where I work as a sous chef is usually safe territory. But when I heard whispers about my mother attending one of the functions we were catering, I'd grabbed a pen and a stack of Post-its for writing out my suicide note cum last will and testament. I couldn't bear the idea of dealing with my mother while I was dealing with reaching my fiftieth flipping decade.

I'm not saying forty is old, but it's a lifetime from twenty. I use the age of twenty, not because it's the exact age of the Asshole Professor's new squeeze—well, not totally. It's also the age I was when I met Stephen's father.

I'd begun receiving responses from my surveys, and they suggested things like tolerance and accepting your mate's flaws. When I was twenty, that might have seemed easier than now. At flipping forty, I was too cynical and jaded. I could accept a man leaving the toilet seat up, but it's hard to accept men with commitment phobias. They don't stick around long enough to practice tolerating them.

Normally, I have a sunny disposition and I'm often described as perky. While it annoys me, it's fairly accurate. But this aging thing was doing a real number on me. Why should this birthday matter more than the others? Was this really only about turning forty, or was my mood caused by a general dissatisfaction with my life?

Connie had suggested self-examination. Figuring it couldn't hurt and seemed like a better use of Post-it notes, I wrote out a summation of my life to date, then stuck it beside my self-portrait on the bathroom mirror.

1. A failed marriage
2. My recent breakup
3. $1,000 in savings and $1,963 in checking
4. A wonderful son
5. My job as executive sous chef
6. Fabulous friends

Okay, on the surface my life might not look so bad.

But once you know the details, you'll agree I was knee-deep in suckiness.

Item #1. Sure, my broken marriage wasn't my fault. What led me to choose a mate who wouldn't stick? Did I have awful taste in men, or was there something wrong with me?

Item #2. Three weeks ago, the asshole I thought might be husband number two dumped me. Even worse, he kept my favorite iron skillet. I'd already left seven voice messages that he hadn't returned. Mental note: *Get it back!*

Item #3. Financially, I wasn't in horrible shape, but the only designer clothing I could afford was sold at Wal-Mart or Target. How long would $2,963 last, considering rent was due (over $900 a month!), not to mention utilities and credit card bills? Raising a kid is expensive, and my child support payments didn't come close to what I spend.

Item #4. My son, Stephen, is not simply wonderful, he's the cherry on top of the whipped cream of my life. However, he needs college tuition and he rarely speaks to me. When he does, it's in French. *Tres sucki, non?*

Item #5. While I love my job and I adore cooking, I don't love it quite so much when it requires creating three thousand identical Southwestern chicken breasts.

Item #6. My friends are my lifeline. They give meaning to my existence. When I'm with them, I can forget I'm a woman with responsibilities and simply enjoy being myself. And when I'm hurt or discouraged, they're always there to pick me up.

Lately, the hurts way outnumbered the ups. Sucky. Sucky. Sucky.

Needing something to cheer me up, I went into the restroom stall, yanked on the roll of paper, and then dragged it back to the sink where I began making toilet paper origami. I was actually pretty good at it.

Origami is like cooking. If you follow the recipe, you know exactly what you'll get. Too bad life doesn't come with instructions. With origami and cooking, I feel a sense of control. If my life could be like that, then all I'd have to do is follow the rules and everything would turn out okay. Lately I'd been following the directions for creating an origami fish. I grinned when it almost came out like I wanted. Just one more fold and —

The pounding on the bathroom door resumed and I jumped.

"You've got to come out of there sometime, Jill," said Big E, the pastry chef, as he banged on the door again.

"Has Mom left yet?"

"You know, she's a very nice woman."

Snort. Like he knew anything about my mother?

If you stick your finger in an electric socket, it will give you an idea of my reaction to dealing with my mom. Basically, my hair stands on end and painful vibes ping-pong through my nerve endings.

So there I was, hiding in the bathroom, hoping she'd give up and go away and knowing that was about as likely as the Federal Reserve announcing the new interest rates are ninety days same as cash.

One of the best things about working for a large hotel is that Mom hasn't yet found the employee bathrooms.

However, I learned persistence from my mother. It's both her greatest trait and her worst. I knew why she was there—she'd found me another man. She wouldn't give up until I reported in.

I considered washing my hands again before leaving the restroom, but I'd already done that six times and my hands had puckered. I grabbed my Post-its off the mirror and stuck them in my pocket. Time to face the dating squad.

Big E smirked as I left the bathroom. I asked, "Where is she?"

"The kitchen."

I girded my loins. My sucky life was about to sink to a new low. Mom would try the patience of a saint. She has good intentions, and I certainly could have done worse in the parent stakes. The problem is, she lives in her own little world and it bears no resemblance to reality. Until a few years ago that wasn't an issue because my dad was wealthy enough that reality never crept near her.

Things, however, had changed, and once reality bit her on the butt in the form of a criminal indictment against Dad, rather than rise to the occasion, she retreated even further into her fantasy world. My father did what he could to protect her from his prison cell and I tried my best to hold up my end. But it wasn't easy.

Figuring that since I was going to hear about whatever guy she'd found anyway, I might as well get it over with, so I took a deep breath, then peeked into the kitchen. Mom was standing in the channel, blocking the way.

I straightened my uniform and then stepped forward. "Why are you standing in the middle of the room, Mom, keeping everyone from doing their jobs? You know you're not supposed to be back here."

"I wanted to talk with you."

Talk? I knew what she wanted to talk about and I dreaded hearing about the man of her dreams for me. "Talking is forbidden during working hours, Mom."

There were snickers all around at that comment and I sent Jaime, the grill man, a dirty look.

"Well, what am I supposed to do when you don't answer my phone calls?"

"You could leave a message so I'll know to call you back." Try the patience of a saint? She'd try the patience of the devil. She was always after me, trying to introduce me to some guy who she thought would be perfect for me, and they were always perfectly *wrong* for me.

The cook elbowed me, trying to get to his station.

I stepped aside, nearly landing in Fang, the nickname given the sixty-quart standing mixer.

I'd just turned forty flipping years old and I didn't have that much time left anymore—certainly not for dealing with my mother. "How did you get in here?"

"I was at the Rosemoors' fiftieth wedding anniversary party."

"You know the Rosemoors?"

"I do now." She lowered her voice to a stage whisper. "I crashed."

I grabbed her arm and dragged her out of the kitchen and into a small storage room before I lost my job. "Are you trying to get me fired?"

She looked at me cluelessly and I felt a little guilty. Okay, a lot guilty. My nerve endings began doing the Macarena.

Just then, a deliveryman arrived at the door, pulling a dolly laden with crates. I sucked in my stomach and crammed my back end into a shelf so he could get past us. "Please don't come here again, Mom. My boss frowns on visitors."

"I wouldn't want to do anything that would jeopardize your job, Jill."

As the deliveryman left, I had to climb on one of his crates in order to breathe again. "I know you wouldn't, just don't come here again. Okay?"

She nodded.

The pastry chef started into the room, after

supplies, but changed his mind when he saw us and retraced his steps. Smart guy.

My mother seemed oblivious to the interruptions. My friends said she reminded them of a strange combination of Debbie Reynolds and Marlo Thomas. I fought a brief annoyance that she maintained the appearance of the perfect upper-class society woman, neatly dressed, and not at all stressed-out like me.

And my stress level was climbing.

"Where's Jill?" called someone from the kitchen.

I had to get back to work. If Mom would hurry up and tell me about this latest guy, then I could get rid of her. "What do you need?"

"Your help with the warden. I think he has it in for your father."

Surely she didn't want me to date the prison warden? My father had been CEO of a huge corporation before the Enron scandal. Thanks to similar bookkeeping methods, Dad calls the state pen home for the next five to seven years. I didn't have Stephen's college tuition because Dad hid most of their assets in overseas banks.

I had still been in the recovery room after Stephen's birth when Dad first promised to handle his college expenses. So you can just imagine my reaction (spontaneous combustion) when Dad suggested after he was sentenced, "Maybe Stephen can wait for college until after I get out of prison?"

The last thing I needed to hear at the moment was

that Dad was having trouble while in prison or that his release would be delayed. My stomach knotted. "What happened with the warden?"

"Our fiftieth wedding anniversary is next month. All I want is to have a picture of us in the paper. Is that too much to ask?"

"What does that have to do with the warden?" Or dating the warden? It was mind-boggling how my parents had stayed together for fifty years. Talking with either of them for fifty minutes was enough to make me wish I had a prescription for Xanax. And, since my divorce, I couldn't sustain a relationship for fifty weeks. Was there some secret relationship recipe I hadn't been let in on? I sure hoped my surveys would give me the answer.

"Oh, Jill." Mom shook her head. "I'm just beside myself. That warden refused—he refused!—to allow my photographer's crew in to check for lighting and the best location for the shot. Can you imagine?"

I couldn't imagine what she was talking about. "Your photographer's crew?"

"For our photo for the paper. The warden was quite rude when I was making arrangements to have your father fitted for a tuxedo. I have half a mind to call the governor's office. He and your father were always very good friends."

I caught on that Mom wanted anniversary pictures but she'd lost me at the tux. "Dad needs a tuxedo . . ."

"For the photos." Mom nodded. "I'm not nearly

half as good at communicating as you are, Jill. I was hoping you'd talk with the warden and see if you can straighten this out for me?"

Yup, she evidently wanted to set me up with the warden at the prison where my father was serving time. Good God. "I could call him, but I doubt he'd agree to it, Mom."

"If you were to pay him a visit? In person? And maybe you could wear your cute pink skirt."

I got it now. She thought if I wore the pink skirt I hadn't worn in public for at least ten years, enough of my legs would show that it would either get me a date . . . or distract the warden. "Shall I bring a metal file and a lock-picking kit, too?"

"Don't be facetious. This is very important to me, Jill." Her lips thinned in that *you've hurt me now* expression I was too-intimately familiar with.

"I don't have time to go to the prison, but I'll call the warden and see what I can do." Was it possible that for once she hadn't wanted to lecture me about needing a man? Maybe she thought I was over the hill? Always on the lookout for the silver lining, I decided there were some decided perks to turning forty.

"Jill, I need you!" called someone from the kitchen. From the sounds of it, a man who truly needed *me*.

Wanting to hurry things along, I turned to leave. "I absolutely have to get back to work now. I'll walk with you to the banquet room."

Mom touched my arm as we reached the hall leading to the room where the Rosemoors' party was being held. "You've always been such a good daughter. Your problems would all be solved if only you'd find a new husband—" She interrupted herself. "Oh, that reminds me. I've found you a man!"

Of course she had. How silly of me to have thought she'd given up on her manhunt, even for a moment. "Who now?"

"This one's your type. I'm sure of it. I met him at the party just now." She signaled for me to join her at the swinging door opening from the hallway into the banquet room. "Come over here and I'll point him out."

I did as she asked, wondering if he was a corporate executive, the president of something, or what charity he donated large sums to. "Where is he?"

She opened the swinging door a crack, then pointed to a very tall and very attractive man standing near an older man and woman.

"Is he talking with Mr. and Mrs. Rosemoor?"

"Yes, he's their only son and best of all, he's single!"

I knew there had to be a catch because he actually *looked* interesting. "What's he do for a living?"

"He's a zookeeper." Mom beamed at me. "He promised to wait so I could introduce you."

"I can't go out there, Mom. I have a job to do."

"He seems very sweet."

I watched him interacting with his parents for a moment and wondered if Mom was right for once. He wasn't bad looking. Until . . .

His mother licked the corner of her napkin, reached over, and wiped off his mouth. My jaw dropped, but it wasn't over! Next, she pulled out a comb and smoothed his hair.

And he held still for it.

"Mrs. Rosemoor said he'd be on his feet again soon. Losing his job at the zoo is only a tiny setback."

This begged the question, other than finally getting my mother off my back, how would becoming involved with an unemployed, zoo-keeping mama's boy solve all my problems?

ও ও ও

One of the things I've come to value as I ripen (a.k.a. mature), is quiet time to spend alone. After work, I came home to a peaceful apartment because Stephen was with his fa—other mother and he wouldn't be home until morning. Since my ex's sex change was completed last year, our relationship had devolved into *competitive mothering*. If Stormy could afford Stephen's tuition, I'd even consider letting her win. Unfortunately, she's still paying for her surgery and likely will be for the next ten years.

I took a seat at my writing desk and thumbed

through the stack of survey responses from the couples celebrating significant anniversaries.

I grinned at one respondent's answer to what makes her marriage last. She answered, "Hot sex." Farther down the survey, her answer under her spouse's character traits said, "Sensitive lover."

Another response came from a woman who hadn't had sex since 1990, but stated that her husband had never been any good anyway. Sounded like my non-relationship with Stephen's father.

As I scanned the stack, I saw there were two golf widows, three military wives, and several others whose husbands traveled as part of their jobs.

I was left with a series of questions:

How would I find anything useful from such diverse women?

How had any of these marriages lasted?

How had Mom and Dad's marriage lasted for so long?

What makes successful marriages tick?

As much as Mom's attempts at matchmaking annoyed me, I wanted to find someone. Although I had many people around me and I wasn't lonely, I wanted to be in a good relationship.

I missed the close friendship of a man. I missed the emotional intimacy. And I really missed having an escort. I'd realized that after the Asshole Professor had dumped me. The sex hadn't been that great and there wasn't much in the intimacy department, but I always had a date to take with me to social functions. Plus, there was the side benefit of not worrying about Stephen's tuition.

What I missed most, however, was my skillet. It was perfect. It was iron. It was well seasoned. I felt naked without it. And the jerk hadn't returned it or my phone calls.

I was tired of doing everything by the rules, by doing things the right way, when all it got me was nowhere.

Being forty flipping years old wouldn't be so bad if it meant I could do things differently, if I no longer believed it was so damned important to be a good girl.

I was no longer a girl.

I was ripe, dammit.

Maybe it was time to take chances, time to leap out of my usual comfort zone, time to act out in general! I wanted to act out, act up, and kick up my heels a little.

No matter how many times I looked at the survey responses, nothing seemed to jump out at me until . . . Wait a sec. All of the responses that ranked their martial happiness as awesome had one thing, and only one thing, in common.

They all had absentee husbands!

Could the answer to marital happiness be to marry a traveling salesman?

Could solving my problems be this easy?

I wanted to cheer, but at that moment, the phone rang. I checked the caller ID and it was Connie. I couldn't wait to tell her about the scheme that was percolating in my head.

I didn't bother with preliminary pleasantries. "I have a great idea!"

"So do I," purred Connie. "I've thought of the perfect thing to cheer you up. Have you gotten your skillet back yet?"

"No . . ."

"You still have the key to his condo?"

"Yeah? Are we going to break in?"

"You got it. I've been watching his place and the coast is clear. Wait for me outside. I'll be there in ten minutes. Don't forget the key!"

"What? Have you become some kind of ex-boy-friend stalker?"

"No. A skillet-getter-backer."

"We can't break into his condo."

"You've got a key. That's not breaking and entering. Besides, he's got your skillet. There's probably some statute about unlawful possession. We're not stealing anything. Unlocking is legal."

"What if he changed the lock?"

"Then we'll leave. I promise not to smash windows. Well, unless there's a good reason. You can tell me about your great idea when I pick you up. Be there in a minute!"

"Wait," I said again, but she'd hung up. I was hoping she'd called to invite me to a party or something glamorous, not to commence a life of crime. On the other hand, within the hour I could have my skillet back. Wasn't I just contemplating kicking up my heels and moving outside my comfort zone? Unlocking and entering definitely qualified as acting out.

What would Connie think of my idea and the glimmer of a Salesman a.k.a. Tuition Plan that my subconscious had just about fully hatched? I couldn't think of anything better for improving my mood and returning my optimism.

Twenty minutes later, I unlocked the Asshole Professor's front door.

"Hurry up," said Connie as I stood still, listening for any sound indicating he might be home. All I could hear was my heart throbbing in my ears. "Shh."

She pushed past me. "Quit shushing me. I told you he's gone."

I followed her inside and closed the door.

She made a beeline to the bar. "Get your skillet and I'll make us a drinkie winkie." After fumbling around in the cupboard, she pulled out a bottle. "Sour apple martini sound good to you?"

"A sour apple martini sounds delicious." It was the perfect accompaniment to breaking and entering. I definitely needed a drink. His condo had a kitchen open to a living area with a wet bar on the opposite wall. I walked over to the kitchen counter and laid down my purse.

While Connie began mixing our drinks, I pulled open the drawer where the pots and pans were kept just below the cooktop. My forehead wrinkled when I didn't see my skillet. I moved pans around. No luck.

Quickly closing that drawer, I opened the one below it. My skillet wasn't there, either. "I can't find it."

"Keep looking. He probably moved it somewhere to keep it safe for you."

I threw open cupboards, doors, drawers, anything and everything. I tossed towels, hot pads, and utensils on the floor. Hiking my skirt to hip level, I placed my knee on the counter and vaulted up. Feeling like a gymnast, I searched the cabinets where he stored rarely used items. "It's not here."

Connie walked into the kitchen area, raised an eyebrow as she looked at the mess I made, then calmly handed my martini up to me. "Drink up and tell me about your great idea."

I took a sip, allowing the tartness to linger a moment before I slithered back to the floor, my dismount anything but graceful. "It's about my survey responses."

"Have you gotten many?" Connie began rifling through the cupboard behind her.

"Twenty-seven."

"I bet they all had hot sex." She pulled out a frying pan. "Is this yours?"

"No." I shook my head and she replaced it in the cupboard. "So far the surveys haven't said too much about sex, except for the lack of it." I addressed her posterior because she'd burrowed almost all the way into the cabinet. "The only responses with anything in common have a husband who is never home. Traveling salesmen, golf widows, even a restaurant site selector—the guys are always gone."

"Ohhhh. Traveling salesmen?" She pulled her head out of the cupboard. "You could do a lot with a traveling salesman."

"That's what I was thinking!" I stuffed some utensils back in a drawer, then began stacking the pots I'd pulled out.

"With your job, you have lots of opportunities for meeting salesmen." She emerged from the cabinet and began going through the pantry.

"There always seems to be a sales convention of some sort going on." I nodded, getting into the idea. "I've been worrying about tuition for Stephen. So, here's my thinking. A traveling salesman is the perfect answer to all my concerns. One woman wrote that she had one week on and three weeks off each month, so I'm thinking one week of sizzling sex and then he's gone again, leaving me to do my own thing. He sends home his paycheck and Stephen's tuition is covered."

"I love it." Connie tossed back the last of her martini.

I loved it myself. Maybe the surveys really had

given me the answer I was looking for. Surely I'd have lots of salesmen to choose from. It was only a matter of applying myself to meeting as many as possible.

"Have you considered holding auditions?"

"What kind?"

"Sexual auditions. With all the bad luck you've had in the bedroom, let me tell you, the last thing you want is a man who's not sexually compatible."

"Great idea." Connie had bragged about Mind-Blowing Sex ever since I'd known her. I never got any and wondered if I ever would. This could be my shot at it.

A muffled thud and the sound of the front door lock turning made Connie shriek. She grabbed her purse and mine, then dragged me by the arm to the sliding door exiting onto a patio.

I glanced back through the hedges we'd ducked behind and took in the disorder we'd created, just as the Asshole Professor stepped into the kitchen. He didn't appear to see us as we sneaked behind shrubbery and made our way back to the car. I wondered if he'd know it was me or think some mystery lush had raided his wet bar.

"Do you think he'll call the police?"

"We didn't steal anything." Connie shrugged as she started the car. "What's he going to say? 'Hello, Officer. I want to report a mess?'"

She had a point. Although I was disappointed

about not finding my wayward skillet, I was pretty revved about the decision I'd made. The answer to all my problems was to hunt down the perfect traveling salesman. I could become a salesman groupie.

CHAPTER TWO

Dear Unhappily Single Woman,

Are you nuts? Instead of sending out surveys, you should be counting your blessings!

My husband retired a couple of years ago and has been under my feet 24/7 until I insisted he find a hobby because he drove me nuts. He started working out at the spa. Now, after thirty-two of the best years of my life, the louse left me for a slut half his age. His personal trainer!

I hope she has better luck training him than I did.

You want the truth? Men are just children in larger bodies. Honey, you don't want the heartache. Stay single and invest in a Rocket Propulsion Vibramatic Model XXX19.

Yours sincerely,

Buffy Gordan–Hough

Over the next week, more survey responses trickled in. I sat at my desk in the corner of my dining room, riffling through the survey responses like Midas counting gold coins and daydreaming about auditions and M.B.S. (Mind Blowing Sex).

After reading a survey questioning my sanity for wanting a man at all, doubts about my traveling salesman plan crept in.

It did seem sort of harebrained. Would setting my sights on a salesman classify me as a gold digger? What made me think a relationship with a salesman would be any better than the ones I'd already been involved in? And, bottom line, was I really that desperate yet?

I guess I was. While the idea seemed nutty on the surface, it appealed to my sense of adventure—and Stephen's college tuition might be the payoff.

I'm not sure if other people have a secret dream, but I did. A dream that sort of embarrassed me, which is why it was a secret. I once asked Connie if she had a secret dream and Connie reassured me that of course she does. She dreams of winning the lottery and having sex with lots of younger men.

That isn't the kind of secret dream I mean. Her fantasy is the kind that could come true, or is at least more likely to come true. After all, someone has to win the lottery.

I pulled my wallet from my handbag, stuck my hand in the little pocket behind the change purse, a

pocket you wouldn't realize was there unless you'd ex-
plored the wallet carefully, then slid out the magazine
photo of my dream.

It was a house in Lexington, Kentucky, surrounded
by a white picket fence. Between the house and the
fence was lots and lots of Kentucky bluegrass.

Other people might fantasize about winning the
lottery, but I dream of white picket fences. Nevada
doesn't especially run to houses with picket fences, at
least not the sort surrounded by bluegrass.

I'd pulled out the photo so many times that the
edges had frayed and a crease at the corner fell off in
my hands. Perhaps I should take it to be laminated?
Technically, the house wasn't my dream it was what the
house symbolized. I didn't actually need a picket fence,
or bluegrass, or this particular house. What I craved
was the safety and security and the feeling of home and
peacefulness that stole over me whenever I looked at it.

Now that I was forty flipping years old, my dream
seemed farther away than ever.

I was angry. I was alone. And I was scared.

It was time to take myself and my dreams seriously.
I'd scheme, plan, devise, forecast, concoct, hatch, frame,
and design.

I'd make accountant types seem like screw-offs and
anal compulsives seem relaxed, and mostly, I'd be more
organized than Susan, who's the most together person
I've ever met. If I didn't love her, she'd scare me half

to death.

And, dammit, I'd find the perfect traveling salesman to pay for Stephen's schooling and provide me with M.B.S.

I pushed the growing stack of surveys away and gave the newspaper a fast scan. For once no family member was featured in it. A few months back, I flinched every time I saw the paper because I knew my dad would be front-page news.

I heard the front door open and Stephen called out, "I'm home, *Maman*."

"Welcome home," I answered as he neared and pressed a quick smooch to my cheek. "Did you have a good time?"

He rolled his eyes. I hadn't truly expected an answer.

Although I wanted him to spend time with his fa— other mother, knowing he was back gave me a sense of security. Even though he's a head taller than me, I like having my chickling safe at home.

I always worry when he's gone, even when there's nothing specific to worry about. However, now that my ex has her own entertainment business (too bad it isn't successful enough to run to college tuition), occasionally she fills in for sick or missing employees. I insist that she return Stephen home on those occasions and not take him with her while she does her cross-dressing diva act. Stephen has enough confusion over the whole sex change issue. I know I do.

The good news was I'd almost stopped cringing whenever I saw Stephen's blue hair. The bad news was that the French beret perched jauntily atop said blue hair still made me cringe.

"S'up?"

At least he hadn't added *Maman*. The mix of high school slang with street French made conversation with him confusing—that is, whenever he decided to converse. He'd actually found a way to give his grunts a French accent.

"I'm getting ready to run some errands. Want to come along?"

"Can you get me some new pastels?"

I looked at him closely. At the sweet nose I'd kissed a zillion times that had now bloomed into youthful manhood. At the cat-green eyes that seemed to capture more life and energy from his surroundings than any other eyes I'd ever known. At his strong chin that so reminded me of the man who'd been his father. "Do you have an inner woman aching to break out?"

He rolled his eyes. "Just because Stormy—"

"You've told me this before. *Just because Stormy had an inner woman doesn't mean her son does, too.* But pastels?"

"I'm working on a new version of *Las Vegas après Holocaust*, Mom. I ran out of orange and black."

Did I mention his artwork generally gives me nightmares?

"I'm going to Target. Will they have pastels?"

French grunt.

"Come with?"

More eye rolling.

"I can't be expected to pick the right kind of art supplies. You said so yourself. Besides, I might need a big strong man like you to help little ol' me load my purchases in the Animal."

The Animal is the name of my Saturn ever since Stephen got a learner's permit and on his first outing drove into the McDonald's drive-thru window. Literally into.

Insurance paid to fix McDonald's but not the Saturn. Fortunately, it still runs. Unfortunately, with the combination of dents, rust, and green paint, it now looks like a tarantula on PCP.

"I'll come. Just don't talk to me."

"That's hard, Stephen. What if there's some danger? I'll need to warn you. Even if it's only to say, 'Watch out for the Bounty avalanche.'"

French grunt.

I shrugged, grabbed my keys, and we headed out the door.

Our trip to Target began as expected.

I like going out with my son. I really do. Honest. Even when he walks ten paces in front of me so he can pretend we aren't together.

Before long I realized I'd left my list at home and

now I wandered aimlessly wondering what the hell it was I needed besides Stephen's pastels.

After Stephen chose his pastels, I grabbed a packet of laminating sticky paper to see if I could do some repair work on my dream house photo. As we walked amicably down the aisles in pursuit of whatever it was I'd forgotten, I decided it was a good time to find out about his report card. Since he spent the night before with his fa— other mother, he'd managed to avoid me so far.

"Did you get your grades on Friday?"

French grunt.

"So, how'd you do?"

"Got an A in French."

"Oh, that's good." Maybe he'd turned a new leaf and his grades had skyrocketed?

"*Mais oui.*"

"Any other As?" I couldn't keep the hopeful note out of my voice.

"Art."

He stopped to gaze at a computer game display, indicating our discussion was over. I, however, am never one to take a broad hint, especially not when in pursuit of my son's grades. "How do the rest look?"

"Two Cs and two Ds."

My stomach churned. Definitely no hope for a scholarship reprieve. Unless . . . "Water polo?"

Stephen rolled his eyes, then walked back up the aisle.

I rushed to catch up with him. "Darts?"

No response.

Just then a cute pajama set caught my eye. Immediately behind it was a colorful bra display. I needed another bra. Hey, there's a chance it *could* have been on my list.

As a decoy, I quickly grabbed the cute pj's, which I had no intention of buying. Stephen was more likely to cooperate while I shopped for pj's than if he thought I was looking at bras. "Stay right here. I need to check this out and I'll be right back."

This time his grunt didn't sound so French. It was more guttural, but he remained in place, which was all I wanted.

I darted to the bras. They were made of cotton, didn't have any froufrou lace, and I particularly liked the bright colors. Most especially, I loved the price.

It didn't take long to become absorbed in choosing which color I liked best. I didn't look up until I heard the sound of Stephen's voice.

He was in conversation with a man. I couldn't see his face. I selected one of the bras, then headed in their direction.

As I moved around the pajama rack, bits of the man came into view. I came up behind him and noted his close-fitting black T-shirt and black jeans. I admired the muscular tightness that formed the shape of an award-winning male physique. Whoa. Even from the rear, this man exuded confidence. His posture was relaxed and yet there was a hint he would spring at the first sign of danger.

Curious how Stephen knew a man like this, I approached, unable to take my eyes off him. Wide shoulders. Oh, yeah. Trim waist. Oh, yeah. Dark hair. Oh, yeah. Dark eyes with incredibly long lashes just like George Clooney's. Ah, shit.

It was Stephen's third-grade teacher, Mr. Davin Wesley. Stephen had adored him but he'd been a total pain in my parental butt.

Eight years ago, Mr. Wesley had been an attractive man. But eight years of maturing had done incredible things to him. Who would expect the young, eager teacher to now appear more suited to a boardroom? The few crinkles age had sprinkled in the corners of his eyes didn't make him look older. Instead, they added character. His chiseled nose was still straight and strong, but now it fit his face in a way it hadn't before. The youth had left his cheeks, leaving sexy planes in their stead. And his lips . . .

I shook my head, determined to remember how Stephen had told this guy about seeing his father wearing my peekaboo nightie. Davin Wesley knew too many intimate details about my past. Intimate and humiliating details.

He was annoying. He was controlling. Hell, if I thought about it long enough, I might find some way to blame Mr. Wesley for most of my mother/son problems.

"Hullo," I said in as snooty a tone as I could muster. It must not have worked, though, because he smiled at me.

He was one of those men with really white teeth and I wondered whether he bleached them or if they were natural. I also wished he had asparagus or some other noxious vegetable caught between his teeth. Sadly that wasn't the case.

Not wanting to further embarrass Stephen by discussing his grades in front of his ex-teacher, I sought some safe subject I could turn our conversation to—like the weather. However, this being Nevada, there's usually not much to talk about in that regard.

I didn't need to change the subject, though, because Mr. Wesley directed his attention back to Stephen. "You're a senior now, aren't you? Are you busy applying to colleges?"

"I'm trying to decide which to apply to," said Stephen.

My stomach churned. College. Tuition.

"You're still painting, aren't you?"

"*Oui.* I want to be an artist."

"Have you considered the Massachusetts College of Art and the School of Visual Arts? They're both top art schools."

"Thanks for the suggestions."

"My class would enjoy having you demonstrate how to use pastels. Would you consider speaking to them?" Mr. Wesley smiled while I mentally calculated the tuition at top art schools.

Stephen glowed. There was little he enjoyed more than talking art. "Sure."

"I knew when I saw your entry that it would be a winner at the Henderson ArtFest."

"You went to the festival?" Stephen asked. "Did you know all of my artwork sold out?"

"Awesome." Davin nodded, said to me, "I bet you're proud."

"I've been bragging about it for weeks. Stephen is very talented."

"He is. I suspect he gets that from you?"

I chuckled. "No way. I'm an artist with a pastry brush, not a paintbrush."

He leaned his head to one side and looked at me intently. Like he was interested in what I was saying. "It seems to me that a gift for art of whatever kind is something you both share. I hear you're a famous chef."

"I'm not famous, but I enjoy my job as sous chef at La Papillon."

"I'm impressed. I bet you're proud of your mother, too, Stephen."

"*Oui*. Mom's a great cook."

Davin glanced my way again. "Oh, yeah?" His gaze lowered and I realized I was standing there with the fuchsia bra I'd selected clutched to my stomach. I quickly yanked it behind my back, but not before he noticed, because his lips slowly turned up in a lopsided smile as if he was fighting back a laugh. It was damned sexy.

"I like to think I'm a good cook," I replied with as much dignity as I could muster. However, it's hard to be dignified when you're holding a fuchsia bra in public.

Davin's eyes twinkled mischievously. "I like to think I'm a good taster."

Was he hinting he wanted to taste some of my cooking? Was he flirting with me? *Say something*, I said to myself. *Say something so you won't seem like a total dweeb standing here with your mouth drooping open and lingerie hidden behind your back.* I blurted, "And all this time, I thought you were a teacher."

"Between tasting engagements, I try to get my third graders interested in something other than snickering over body functions. Is there any chance for a tasting engagement with you two?"

Speaking of body functions, before I could reply two young women stopped in their tracks to ogle Davin. They were probably wondering how his body functioned, based on the way one of them—the youngest one—stared at his mouth.

Did I forget to mention his lips? Besides the George Clooney eyes, it was Davin Wesley's best trait. His lips speak directly to a woman's inner lust. You can't help but imagine what it would feel like to have *those* lips touching you, teasing you. Considering the way the young woman was clutching her shirt, that's exactly what was on her mind, too.

She nudged her friend and the two of them approached.

Okay, they made a beeline so fast they could have competed in a track meet. They were all dimples and grins as they said in singsong unison, "Hi, Davin."

He'd been smiling impishly at Stephen, who seemed particularly pleased with himself for some odd reason, so Davin hadn't noticed the women until they'd spoken. He turned and addressed them, "How are you doing, Jessica and Tanya?"

"Fine. It seems odd to see you outside the classroom," said the younger woman. She was blond, blue and dewy-eyed, and you could tell she had an enormous crush on the teacher. I'd almost forgotten what it was like to be that young and that obvious. Her friend was dark-haired, slender, and made me think of deer and gazelles.

The blonde smiled and glanced first at Stephen, then oddly at me. What did she think, that I was competition? Hardly. Like the Asshole Professor, Davin Wesley apparently attracted much younger women. Their combined ages couldn't add up to much more than my forty flipping years.

"Speaking of the classroom, I'd like you to meet Stephen Storm and his mother, Jill . . ." He looked at me, "You haven't remarried, have you?"

I shook my head.

He smiled again. Warmly. Maybe he really had been flirting with me?

"Jill Storm," he continued, now addressing the

women, while I was still reacting to the warmth of his smile. No wonder women tripped over themselves to come talk to him.

"I've invited Stephen to talk to the class," he said.

"That's great," said the blonde, extending her hand to shake Stephen's. "I'm interning in Davin's class right now."

"*Bien*," replied my son, who seemed somewhat dazzled by the two attractive young women—closer, I might add, to his age than to Davin's.

Davin then introduced the blonde as Jessica and her cohort as another teacher at his school. Jessica kept slanting seductive glances at him, but he didn't seem to notice. I caught Tanya taking a quick peek at his posterior and, based on the grin she shot me, she didn't seem the least ashamed about being caught. At least I had done it from a discreet distance.

Then Davin caught my eye and I realized, based on the barest hint of a blush on his tanned face, that he was aware of Tanya's peek, too. With a sweep of his long eyelashes, he somehow conveyed an apology for our conversation being interrupted. How the hell did he do that?

"It's such a pleasure to meet you, Stephen," said Jessica. "I'm a huge fan of your artwork."

"You've seen it?" Stephen's tone was as excited as the look on his face.

"Sure." The blonde glanced at Davin through

upturned lashes, and he seemed to signal a warning to her as she continued, "In the classroom. All those paint—"

She stopped midword at Davin's embarrassed expression. He broke in, "You're one of my star pupils, Stephen. I still have the still life you did of the fruit bowl on the playground slide."

Stephen grinned, but my mind was working overtime. Davin hadn't wanted Jessica to finish her sentence about Stephen's paintings.

Oh, shit. It had to mean that Davin was the customer who bought four of Stephen's six paintings on exhibit at the art festival. Davin didn't want Stephen to know he'd been the one.

Buying them had been an extremely nice gesture. No matter how I tried, I couldn't find an ulterior motive for Davin, other than he wanted to provide moral support to his ex-student. Maybe he simply wanted to brag?

The three of them started chatting about Stephen's upcoming visit, and about teaching, and about school, and blah blah blah, while my mind wandered.

Normally I love spending time at Target. Discount stores make life for single and working parents possible because they can shop for a myriad of items at once for everyday low prices. The nation and the economy should be grateful. And while normally I could spend a good half hour waxing eloquent over discount stores, and *Tar-je'* in particular, right then all I wanted was to pay for our items and leave rather than listen to Davin Wesley droning on.

It's not like he's my type, or that I resented being interrupted midflirt. Although he's a decent teacher, he belongs to the class of teachers who think the children belong to them and they merely lend their budding geniuses to the care of the parents. When Stephen was in Mr. Wesley's class, he was such a control freak that I half-expected a parental report card. He sent reams of paperwork home and not only did his students have plenty of homework, the parents did, as well.

I didn't want to waste my time standing there witnessing Jessica and Tanya's attempts to snag Davin's attention.

"I'm sorry to interrupt, but I'm afraid we need to run now," I said, politely, because he was being kind to my son.

"You didn't interrupt." Davin looked a little disappointed. "I need to head out soon, too." He smiled at the young women. "It was nice running into you."

Then he turned away from them and focused his attention back on Stephen—and shot me one of those warm smiles again.

Wanting to direct my gaze at anything other than his come-hither lips, I watched the young teachers depart. Maybe my opinion about him had been a little harsh?

He did seem to be a good influence on Stephen,

who needs strong men in his life.

Davin is strong, if you consider being opinionated a strength. He's a few years younger than me and, as I've mentioned, very attractive in a sexy just-got-out-of-bed way, making him a great role model for me—and the young teachers—if not for Stephen.

I hoped Davin didn't think he was a man trapped in a woman's body. He didn't seem the type, although Daniel hadn't either and look what happened.

However, Davin Wesley was practically a poster child for the opposite of what I was looking for in a man. Not only was he bossy, he was a total homebody. This was a guy whose sense of adventure was teaching third grade for the past decade, and on a teacher's salary he couldn't afford college tuition, either. If that wasn't enough, he was way too young for me—even if he was too old for Jessica and Tanya.

Davin pulled a business card from his wallet, and handed it to Stephen. "Call me to schedule a visit."

"Okay."

"It was very nice seeing you again, Jill." Davin's smile seemed genuine.

"You, too." I knew he was hoping I'd ask him over to taste my cooking, but finding him sexy wasn't enough. Even though I was on the make, I had a definite target of my own. What point was there in flirting with Davin when I wasn't interested?

Stephen nudged his ex-teacher, as if he was

encouraging him.

Davin patted Stephen on the shoulder but addressed me. "You never answered my question, you know."

"What question?" I knew exactly what he meant and I hoped the heat rising from my neck to my face wasn't noticeable.

"About the three of us getting together for a meal?"

"Oh. Yeah. We'll have to do that sometime." Vague. Deliberately vague. "Well, gotta run. See you around."

As we turned, Davin made a parting shot. "Yes. You'll be seeing me around."

Why did that sound more like a threat than a pleasantry?

Stephen and I headed toward the checkout and the grin on Stephen's face could not have been bigger. Maybe Davin Wesley wasn't too awful since he genuinely cared about his students.

And perhaps, after all these years, I could admit that he had been right about me back then. The last time I saw him, shortly before school let out for the year, Mr. Wesley called me a deadbeat mother—well, not in those words. But his intent had been clear during our parent/teacher conference when he mentioned I wasn't giving Stephen enough attention.

The problems between Daniel and I had first surfaced when Stephen entered third grade. Daniel's admission that he wasn't happy in our marriage had devastated me. That he wanted to live his life as Stormy Daniels rather than Daniel Storm nearly did me in.

As a result, I couldn't spend enough time with Stephen—not with going back to school and money worries. I tried to make it up to him, but making up never seems to be as good as having been there in the first place. I could spend the rest of my life making up and it would never be good enough. Even now, Stephen spent more time chatting with his ex-teacher, had strung more words together at once, than he'd said to me all together in weeks.

I didn't know how to fix it, wasn't sure if I could, but one thing within my power was to make sure Stephen had a good education.

I'd find a way.

I'd find a nice traveling salesman, with oodles of moolah for tuition, and all would be well with my world.

And sexy control freaks like Davin Wesley could kiss my aspic.

CHAPTER THREE

Dear Jill,

What a terrific idea. Please share your survey results with those of us who've sent you information.

My personal philosophy is once you find Mr. Right, pull out all stops to snare him. Don't worry so much about learning the secrets to a successful relationship. Love is the answer!

If you love a man, you do what it takes to make the relationship work. Every woman looks for something different in a man. What works for me might not work for you.

Viva la difference and happy man hunting,

Yours truly,

Marion S. Jones

Renowned Five Star Master Chef, Albert Radkin, author of two best-selling cookbooks, internationally recognized for his take on Southwestern cuisine, was drunk. Again.

As the chef at La Papillon Casino and Hotel, he's my boss and also the biggest lush I've ever encountered. Considering I work in the food service industry, that's saying a lot.

He was slumped over his desk, which wasn't unusual, but it did give me problems. I wanted the list of upcoming banquets clipped to the clipboard under his left arm. His head rested on his right arm, so maybe it wouldn't be too difficult.

I tiptoed closer to the desk, hoping not to wake him, although I didn't think it likely. Leaning over the desk, I inched my hand toward the clipboard. I took another step closer and my fingertips came in contact with the banquet list.

I checked Albert's face. He hadn't moved at all. Using my forefinger and thumb, I pinched his uniform sleeve, then lifted his left arm. As I yanked the clipboard out, I must have joggled his arm too much, because Albert awoke.

Well, I use the word *awoke* loosely. He momentarily emerged from his stupor. His patriotic eyes opened—blue eyes, extremely bloodshot—and he slurred, "'Lo, Ms. Morganstern."

My teeth gritted. I hate being called Morganstern.

"The name's Morgan Storm."

"S'right." He pulled himself upright. "You're looking lovely today. Want to bear my children?"

I sighed. Whenever he was drunk, which was more often than not, for some reason he always wanted me to carry his children. Maybe he thought the mix of his culinary genius with my culinary near-brilliance would result in a culinary supergenius.

Thankfully, he slumped back down and began to snore, so I backed out of the room.

As I scanned the list, I realized it didn't have the information I needed. There were several sales conferences, but how to choose the best one for finding a possible mate? Which would be most likely to have lots of men to choose from?

I would have to go see the catering manager. However, I couldn't go without a bribe.

I had to promise Big E that I wouldn't lock myself in the restroom again before he gave me a basket filled with his incredibly light, tasty, and delicious pastries. He was a truly tough guy, about six feet, four inches tall, and looked exactly like he belonged on a Harley, right down to a missing front tooth and pinkie finger. He swore like a biker, too, but he was an artist. No one made pastries like him. No one.

Despite the tough exterior, I'll never forget the time his starter kicked the bucket and Big E wept for hours. Yeast can be a tough mistress.

So, now armed with suitable gastronomic persuasion, I left the kitchen and headed for sales.

Glamorous, sophisticated, and intelligent, Mandy Webster, the catering manager, was the type of woman that women loved to hate. She could swap clothes with a fashion model and look even better than they did. Men adored her and women avoided her, including me.

But she had what I needed—intimate knowledge of the sales conferences that would be most likely to a) have plenty of men, b) have plenty of men who were the right age, and c) have plenty of men who were the right age and were single. She'd know which conferences I should crash to find the salesman of my schemes, I mean, dreams.

Mandy had a small office in the administrative area of the hotel. When she saw me, she greeted me warmly and ushered me inside. For some reason, probably related to karma, she was always excited to see me, which made me feel badly about wanting to hate her.

"I brought you some pastries." I handed her the basket, then took a seat.

Her face lit up with undisguised hunger. "Oh. I love these. Thank you!"

I felt a little guilty since I was appealing to her well-known carbohydrate addiction, but all's fair in love and payola.

She took a seat behind her desk, grabbed a pastry, and took a bite. "Is there something I can help you with?"

Well, yeah. What did she think I brought the crullers for? I wasn't sure, however, whether to act like this was pure business or to 'fess up to my plan. I eyed her as she munched, and she was even gorgeous while engorging.

"I bet you never have men trouble," I blurted. It didn't come out exactly the way I wanted, but she smiled ruefully and her eyes oozed concern.

"Sure, I do. Don't you think most women do?"

"Yeah, but with the way you look . . ." I waved my palm.

"The kind of guys who interest me most are the sort who are intimidated by my looks."

My jaw dropped. I know it did. "What kind of guys interest you most?"

"Geeks. Computer geeks." She sighed. "What can I say? I love smart men."

I felt as if I'd bitten into a bitter lemon. After all this time being jealous of her, and resenting her, it turned out . . . she was *nice*.

"I'm hoping you can help me, Mandy. I have this plan . . ." Maybe my plan was stupid? Maybe she'd think I was stupid?

She leaned forward. "A plan to do with men?"

I nodded. "Okay, you'll probably think it's insane, but I sent out surveys to women who've been married for twenty-five or more years, and the answer to a successful marriage, at least from what I've gleaned so far, is a man who travels for a living."

"Really?"

"It looks that way." I shrugged. "So I want to meet traveling salesmen . . . and we have so many sales conferences."

"I love this!" Mandy, who was normally perky, now literally vibrated in her chair. "How can I help?"

I showed her the clipboard of upcoming banquets. "Which of these would be the best for me to crash?"

She took the list and scanned it quickly, then turned to her computer. Within minutes, she'd printed out a list and handed it to me.

"These six are your best bets."

I glanced at the list and the first item caught my attention. "Easel salesmen?"

"Go figure. They're almost all men. Cute, too."

"Sounds great. I just hope I can pull this off."

"What are you worried about?"

"I've never set out to pick up men before. I mean I know I can do it, but I'm not really sure what to say." It wasn't like I could walk up to a cute easel salesman and say *wanna get married and pay my son's college tuition?* Maybe I should mention monkey sex?

"You can ask them about their jobs. That always works. Men love talking about themselves."

"I can do that. Any other tips?"

"Well, if all else fails," Mandy said breathlessly, "you can always use my best line."

"You have a best line? I don't even have a not-best line. Tell!"

"I'll tell you, but you have to promise not to use it unless it's an emergency."

"Got it. Only in an emergency." Like my situation now wasn't an emergency? Help! I need college tuition.

"And you need to be careful who you use it on. It can't be used lightly."

I made an *X* over my chest. "Cross my heart."

"Remember, only use this on a guy you are seriously interested in."

"Promise."

She looked around, as if worried that someone would overhear, then came from behind her desk to whisper in my ear.

After she was finished, I leaned back in my chair and marveled at her brilliance. It was one hell of a great line.

❧ ❧ ❧

You had to hand it to the Easel Boys, they certainly knew how to do a cocktail party right. And Mandy really knew her stuff, I thought, as I glanced around the elegantly decorated ballroom. It was filled with cute guys.

A string quartet played graceful music in one corner, while the back wall was lined with hot and cold appetizers and Julio, my favorite line cook, sliced roast beef and ham for easel salesmen as they came down the line. Several waiters hovered about the room, carrying trays filled with red and white wine for the Easel Boys' consumption.

And I could say *Easel Boys* confidently. Besides me, there were two, count 'em, two other women in the room. Who'da thunk there could be that many easel salesmen? I glanced up to heaven and said a silent thank-you.

I did some reconnaissance, checking out salesmen who looked interesting or appealing in some way. I came up with seven possibles, then recircled the room to make sure none of the seven wore physical matrimonial evidence (i.e., wedding rings). This reduced the number of possibles to three.

The first reminded me of a younger Mel Gibson. The second looked a bit like a middle-aged, Daniel Craig, the latest James Bond. The third looked like a CNN News announcer, but I wouldn't hold that against him.

I felt positively giddy with female power. The skirt I was wearing looked awesome, I had killer shoes, and an adequate amount of bodacious bosom was revealed by my blouse. Not only that, but I was armed with a sure-fire plan and, should it fail, I had Mandy's emergency line.

I approached the first guy as he left the serving line. "Hi, I'm Jill Morgan Storm. I was wondering if you could help me?"

I stuck out my hand for him to shake and he co-operated after moving his food-laden plate into his left hand. "I'd be happy to help."

He looked proud and pleased to be asked. This was going to be easier than I'd imagined. "I'm thinking of a career change. Are you an easel salesman?"

He nodded.

"Do you like it?"

"Love it. Are you in sales?"

"Sort of. I work for the hotel."

"What do you do?"

"I'm a sous chef." I searched for something to say that would get him to start talking in longer sentences. "I never realized there were so many easel salesmen. Who do you sell easels to?"

"Just about everyone. My company sells a full line of presentation and display easels to distributors, office supply companies, advertising and marketing companies, hotel conference centers, and even artist supply companies."

"Wow." That was so much more than I wanted to know.

"We also sell other items, such as dry-erase boards, interactive marker boards, chalkboards."

"I see." I did see. As he continued yammering about different presentation products, my eyes began to glaze and I saw that he was a total bore and the only thing more boring I could think of was to actually work as an easel salesman.

But if I only had to tolerate him coming home once a week, maybe I could deal with it? Maybe I could change the subject? "So, are you a Las Vegas native?"

"Nah, I'm from Omaha. Here for the convention and to get in a little slot machine action. How about you?"

"Oh, I don't gamble." I especially didn't gamble on the easel salesmen all living out of state. How was I going to date them? "Don't any of you guys live in Las Vegas?"

"Yeah. There are sales reps from all over. In fact, the number-one salesperson from this region is standing over there by the bar."

I turned my head where he indicated, and happy days, It was my second choice easel sales rep, Mr. James Bond look-alike. Maybe he'd be more interesting than this guy. "Thanks," I said as I headed toward my next victim . . . er . . . possible.

Feeling much more brave this time, I walked up to him and said, "Hi. I hear you're from Vegas."

"That's right. How'd you know?" He smiled and I rather liked the way his eyes seemed to smile, as well.

"A guy over there said you were. I'm Jill Morgan Storm and I wonder if you can help me?"

"Nice to meet you, Jill. I'm Anthony Winston. I'd love to help, but first, can I get you a drink?"

This was more like it. "What are you having?"

"Oh, this is just a Coke," he said. "I don't drink much."

Better and better.

We chatted for a while and it went according to plan. He hadn't launched into a spiel about his products. And he seemed genuinely interested when I mentioned I was the hotel sous chef.

"Do you have any specialties—" he was asking when another easel boy joined us. "Hey, Tony. Who you chatting with?"

I automatically checked for the matrimonial evidence and a thin gold band flashed, *not eligible*.

"This joker works at 5N with me. Jerry, meet Jill," replied Tony. "She's the chef."

"Here to look after us salesmen?"

"You could say that," I replied. "I like to make sure all our patrons are well fed." I wanted to get back to my *tête-à-tête* with Tony and turned away, but Jerry didn't seem to take a hint.

"The appetizers are great. I really liked those little pinwheel thingies. Did you make them?"

"It was my recipe."

"They're good."

"Thank you."

"You're welcome."

Go away.

"Tony, you were going to tell me about selling

easels."

"You asked the right guy," interrupted Jerry who punched Tony on the arm. "He's the region's best."

"Really." I looked at Tony through my lashes. "I always did like the best."

Tony blushed and Jerry laughed.

"I can see I'm butting in," said Jerry.

I didn't say anything, thinking he'd finally gotten the hint, but Tony opened his mouth to object. Quickly grabbing one of the stuffed mushrooms from Jerry's plate, I stuffed it in Tony's mouth. "Try this."

Jerry yanked his plate behind his back and looked at me as if I'd stolen candy from a baby. "Well, um, nice to meet you." He backed away toward a group of men standing near the string quartet.

"Do you like the stuffed mushroom?" I asked innocently.

Tony took the napkin from around his Coke and blotted his lips. "Very good."

Now that I had him back to myself, I wasn't sure what to say. And I could tell from the way he was looking at me that I'd better get to the point soon. Unfortunately, every word of my plan evaporated from my brain and I was unable to think of a conversational gambit. Surely I didn't need to use Mandy's emergency line, yet? So I asked the only other thing I could think of. "Are you single?"

"Divorced."

"Me, too."

He had really nice hazel eyes and I liked the way they seemed to glitter with interest, as if he really saw me, not just the hotel sous chef.

Two other salesmen came up and clapped him on the back, congratulating him for making number one. While they chatted about selling easels, I continued watching Tony. He seemed very nice, like someone I'd really enjoy spending one week out of four with.

Unfortunately, he seemed very popular. I began to feel a little desperate, as if I'd never get his attention again. But he must have been feeling the same way, because he said, "Excuse me. I need to ask Jill a question."

He separated himself from the others, took my arm, and walked me toward a dark corner of the ballroom. I liked him more and more.

"Thanks for going along with me," he said. "Those two guys are my chief competitors and they really get on my nerves."

"My pleasure." Now I truly was at a loss for what to say. I'd asked about his job, his marital status. What else was left but Mandy's line?

It was definitely an emergency.

My forehead beaded with nervous perspiration. Could I say something like that? I appeared to be at risk of losing my best tuition candidate, so I opened my mouth to force the words from my mouth: *If you play your cards right, I'll let you be my love slave*, but he spoke first.

"Say, I know this is fast, but would you consider having dinner with me some time?" he asked.

What a relief. I might talk a good game, but I don't have the steel *cojones* needed to carry off a line like Mandy's.

I smiled at Tony. This I could handle. I peeked up at him through my eyelashes. Maybe even a dimple or two. This I could do. "I'd love to have dinner with you."

CHAPTER FOUR

Survey Comments:

My husband's job requires 40 percent travel. This means he's actually gone 70 percent of the time.

Since he isn't home often, when he arrives I want everything in place to make him feel happy and comfortable. I want "home" to be a place he longs to return to.

I've found that preparation is every bit as important as participation. I start three days before he's due home. I do everything, from cooking ahead to cleaning beneath the refrigerator to bikini waxing. Once he walks in the door, I'm not distracted by household chores. This is the true secret to our successful and blissful relationship. My motto: Always Ready!

Good luck!

Yavonne Goodnight

Pre-date rituals can be more important than the date itself.

Think about it.

You know how excited you get when you're about to go out with a really cool guy? Your blood seems to rush more smoothly through your veins.

There's a high-pitched buzz of excitement in your head, making you feel more clever, more attractive, more everything.

You're happy.

Are those birds chirping in the trees?

Your heart seems to expand.

The entire world is painted in rosy hues.

Jokes are funnier. You laugh more.

And the reason you get so excited is because this guy might be *the one*. The guy you'll want to spend the rest of your days and nights with.

At least, that's how it is with me.

But the majority of first dates end up being duds.

Not that I'm complaining, mind you. It's the odds.

How can you expect to find Mr. Perfect without discarding a lot of Mr. Grosses along the way?

I'm looking for a knight in shining armor who will sweep me off my feet and pay my son's college tuition. What I generally get is a toad in dirty underwear who expects me to do his laundry and prepare sumptuous meals for him because I'm, like, *a chef*.

After rejoining the dating pool, I've learned to enjoy preparing for a date because sometimes it's the only pleasure that lasts.

If it sounds like I'm jaded, I am.

Almost all of my female friends, I've noticed through the years, spend at least three hours getting ready before a first date. Some spend days. They'd spend weeks if they had that much notice, but most guys don't think that far ahead.

Three days before my date with hubba-hubba-Tony a.k.a. Easel Boy, I began preparations by power shopping for the ideal outfit. The next day I found the perfect, sexy-strappy shoes.

When I began my preparations early on the afternoon of The Date, my goal was to eke every bit of pleasure out of getting ready. My schedule was filled to the brim with activities such as manicure, pedicure, body-hair removal, and bubble bath.

While I was excited about Tony and my Tuition Plan, it wasn't likely that the first salesman I auditioned would be a winner. I'm not that lucky.

At worst, preparing for The Date would leave me relaxed and feeling my best for two hours over dinner with an attractive Mr. Creep-Me-Out. At best, we'd hit it off, I'd continue thinking he might be Mr. Perfect, and date number two would be in the bag.

So I was standing in the kitchen, determined to gain pleasure from my pre-date rituals, hard at work so

I could adequately pamper myself, when my son stuck his nose out of his bedroom.

"Whaccha up to, *Maman*?"

I didn't cringe, not even a little. Maybe the French expression was growing on me? Nah. Sticking the cucumber into the food processor, I said, "I'm making a mud facial."

He looked at the bag of 100 percent clay litter sitting on the counter beside the food processor. "We don't have a cat."

"It's for my facial. Mixing it with liquid will turn it into mud."

"*Le ick*." He held up his hands as he backed away. "Just so long as you don't consider it an ingredient for dinner."

"You're having pizza, so you're safe."

"Delivery?"

"Yup." I added some water to the cucumber slices, then hit the puree switch. Within seconds, my fresh cucumber was a lovely green froth.

"Can you order a large pizza? That way I can have a friend over."

"You got it."

I should have paid more attention to him. Instead, I was concentrating on adding the green froth to a bowl of litter. I hadn't made this facial before, and it seemed a little odd to use litter on my face, but mud facials are made of clay and since the brand of kitty litter was 100 percent clay, I didn't see why it wouldn't work like a charm. The facial mixture came out a bit lumpy, but it probably needed to steep a while.

Since I had other things on my agenda, I abandoned the facial goo and headed to the bathroom. Once I wrapped my hair in mayo and Saran Wrap, I returned to the kitchen and stirred the facial. It was getting muddier and less lumpy. Figuring it needed more steeping, I returned to the bathroom and began my pedicure.

After moisturizing them in the bathtub, I then sanded and powdered and generally loved my feet. I once read an article in *Cosmo* that said women who loved their feet were happier. I wasn't sure if I agreed but figured it wouldn't hurt to find out. I even had those cute, bright pink foam pads for separating my toes, which I used while painting my toenails.

I walked on my heels—holding my toes in the air as much as possible—back to the kitchen, hoping the foam pads would keep the polish from smearing. I checked the mud facial. There were decidedly fewer clumps and some of the clumps might be cucumber peel, so I took it to the living room mirror and began applying the green mud to my face.

While I was smearing the stuff on, Stephen came out of his lair again and took one look at me. His eyes met mine in the mirror reflection, an expression of horror on his face, then he immediately went back inside his room, like a turtle retracting for safety.

I looked at my image and agreed; I was pretty scary. From the mayo and plastic covering my head, the thick, green, lumpy goop on my face, my well-worn and oversized COOKS DO IT HOTTER T-shirt (with a number of rips and gouges caused by a run-in with a staple gun), down to the rain forest I call my legs and the hot pink toe separators, I was the spitting image of Sasquatch. At least I'd be beautiful by tonight.

I shrugged and continued applying the goop. It was already drying near my hairline and turning an interesting shade of forest green. Maybe not Sasquatch. Perhaps a visitor from Mars?

The doorbell rang. Figuring it was Stephen's friend arriving for dinner, I threw open the door.

Mr. Davin Wesley!

How did he always manage to look so . . . muscular, as if his chest strained against his button-down shirt?

A glop of mayo slid down my neck.

I slammed the door shut.

What the hell was he doing here? My heart hammered. Blood rushed to my head. My hands flew up in the air. (I'd never honestly believed this happens to people when they're surprised, but guess what? It does.)

Okay. Calm down.

Screw that.

"Stephen!" I shouted.

"*Oui.*"

"Who the hel—ahem—who did you invite for dinner?"

"Mr. Wesley. I told you I was inviting him."

Ah, no, he'd said a friend. *Devil* Wesley had never been mentioned. I shoulda known he'd turn up at the worst possible moment.

There was no way Wesley was getting a second glimpse of me looking like Frankenstein hopped up on steroids. I hobbled (the foam toe pads prevented me from running from the scene of my recent humiliation) to the bathroom, yelling, "He's here. Go let him in."

I quickly closed the bathroom door and any hope I might have entertained that Davin hadn't had a good look at me died as I heard his maniacal laughter when Stephen let him in. All the way at the back of my apartment. On the other side of the bathroom door.

It was bad enough that anyone other than a blood relative saw me looking like the undead, but to have it be *him*—a man I disliked and who already had an extremely low opinion of me—made it worse. Much worse.

I had no other recourse but to set a goal. The next time he saw me, when I exited the bathroom, I'd be so incredibly gorgeous it would totally drive the other image of me permanently out of his head. In fact, he'd probably be unable to keep himself from shouting *Va-va-va-voom* while attempting to hide an instant erection.

It was the only solution.

I looked at my face in the mirror over the sink. I had a lot of work to do. Why hadn't I insisted on a face-lift to go with my new boobs? The Asshole Professor could have afforded it.

Even worse, I didn't have any other clothes in the bathroom. I searched through the linen closet, seeking something other than a threadbare towel. I came up empty, well, except for the colander I'd been looking for last week. How the hell had it gotten mixed in with the washcloths?

Okay, I'd have to wear the T-shirt, but at least the rest of me could look fabulous.

While the facial continued steeping—and by this point I was wondering how soon I should take it off. Could it stain my face?—the next item on my agenda was tending to the rain forest that had taken over my legs. After my breakup with the Asshole Professor, I'd gotten a bit lax about shaving my lower limbs (I did keep my upper limbs in tip-top smooth shape, natch). I like to think of this sacrifice as my contribution to the world's ecology. Think of the petroleum products that weren't consumed by Bic.

With only a little trepidation, I examined my legs. Thankfully, no jungle animals had claimed them as a habitat. Wanting to do things right for my upcoming date, I'd purchased a jar of leg wax. Well, kind of leg wax. Figuring I'd give myself third-degree burns, I bought the kind that you didn't have to heat and that mentioned the word *honey* on the label. Sounded good to me.

Pure. Wholesome.

I carefully prepared the cloths I'd need for strip-mining the rain forest, and began. It worked very well and, while very sticky, my legs were presentable in no time. Feeling flush with success, I decided to give myself a bikini wax.

There should have been a warning on the label.

"AAIIiieeeEEEEaaaaiiiEEEEEiii." That's a close approximation to the sound that catapulted itself through my larynx, having removed some of the soft skin (necessary skin, in my humble opinion) in that tender area where my leg met my body.

Within seconds, Stephen pounded on the bathroom door. "Are you okay, Mom?"

Between screams, I managed to reassure him that it wasn't necessary to call 9-1-1.

I was even alert enough to note that he'd dropped the French-isms temporarily. After my high-pitched operetta ceased, and the vision had returned to my eyes, I couldn't figure out how to get the rest of the cloth and pseudo-wax off, because there was no way I was yanking it the rest of the way. I turned on the shower, waited for the water to run warm, then jumped in.

"AAIIiieeeEEEEaaaaiiiEEEEEiii." Again, I have to applaud myself for my awareness, despite pain akin to having your ovaries ripped from your body via your throat. I realized how very similar my caterwauling was to a female cat in heat, except I was louder.

More thundering on the bathroom door.

However, this time the door was flung open.

Of course it was my nemesis, yelling something about calling a doctor or carrying me to the hospital and a suicide watch.

Between yowls, I said, "Get the hell out of here," while I tried to hide behind the less-than-opaque shower curtain, and wondered why I hadn't first removed the mayo and plastic from my hair.

Again the maniacal laughter, but he *was* smart enough to make a fast get away. There wasn't time for anger now; I was too consumed with agony.

Once I stopped screaming for the second time—amazed at how painful water meeting skin stripped from the body could truly be—I managed to remove most of the waxing product and the cloth. After a quick wash of my hair, careful to keep soapy water from contacting my nether regions, I climbed out of the shower, a mere shell of my former self. I say a shell primarily because I quickly learned that walking was nearly as painful as the water had been. I mastered an odd, spider-walk, where I stuck my injured leg out, far far out, ahead of my body, slung my body forward until it nearly met my leg, then began again. It was pretty scary.

I wondered if women had died from this. Was I the latest on a long list of women who'd sacrificed their health all in the name of beauty?

How was I going to be able to work in this condition?

Even worse, I couldn't think of anything more dreadful than the idea of having sex, much less auditioning a traveling salesman. Maybe I needed to cancel The Date?

I considered my options and the obstacles in front of me. I'd eventually have to leave the bathroom, either to cancel The Date or go on The Date, so either way, I'd have to face my nemesis while dressed in a towel or my holey T-shirt. But . . . I had a tube of antibiotic ointment infused with Novocain pain reliever in the medicine cabinet behind the mirror over the sink.

I grabbed the tube and a box of adhesive bandages and went to work on my injury. After applying half the tube to my owie, I slapped a bandage on it. Since I'd been so generous with the ointment, the bandage didn't want to stick. I grabbed another bandage. And another. And another.

After applying eleven bandages, I figured it had done the trick. Now to see whether I could walk.

I took a tentative step.

At first I could only spider-creep my way to the door. However, after a little practice (or maybe the Novocain finally kicked in), I mastered something like my normal gait. Kinda.

After pacing the bathroom six more times, I decided I could walk semi-normally as long as I took it slowly.

So what if I didn't get to audition Tony tonight? I could enjoy the pleasure of his company and get to know him better. I could audition him on personality traits rather than sexual prowess. M.B.S. could wait until date number two.

It didn't take long to dry and style my hair, put on my makeup, and wrap myself in a towel. I was as gorgeous as I could make myself and ready for The Date—well, except for clothes.

Taking one last look at myself in the mirror, I was pleased with my appearance. While Wesley might not have an instant erection, I looked pretty damn good. And maybe the towel would make me look sexy?

I stealthily unlatched the door, pulled it open very slowly, hoping it wouldn't creak as it often does. I peeked out, but didn't see either Stephen or his fiendish ex-teacher. Turning my head, I saw Stephen's door was open wide, revealing an empty room. I stepped from the bathroom. Where the hell were they?

Hitching the towel up higher, I stalked through the apartment and didn't find either of them, before giving up and returning to my bedroom.

It was just as well they weren't here. After all, I didn't want Wesley to see me in only a threadbare towel, and Stephen would probably have made some sarcastic French comment anyway.

I took my time slipping on the new outfit I'd bought for The Date. The skirt was short, very short, as short as the pink one my mother is so fond of when it comes to matchmaking me with unsuitable men. My new one was a lovely shade of dark blue chiffon and it was flirty and youthful and I knew, without a doubt, that I looked fantastic in it.

I pulled on the matching camisole, then covered that in a see-through chiffon over shirt. After slipping on my new strappy shoes, I took a look in the full-length mirror inside my closet door. Oh, wow. I might be forty flipping years old, but I didn't look it in this outfit. If it didn't knock any number of traveling salesmen's socks off, I couldn't imagine what would. And, it would definitely erase any unpleasant earlier images of me, should my son and his loony teacher have returned.

I quickly put on faux diamond ear studs, a tiny chain and locket, and dabbed on the barest hint of Opium as the finishing touches before emerging from my bedroom.

From the smell, I could tell the pizza had arrived. As I entered the kitchen, two low male whistles greeted me.

Bingo!

From the grins on their faces, I could tell my outfit was a big hit.

"You like?" I asked, spinning.

"*Tres bien, Maman.*"

"Planning to break some hearts tonight?" asked Wesley.

"I sure hope so." When I grabbed my handbag

from the kitchen counter, I noticed the teacher was doing something to my sink. "What are you doing?"

"Fixing your faucet." He'd taken it apart and was apparently in the process of replacing the little screen filter. "Stephen told me it's been spitting at you lately."

"I was planning to do it." I was feeling defensive, which was silly since it wasn't a big deal.

"I like fixing things," Wesley added.

"The original Mr. Fix-It, huh?" But then, my gaze landed on the yellow cardboard lightbulb package sitting beside the sink. I looked up. He'd replaced the bulb that had been out for several months. Something else I'd been planning to get around to . . . eventually.

Now I really felt defensive. He already thought poorly of me and now he seemed to think I was doing a bad job of taking care of Stephen and myself. "I've been taking care of this stuff for a long time."

"I thought you could use the help." He sounded pleased with himself, as if I should act all girly about it. Like that would ever happen.

He didn't get it. I didn't need someone tromping on what little confidence I had in my abilities. I didn't want or need help from him. I needed college tuition, not a caretaker, even if said caretaker looked kind of desirable with his sleeves rolled up to his elbows and a pair of pliers in his hands.

"Should I wait up for you?" My son, the peacemaker, finished putting slices of pizza on a plate for each of them and apparently noticed that I was fighting an urge to order Wesley out of my kitchen.

Deciding to let the issue slide—I mean, if some control freak wants to fix your sink and replace your lightbulbs, you might as well let him, especially when your kid seems to like him so much—I replied, "Wait up if you want. I expect to be home fairly early, definitely before midnight."

Davin frowned. "Not much of a night on the town."

"It's plenty for me. I can accomplish a lot in four to five hours." I turned to leave.

"Shouldn't you tell us where you'll be? How well do you know this guy?" asked the-teacher-from-Hades.

"It's none of your business, but Stephen knows where I'm going. Don't you, hon?" It's where I always meet people I don't know well because I know the guys who work there. I consider it a "safe spot," so I'd arranged to meet Tony there just in case he turned out to be a psychopath or simply got on my nerves.

Stephen nodded. "Patisserie?"

"Don't tell him! Mr. Wesley will probably try to horn in on my date or screw it up."

"Davin. And I wouldn't." He waved a slice of pizza at me. "Screw up your date, I mean."

"What about horning in? You didn't mention not doing that."

He showed his teeth when he smiled, but he didn't

respond.

"Night, *Maman*. Have fun!"

As I closed the door, I heard Davin mutter, "Keep your shoes on, Cinderella."

∾ ∾ ∾

Tony and I were to meet at the restaurant at seven o'clock on the dot. Patisserie was a local hot spot, trendy, near the Strip, and the food was well prepared. A cook I used to work with at the hotel, Kurt, had opened it. I probably knew half the kitchen staff, because he'd stolen most of them from the hotel. No matter how The Date went, I'd have a great dinner.

The maître d', Carlos, recognized me when I came in and gave me a quick hug. "I'll let Kurt know you're dining with us tonight."

"I'm meeting a date, so there's no need."

"Is his name Tony?" Carlos scowled slightly. Hmm.

"Yes. Is he here already?"

"I seated him by the kitchen. I'll move you to a better table right away. He asked for something nicer, but I assured him it wasn't possible without a reservation." Carlos rubbed his fingers together in a time-honored gesture meaning Tony hadn't coughed up the bucks to merit one of the good tables.

"Stiffed you, huh? I'll have to train him better.

Lead me to your best table, please." I offered him a twenty, but Tony waved it away.

"Are you sure you really want to meet this guy?"

"Hey, Tony is nice."

Again Carlos scowled.

"Isn't he?" Tony seemed sweet when I met him, but maybe my first impression was wrong?

"Yeah. He's nice enough. Just not your type." Carlos nudged me with his shoulder as he led me to the table. "Now me, I'm your type."

So that was what his hints were about. A little male posturing. Since Carlos was *very* married, I ignored his flirtations as he seated me. He then went to fetch Tony from whatever dining-hell he'd been subjected to. I sniffed the flower centerpiece while I waited for my date.

A couple of minutes later, Tony approached. He was every bit as cute as I remembered. I hadn't been deluding myself, which was a thought that had occurred to me when I was on my way to meet him. My eyes focused on something in Tony's hand. A box? Maybe he'd brought me a gift?

He arrived at my table, leaned over and bussed my cheek. "Hi."

"Hi." My eyes narrowed. He wasn't carrying a box. It was a stack of photos. Who brings photos on a date? "Did you have any problem finding the restaurant?"

"No. Looks like a nice place."

"It's one of my favorites." No need to mention it's one of my *safe spots*. "So, how are easel sales?"

"Going great. How's cooking?"

"Just fine." I wasn't quite sure how to get a conversation going and sought some safe subject. I mean, what do easel salesmen want to talk about? I knew nothing about easels. As I opened my mouth to stick my foot in it by mentioning religion or politics, our waiter approached. "Can I get you a bottle of wine tonight?"

He ran through the list of specials and Tony and I quickly placed our orders.

Do you ever have one of those moments, not exactly déjà vu, but where you know that what is coming isn't going to be good?

It happened to me when Tony, who had been sitting opposite me at the table, changed chairs to sit beside me, photos in hand.

"This is my kid, Charlie. Isn't he cute?"

I looked at the photo he held up. Charlie had an uncanny resemblance to Eddie Munster. "Very cute. How old is he?"

"Five. This one's a picture of him in front of our . . . I mean, what used to be our house. I live in an apartment now."

His boy was only five? Amazing. What with the peach fuzz mustache, he looked about fourteen. "Nice house."

"Bridget got it in the divorce." He seemed sort of

choked up as he looked at the house photo. I could understand where he was coming from since we obviously shared a passion for houses—dream or lost.

"I have a son, too. Stephen." It wasn't much of a conversation starter, but it was the best I could do at the time. Since Tony was upset, I was hoping to get him on another subject. But none of my attempts worked. By the time our entrées arrived, he'd hit his stride.

"I miss my kid. I miss my house. I miss my wife. I miss my life!"

When dessert arrived, I realized I'd hit the low point in my dating life, because my date was blubbering. Literally. Crying into his Crème Brûlée.

"I want my life back. Why did she have to kick me out? Why? Why?"

With each "why," he smashed his forehead with his spoon. "Now, now." I forced the spoon from his fingers and patted his back, not knowing what else to do.

But he continued blubbering. Other diners were beginning to stare and were looking at me as if I'd done something to upset the poor man. One woman glared at me, so I held up my hands in an exaggerated shrug to let her know I wasn't responsible.

She turned away, but it was too much. I had to escape. Grabbing my handbag, I popped up from the table. "Gotta go visit the little girls' room."

My tone came out a lot more frantic than I'd hoped, but if this wasn't an emergency, what was? I'd have done almost anything to get away. I'd have yelled fire if Kurt wouldn't have doused me in fire extinguisher foam as retribution. As I trotted to the restroom, toilet paper origami called to me.

By the time I'd applied more lipstick and gone through *every* freshening-up routine I could think of, I remembered my cell phone. I dialed my home number.

The phone was answered on the second ring. "Thunder Storm residence," said the voice.

At first I thought I'd called the wrong number, but the voice sounded sickeningly familiar. "Is this Davin? What are you doing answering the phone? Where's Stephen?"

"He's in the bathroom. How's your date going?"

Like I was going to discuss it with him? "None of your business. Any chance Stephen is coming out soon?"

"Considering how much time the two of you spend in the bathroom, I'm beginning to wonder if there's some genetic flaw at work here, but I'll check."

I heard the sound of him tapping on a door. "Your mom's on the phone. Can you take the call?"

I heard mumbling.

"He asked to call you back in about ten minutes. Okay?"

"Nah. Tell him not to bother. I was just checking in."

"You're okay?

"Just fine! Having the time of my life!" There was no way I was going to admit that my date with Tony was a dud. And what I said to Wesley wasn't a lie if you consider counting bathroom ceiling cracks a ton of laughs. "Gotta run now. Bye!"

I hung up before he could ask more nosy questions. The only thing worrying me was the point he made about the amount of time I seemed to be spending in bathrooms lately. I girded my panties—because I'm not sure if women have loins—and left the restroom.

A quick glance at my table assured me I'd killed enough time in the restroom for Tony to give up and leave without me. My tense shoulders relaxed. I headed toward the exit, only to stop in my tracks. Tension was coiled up so tightly inside of me that I felt like an over-wound spring. There was Tony, blocking the aisle, and a particularly harried-looking waitress.

Each time she tried to slip past him, he stopped her and made her look at another photograph from his nearly endless supply. At least he wasn't crying anymore but the waitress would be soon.

Carlos gestured at me from the restaurant entrance to get Tony outta here. Like I was his keeper? Hell, if it was a choice between me or the waitress, she was Kleenex fodder. I reversed in my tracks and headed for the kitchen and the rear exit.

Unfortunately, a group of angry waitpersons met me and I felt like Beauty's Beast during his run-in with the angry townspeople.

"You gotta get that guy out of here," one called.

I tried to back away.

"Stop her!"

Another cried, "Why the hell did you bring him here?"

Even Kurt joined in. "Out of all the restaurants in all the world, why did you have to bring him into mine?"

So much for my escape route.

I made a swift about-face, lunged for the photo Tony was about to force on the whimpering waitress, and said, "It's time to go."

"But—"

"No buts. I have to go home now." I grabbed his arm and dragged him to the restaurant entrance. Carlos was making get-lost motions with his arms and didn't seem to much care if Tony saw. I didn't much care, either. "And you have to go home now, too."

"You don't want to—"

Again I cut him off as I forced him out the door. "I need to check on my kid."

"Thanks for dinner."

Why was he thanking me? Oh, hell. "Did you pay the bill?"

"No. I thought you did." He started to go back into Patisserie, and I knew if he did I'd never be allowed to eat there again.

"I'll take care of it." I placed my body between him and the entrance. "Don't worry about it. Go. Home. Now."

"You sure?"

"Positive." I was never so positive about anything in my life. When I'd imagined the evening, I'd expected to at least get a free meal out of it, and now all I wanted was to take off my sexy, strappy shoes and go home myself.

"You never saw the rest of my pictures. Want to see them now?" He held out the stack of photos and I could have sworn it had grown taller by another inch.

I shook my head.

"You sure don't want to miss this one. It's one of Charlie dumping a bucket—"

"I've never been so sure of anything in my life. Good night, Tony."

"Night." When he leaned forward to kiss me, I turned my head.

"Well, I'll call you then," he said.

"You do that." And I'd be sure to screen all my calls. Caller ID would be my closest friend and confidant. After he walked away, I reentered Patisserie expecting the worst.

Carlos looked worried until he saw I was alone. "I thought you were going to stiff me, too. I told you the guy was a jerk."

"Actually, you said he was nice enough."

"Didn't I say that he's not your type?"

"True." I gave him my credit card and as I waited for him to process it, I wondered exactly what my type was. Should I give up on traveling salesmen? Was Tony representative of the type?

Surely not. There couldn't be two men with stacks of photo torture. I'd just have to be more selective next time.

CHAPTER FIVE

Dear Jill,

While I enjoy surveys as much as the next person, you can't quantify happiness, much less marital success.

When you walk down the aisle with a man, never forget the vows you'll make, to love him for richer or poorer, better or worse, in health and in sickness.

You have to mean those vows in order to have a successful and long-lasting marriage. Finding a particular type of man won't be a guarantee. Only your heart can make that pledge.

Best of luck to you.

Sincerely,

Caffee McGeintry

Bad dates are actually a good thing. If I say that enough, I might believe it.

Can you imagine what it was like in the days when marriages were arranged and brides rarely met or interacted with their future husbands before the wedding? At least with a bad date, you can rule a man out before vowing to stay with him through better and worse. Or should I say worser?

While I'd had high hopes for my traveling salesman, realistically, the odds were that the first horse out of the starting gate wouldn't be a winner. In fact, the odds, based on my dating history, pretty much indicated that my next good date would occur sometime around 2012.

That's not to say I hadn't been excited about the possibilities with Tony, because I had. I simply was relieved that I didn't have to live with him and his stack of photos.

So there I was on the street outside Patisserie, but 8:14 was wayyyy too early to return home from my *hot* date, especially since the world's sexiest teacher was likely still haunting my apartment. So I did what any healthy-minded woman would do. I called my dear friend Connie.

"Your date can't be over already?!" she exclaimed.

"It ended unexpectedly when Kurt kicked us out of Patisserie."

"Booted, huh?"

"Right on our asses. Wanna meet me for a drink and I'll tell you all about it?"

"Give me fifteen minutes and I'll meet you any-where. I have news, too."

This did not sound good. Her tone was somber. We quickly chose a bar not too far from her place.

Less than half an hour later, I had a Cosmopolitan in my hand and was doing my best to wash away mem-ories of my non-date.

"To think I nearly scalped my yaahaa for this? There's a good chance I'm permanently maimed."

"What happened?"

I waved my hand dismissively because the incident was still too painful. "An amateur bikini wax."

Connie grimaced. "Before or during your date?"

"Before. I'm not sure which was worse."

"At least he didn't pull out a digital camera and in-sist on capturing your moment together."

"I would have died."

Connie seemed a little distracted. She was staring off, zipping and unzipping her purse.

"Tell me your news," I demanded.

She began tearing her napkin into strips. "Mike is coming back to Vegas."

"Shit." Her thieving ex-husband, Mike, had almost done her in emotionally. The last thing she needed was for him to wedge himself back in her life or her daugh-ter's life, for that matter. I suspected he thought there was money in it for him. Maybe he was under the mistaken impression that his daughter was making the big bucks and would share?

Connie seemed to have some kind of homing device when it came to men, and it went both ways. Freeloaders sensed she was a sucker, but they were the type who most intrigued her. She'd be extremely wealthy today if she hadn't said, "What's mine is yours," to any number of men.

Mike was the worst of them. And Connie was still nuts about him. While I wanted a significant other, Connie seemed unable to achieve any kind of happiness without a guy by her side. She never dumped them—they left of their own accord whenever her gravy train ran out.

She still missed Mike, which says it all. And Mike is seriously bad news for Connie.

"Tell me you didn't agree to see him."

"Not exactly." Her gaze didn't meet my eyes.

"Then tell me what exactly."

"He wants to talk. He said he misses me and realizes the mistake he made by leaving me."

I made a Herculean effort not to snort, but wasn't successful. "There's nothing left for you to talk about except repaying the forty thousand dollars' worth of debt he left you."

"He's Rachel's father. I can't refuse to speak to him."

"You can. You should. And if you won't refuse, then I'll be happy to tell him to get lost for you."

"I'm a big girl. I can do it."

"But will you?"

Connie began tearing the napkin strips into tinier bits.

She'd been miserable after he'd splintered her life a second time. I wasn't sure she'd be able to cope with a third. "You know what happened, don't you? Why he's back now?"

Connie shook her head. She was hoping Mike's lies were true, that he couldn't live without her in his life. "He saw Rachel's photo on the cover of *Vogue* and figured his ship had come in. So he's returning to dock—your dock. He wants in on any action."

She pushed the napkin shards away. "You're probably right."

"What probably? You know I am. Has he ever paid the back child support he owes you?"

"No."

There had to be a way to get through to her. "Tell me this. Does he at least have a job?"

"He phoned from Seattle—can you imagine Mike in Seattle?—and said he had a lead on a job here."

Yeah, I had happy daydreams about him being in Seattle, or even Timbuktu—anywhere but in Las Vegas. Then it dawned on me what she had done. "Dammit, Connie, you didn't invite him to stay with you while he looked for work, did you?"

Her bottom lip trembled.

"You're a brilliant woman. Business savvy, articulate, and beautiful."

"You know what they say, lucky in business, unlucky in love."

"That is not what they say and you know it." I grabbed my cell phone. "Give me his number. You're going to call him and tell him he cannot stay with you."

"He said he'd have to call me. He doesn't have a phone."

"Screen your calls. Don't answer them. Then he'll go away and leave you alone."

Connie slumped with relief. I could tell she hadn't been up to dealing with him, but she could cope with the idea of simply not speaking to him at all. In fact, the silent treatment was the only way she'd been able to get over him the last two times when he'd disappeared with the last of her money.

Getting her mind off Mike might help. "How's Rachel?"

Connie smiled. "She's doing great and getting more work than she can handle. Can you believe it? My daughter, the supermodel."

"Mike hasn't tried to sponge off of her?"

"He probably would have, but her number is unlisted."

"There's an idea. Unlist your number."

Connie lifted her drink in a toast. "Here's to unlisted numbers."

છ છ છ

One-hundred and seventy-five dollars poorer from my dinner date, and with my shoes dangling from my index finger, I opened my apartment door with my mind made up after drinks with Connie. Salesmen, okay. Recently divorced men, not okay.

The room was dark, but my stomach sank when I heard a voice that was becoming increasingly annoying say, "You're home early."

"Where's Stephen? Why are you still here?" The lights in my living room were dim, but I made out the form of Davin Wesley sprawled on my sofa. Alone. Long-forgotten images from my youth, of my father waiting up for me, flooded my head.

"I decided I'd better wait for you to get home. Stephen's asleep."

My head shot up. Davin Wesley must still think I was a deadbeat mother. Just where did he get off? It's not like Stephen was a little kid. "You think my son needs a baby-sitter? He hasn't had a sitter for years."

"Can you keep your voice down? Stephen was sick earlier and didn't want to interrupt your date."

That took the wind out of my sails. Stephen had been in the bathroom when I'd called earlier. "Stomach?"

Wesley nodded as I headed for Stephen's room to

check on him.

"Don't disturb him. I just looked in on him and he's fine. Think the pizza upset his stomach?"

"It hasn't before." I sank onto the chair situated kitty-corner to the sofa. "He probably picked up a bug at school."

"That's probably it." Davin rose and stretched, his knit shirt drawing tight across the admirable male torso that housed a less-than-admirable personality. "I'll head out now."

"Thanks for sticking around until I got home." It was very nice of him to care about Stephen, despite the fact that he was even a control freak when it came to my son.

"It's good you had an early night. Bad date?"

"No. Long day." My dates, disasters or otherwise, were absolutely none of his business. I bit back a pretend yawn, hoping it would speed Wesley along.

He took the hint and headed to the door.

I thanked him for looking out for Stephen and, feeling extremely magnanimous, added, "Thanks for the lightbulb and faucet repair."

Davin's gaze furtively darted toward the kitchen then back to my face. His expression softened as he reached up and brushed a strand of hair from my eyes. "You're welcome."

I stepped away. His gesture was too intimate, but he was already walking down the hall.

"Night," he called back.

I locked the door behind him, then quietly snuck into Stephen's bedroom. After my night, I needed a Stephen fix. I needed the centering that looking at him always gives me. Connie had cheered up considerably by the time we parted, but my mood had taken a definite downturn.

Stephen's covers were rumpled at the foot of the bed and his hair was moist at his temples. Fever, poor lamb.

Not wanting to wake him, I gently pulled the sheet up to cover him and watched the gentle rise and fall of his chest with each of his inhalations. I loved watching him sleep and didn't think it was possible to love anyone as much as I loved my son.

When had we stopped being the closest of friends? When had we stopped talking? I was clueless about how to fix our relationship. Was adolescence the cause of our lack of communication? Or was it something I failed to do right or should have done but didn't?

His pediatrician had warned me years ago not to wake a sleeping child, not even to give him medicine, but seeing Stephen so feverish made me want to do something. Anything to let him know I was here for him and I cared.

I forced myself to leave before I did something foolish, like grab his face and cover it in kisses as I'd done when he was younger and uncomplicated enough to welcome it.

CHAPTER SIX

Dear Jill,

Ur survey rocks. My grandmother's got Alzheimer's, but I know how she would answer if she could remember Granddad's name.

She'd say: It's the little moments that count. Savor the little moments, the times U feel especially connected, because odds R, those R all U'll remember when U R old and have lost Ur mind.

Good luck with Ur surveys!

Luv 4evr,

Heather Thompson

The next morning I slept until seven, which is unusual for me since I generally get up while it's still dark. Although I'd planned to sleep until at least nine o'clock, I woke early thanks to nightmares about traveling salesmen chasing Stephen and forcing him to stay in the bathroom and Mandy jumping out of photo albums and insisting she wanted to be Davin Wesley's love slave.

When I puttered into the kitchen to make coffee, I froze in place when I saw the sink. My faucet now sported an ugly growth. I stepped closer. The maniac-fixer had installed some kind of water purifier!

No wonder he'd looked strange when I thanked him for fixing the faucet. Now he was controlling the quality of the water we drank! Men. Give them an inch and they'll take an entire football field. Argh!

After calming down and imbibing some caffeine, I spent the morning fielding phone calls. As I'd advised Connie, I screened my calls, but picked up when it was MaryEllen.

"How was your date last night?" she asked.

"It sucked."

"Did you know Mike's coming back to town?"

And another call from Susan.

"How was your date last night?"

"It sucked."

"Did you know Mike's coming back?"

I didn't pick up the next call, but listened to the

message on the recorder.

"Quit stalking me," said a male voice.

Nothing I'd done could actually be classified as stalking the Asshole Professor, could it? I suppose that breaking into his condo and his liquor cabinet might be construed that way. I thought of it more as skillet stalking.

While I didn't want to break into his home again, I wanted my effing skillet back. I haven't mentioned the other messages he'd left on my voice mail, primarily because a) I was humiliated that he'd figured out it was me who'd broken in, and b) I hadn't figured out yet how to deal with him in the future. One part of me wanted to pretend he didn't exist, but until I had my skillet in my hot little hands, that wasn't an option.

I could correspond only by mail—or maybe an attorney could send him a letter of demand? *Dear Sir, return Jill's skillet or face legal consequences. Signed, Katchum and Lynchum Law Associates*. But what if the lawyer wanted documentation of my attempts to get it back?

Preferring not to document breaking and entering, instead I pulled the pad of Post-its from my handbag and made a new phone log to record my attempts at skillet collection.

After writing down the date and time, I picked up the phone and dialed his home since he'd just called from his office, natch.

"This is Jill. I haven't been avoiding your calls. I've been busy. Please call me back. If I'm not available, leave a date, place, and time when I can collect my skillet. I need it back. Bye."

That hadn't gone too badly.

The next caller was Mandy.

"How was your date last night?

"It sucked."

"Good."

Whoa. That wasn't the reaction I expected. "What do you mean, *good*?"

"Oh, sorry. I wish it had worked out, but have I got a convention for you. It's teeming with cute salesmen, and it's right up your alley."

"This sounds interesting."

"It's a cookware convention!"

Since I was already skillet stalking, it seemed only reasonable to take it a step further and begin skillet salesman stalking. I fought back the urge to yell *cowabunga* as Stephen used to yell during his Mutant Turtle phase, but I settled on a fairly sedate, "Awesome."

"It gets better. The guy who sited the convention is local, single, and incredibly hunky. He's perfect for you."

"Does he look like Mel?"

"You won't believe this, but he looks just like Harrison Ford in his professor getup, right down to the glasses! His name is Aiden Campbell and you have to meet him!"

After we hung up, I grabbed a shower, careful of my faux-wax wounds. As I puttered out of the bathroom, I heard Stephen moving around his room. I poked my head in.

"How are you today?"

"All better."

Considering he was fully dressed and apparently about to head off somewhere, I certainly hoped that was the case. "Let me check you for fever."

My palm almost made contact with his forehead before he caught my arm and pulled it down. "I'm fine, *Maman*."

"Where are you off to?"

"Believe it or not, I'm going to the library."

This was music to my ears. Maybe Stephen was a late starter, but was he now prepared to seriously hunker down and get to work catching up his academic grades? "To the library to study?"

"Sorta. I'm looking up information on the two colleges Mr. Wesley mentioned at Target the other day."

The two extremely expensive art colleges he'd mentioned. I gulped. It must have been a big gulp since Stephen seemed to catch on to the state of my nervous system.

"Do you want me not to apply?"

"No. No. No. Apply."

"What if I get accepted? Can you afford it?"

"We'll cross that road when we get there. Somehow

I'll find the money." I had to. I was a good mother. Good mothers find a way to pay for the things their children need to set up their futures. "Speaking of Mr. Wesley, did you see what he did to the kitchen faucet?"

"Yeah. The water purifier?"

I nodded.

"I told him it was a great idea and that you'd love it. The water tastes good, too." Stephen grabbed his backpack.

Not wanting to admit I hadn't tasted it, except in my coffee, I returned to our previous subject. "Maybe you could apply at a state school, too? And consider a double major? Art and something that'll earn you a living until you're famous?"

I didn't want to discourage him from pursuing fine art, but having skills that put food on the table and a roof over your head is mandatory.

"I'm going to be an artist."

"Of course you are. But it'll take a while to make a living at it, won't it? And in the meantime, you'll want to eat—"

He cut me off. "Thanks for your faith in me. Not. You've never believed I can make it as an artist."

"You'll make it as an artist. I never said you wouldn't."

"What about last month when you asked if I really had to buy more canvases."

"That was about money, not art."

"Like an artist can work without anything to paint on? You don't want me to go to the best art school because you think I suck."

He stormed out of his room before I could formulate a reply. I followed him down the hall, feeling as if I needed to walk on eggshells. "You don't suck. You're extremely talented. Of course I have faith in you!"

Stephen pulled open the front door. "No, you don't. You think I'm going to starve."

"You won't starve. I'll always feed you."

Stephen snorted and banged out the door.

I whimpered. Somehow I always said the wrong thing. He'd actually been so upset with me that he'd dropped his Frenchisms.

How was I going to pay for an art school with annual tuition equal to my yearly wages? If I couldn't, Stephen would be convinced I had no faith in him.

The phone rang and I snatched it up. "Hello?"

"Your father feels he's been abandoned by his family."

The damn phone should have a special ring when it's a call from Mom. Maybe sirens. After my argument with Stephen, all I needed right now was more grief from my mother. I sank down on the living room sofa. "I haven't abandoned Dad. He's in prison"

"He thinks his family could at least visit him every so often." Mom's tone deepened. "He's thinking of changing his will."

"I haven't been to see him for the past week or two

because it's so depressing. It's not him, it's the whole prison setting."

"It's been two months, not two weeks. And what do you think it's like for him? Day in and day out of nothing but orange? You know that color never suited him." Mom coughed.

And I knew it was coming—The Guilt Trip.

"I thought I brought you up better than that."

"Okay. Okay. I'll visit him on my next day off."

"Have you called the warden yet?"

Guilty. Guilty. Guilty as charged. "No. I promise to do it right away."

"Don't forget, Jill. You're only as good as your word."

Shit. No one does guilt better than Mom.

"Your father is lonely." She paused to drive home the point that I'm an awful daughter who neglects her father.

I squirmed, as she planned.

"What are you doing now?"

I sought some excuse that would put her off. I couldn't visit Dad now. After wasting yesterday on date preparation, I had to do some serious housework, not to mention paying bills. I needed to scrub the toilet after Stephen was sick. Since Mom only understands food, though, I said, "I just put a batch of macaroons in the oven."

"Really."

"Uh, yeah." It wasn't a question. Curses. "Plus,

Stephen was sick last night, so I need to strip his bed and clean the bathroom."

"I'll come and help you get it all done, then. That way you can come with me at four o'clock."

"They let prison visitors in that late?"

Mom paused, and from her hesitance, I knew this was going to be a doozy. "Your father asked if you'd come with me and I assured him you would."

"Where?"

"Well. Your father and I believe it's important, our civic duty, to assist the needy and bolster various charitable causes. Because of our good fortune, supporting important causes is an obligation we cannot ignore."

She was in total Our-Lady-of-Society-Speech-Mode. It was hard not to snort. "I thought you do it because you like going to the parties?"

"That's a mere side benefit of knowing we are doing good in our community and for those less fortunate."

There was no point in bringing up the time when she asked my advice on how much to donate to assure herself an invite to the Platinum Charity Ball sponsored by the Friends of the Ailing Pigeons. Talk about an important cause. Yep, what the world needs is more healthy pigeons. "So what's tonight? It's a Sunday, so it can't be a gala event."

"Well."

Again the pause. Whatever she had to say, I knew I wouldn't like it. "Spill."

"Your father is being named Philanthropist of the Year by the Entomologists' Society for his work protecting an endangered species. I have to accept his award."

My mind stopped functioning at the idea of endangered bug scientists. What were they being saved from? Killer praying mantises? But it was nice they were honoring Dad. "Wow. That's great."

"Not really. They're only awarding it to him because they feel guilty over giving me the cold shoulder since he went to prison. Coldhearted biddies."

Whoa. "I thought they were your friends?"

"I'd thought so, too. Jill, I can't show up without emotional support. I need you."

"All you had to do was say that, Mom. Anytime you need me, you know I'll be there for you."

"You're a good daughter. I'll be over in half an hour to help you get things done."

Now I was a good daughter? I thought I was a father abandoner? "Make it an hour, Mom." I had a batch of macaroons to whip up before she arrived.

I entered the kitchen and grabbed a cup from a hook in the cupboard, then faced the water-purifying faucet. Expecting to hate the taste, I poured a tiny amount into the cup and brought it to my lips. Hmmm. It wasn't bad, even though I'd never admit it. Shrugging, I turned and got busy.

While I whipped up some macaroons, Stephen came home, but didn't say anything to me. I wasn't sure if he was still mad or merely sulking. Once the macaroons were cooling on the kitchen counter, I approached Stephen's lair with the goal of stripping his bed and asking him to come with Mom and me to the award presentation. Talk about walking on eggshells. I wasn't exactly sure how to approach the subject.

Stephen yelled, "*Entre vous*," after I tapped on his door.

"I need your sheets," I said as I came in the room. He was busy in the far corner, painting on a canvas.

"I'll help you." He plunked his paintbrush in a cup, then came around to help me remove his sheets.

"Painting, I see," I said as a conversational gambit. He must not be angry with me any longer. Whew.

"*Mai, oui.*"

And his French was back. "Are you in the throes of your muse, or is there any chance you can come out with Mom and me in a few hours?"

"Granmama is coming over?"

"*Oui*, I mean, yes. Your grandfather is receiving an award this evening and I thought you might like to come?"

"I'm kinda busy."

Should I push it? Mom would very much like him to attend and maybe it would give us a little extra time together. Since I'd learned guilt from The Master, I gave it a shot. "What about family solidarity and all that?"

"If you're going to make me, I'll come."

So much for my ability to emulate The Guilt Trip. Stephen saw straight through me. "I'm not going to make you." I shrugged. "I just thought it would be a nice idea to spend some time together."

We finished stripping the bed and, to make up for earlier, plus I really was interested, I approached his easels. "What are you working on?"

"Just a little project."

My brows shot up as I saw what he was doing. It was very impressive. On one easel, he'd tacked up an eight-by-eleven magazine reproduction of the *Mona Lisa*. On his canvas, he was painting the same woman, but with light, cheerful tones. To my untrained eye, it looked as if he was the original artist of both. "A school project?"

"Not exactly."

He took my arm and gently steered me to his door. "If you want me to come with you and Granmama, then I need to get back to work."

"Thanks, Stephen." I quickly bussed his cheek before he had a chance to duck. Within seconds, he'd disappeared behind his closed door, leaving me standing there with my arms full of bedding.

Just as I got the washer going, I heard the doorbell. Normally, knowing it was my mother, I'd hide in the bathroom. Answering the door to her was the lesser of two evils since I hadn't yet cleaned it.

"Hey, Mom."

She gave me an air kiss on each cheek, then shot me The Look as she entered the living room.

"What's the matter?"

"You've got something wrong with your eyes?"

"There's nothing wrong with my eyes." I glanced in the mirror and didn't see anything wrong. "I'm fine, Mom."

She tsked. "You've been crying."

"I haven't been crying! I'm fine."

She gazed up and down my figure, coming to rest on my midriff. Okay, so maybe I should have skipped the biscotti.

What is it with mothers? Mom can never start a normal conversation. She has to find *something* wrong. Speaking of which, I chased behind her as she rushed through my apartment while imaginarily white-gloving the dust on my furniture.

Fortunately, she had thoroughly disinfected my bathroom within seconds of her arrival.

Unfortunately, my self-esteem reached a new sublevel. Evidently my eyes were as swollen as my waistline.

∾ ∾ ∾

Did I mention that my mother doesn't drive? She has a driver to take her to all the places she needs to go to keep up her public image. Nathaniel has worked for her for years. He seemed really old when she first hired him around the time I was twenty. I kept worrying he'd have a stroke or something while toodling her on her jaunts around town. Twenty years later, he looks totally unchanged; just as old and decrepit as back then, but not a day older, either. I've long since decided he is either an Immortal or his appearance is extremely deceptive, because he certainly is very spry. I once saw him lift a one-hundred-and-fifty-pound suitcase full of lead weights that my mother kept referring to as party supplies as if it were as light as a poker chip.

That evening, Stephen was seated in the front with Nathaniel, chatting about Dumas, while Mom and I sat in back. Mom's face appeared pinched and a little pale. It was a no-brainer that she was worried about this particular ceremony.

"Maybe you could call and say you caught Stephen's stomach bug and can't attend?"

"No, dear. That wouldn't be right. It's my duty to be there to accept your father's award. Besides, it'll serve those vultures right. They don't believe I have the balls to show up."

My mother had said the word *balls*? And not in reference to tennis? My, oh, my, the world was changing. I wasn't sure I could deal with this new, strong mother who was emerging. It totally altered my worldview. "Why don't you send me or Stephen up to get it, then?"

"That would be cowardly. No one can say that Zelda Morgan has ever been afraid to face the music. I promised your father and I keep my word." She smiled and squeezed my hand. "Knowing there are at least two friendly and loving faces in the audience will get me through it."

"I'm incredibly proud of you."

Again she smiled, reminding me of the *Mona Lisa* smile that Stephen had so recently reproduced.

Within a few minutes, Mom's Town Car pulled up at the country club.

I'd like to be able to say I had suspicions about my mother's motives, but that wasn't the case. As we entered the country club ballroom, I was more concerned about my mother and her reactions than I was observant.

She led us to a table near the front of the room, where her once-dear friend, Gail Brooks, was seated beside a middle-aged, and particularly unprepossessing and unattractive man. Gail and Mom did the air kiss thing, so maybe she wasn't one of the vultures? Mom didn't seem self-conscious as she introduced us to Gail's son, Jeffy Brooks.

"Nice to meet you." I offered my hand as I was taught before I'd reached kindergarten. He was even less attractive up close than he was from a distance, with a receding hairline, stomach paunch, and wearing what I suspected might have been a 1980s leisure suit.

As Jeffy stood to greet us, Mom quickly slipped into his chair, knocking him out of the way with a not-too-graceful hip butt. "Why don't you young people find a place to sit at the back of the room? I'll sit up here with Gail because it'll be easier to make it to the stage when they announce William's award."

I looked at Mom. She stared back with a firm jaw.

I glanced at Jeffy, then back at her again.

Calculation lit her eyes.

I knew I should have locked myself in the bathroom rather than answer the door to her. My interfering matchmaker of a mother had done it to me again.

And there was no way to get out of it this time, because Jeffy was smiling at me as if I was a nearly naked woman jumping out of the cake at a bachelor party. ARRRRGGGGHHHH.

ↄ ↄ ↄ

"And then Jeffy told me all about his Beanie Baby collection. Even Stephen thought that was extremely peculiar and nixed my idea of introducing him to Stormy."

There's something about sharing life's foibles with my best gal pals that makes everything more right with my world. I feel more captivating, like my life has substance, after talking events over with them. And vice versa, of course.

Let's face it. I'm a forty-flipping-year-old divorcée whose life is boringly filled with bills to pay, worries about my kid, a job that no longer floats my boat, and tales of increasingly awful dates. Like me, do you ever fight an urge to stand up and yell, "When does it get better?"

Our weekly cocktail night allows the four of us to feel amusing, as if our life is interesting to someone other than our mothers, and gives each of us a reason to get up the next morning and keep on keeping on. That night we'd chosen a fern bar close to Susan's home. I know. Fern bars are so 1980s, but there's something comforting about all that plastic greenery.

I took another sip of my cocktail, this time a deliciously biting vodka sour, which I know is no longer trendy, but considering my level of ripeness, I feel perfectly justified saying, "Screw trendy."

MaryEllen turned to Connie. "Have you heard anything more from Mike?"

"He called once. I didn't answer. He hasn't called since." She sounded sad and it broke my heart for her.

"That's great news. Maybe he won't try to steal you blind." I touched her hand, wanting to comfort her. "You did good."

"I know I did the right thing, but I'm so effing tired of being alone, of everyone in my life leaving me. If it weren't for you guys, I wouldn't have anyone."

"We're not going to leave you, Connie," said Susan.

"We love and adore you. I love and adore all of you."

After a round of toasting each other, Connie still didn't appear to be feeling any better.

"You guys are great, but I want sex. I want intimacy. Mike may not stick around, but when he's in my life, I get both in spades."

"But is it worth the cost?" I asked tentatively. It wasn't my place to argue with her, yet she needed someone to help her clarify the situation.

"Maybe it is. Maybe that's the only way I can have both." She pushed back her chair. "You'll excuse me. I have to go. Errands to run, that kind of thing."

What errands could she need to do at this time of night? I got up to go after her, but Susan stopped me, saying, "No. I'll talk with her."

The rest of us left shortly afterward, and I don't know about the others, but I was feeling somewhat philosophical. Maybe Connie was right. Maybe you have to be prepared to pay in order to find happiness and decide how much it's worth to have your needs met.

တ တ တ

When I got home, Stephen was sprawled out on the sofa mainlining Brady Bunch reruns. Since he is an only child, he longs for the chaos and social dynamics of a huge family. I feel vaguely guilty for not providing one, but am self-aware enough to know I'd go insane in a family like that.

"You're not painting?"

He grinned. "I finished. Want to see it?"

"I'd love to."

As we entered his bedroom, I noticed he'd turned the easels around to face the door. I stopped in my tracks. My kid did this? This brilliant, perceptive, gorgeous painting of a woman so like *Mona Lisa*?

I was proud, right down to my painted toenails, but I couldn't figure out how his father and I had somehow merged to create such a talented and, dammit, perfect human being as Stephen.

"You don't like it," he said, due to my extended silence.

I'm not usually quiet for so long, but his talent was overwhelming. "No. I don't like it. I love it. I'm awed by it. I'm . . . I'm struck silent."

It seemed to be the right thing to say (Yes, it's on record, I said the right thing for once in my life!) and he positively glowed.

"Are you entering it in an art show?"

"Mr. Wesley wants me to, but I'm not sure yet."

"He saw it?"

"He came over when I finished."

Great. Wesley had been here tonight and racked up new ammunition to sling my way about being an absent parent. I wanted to ask if Mr. Butt-In-Ski fixed anything else while he was here, but didn't want to piss off my kid.

I studied Stephen's rendering of Mona and wondered if she, too, worried about her mothering skills or if they came naturally to her. Something about the lines around her eyes told me she'd understand. "If you enter the painting in a contest, it's a sure winner."

"Could be."

He stared at his work, distracted, and appeared to be battling with some inner demons. I'm intimately familiar with inner demons, so I didn't push.

"This weekend I have to go visit your grandfather, but otherwise I don't have plans. Want to do something just the two of us?"

"I'm kinda busy and waiting to hear back from a friend about a project we're doing together. Plus Saturday is Stormy's night."

"Sorry. I forgot he'd switched nights this week."

"She called and asked me to remind you. That reminds me. I almost forgot. You had a couple of phone calls."

He pulled a pad of paper from his nightstand.

"Jeffy Brooks called. When I offered to take a message for you, he asked if I wanted to come see his Beanies."

"I hope you told him no!"

"I told him my mother didn't allow me to date older men."

It took me a second—okay, a full minute—before

I realized that was a joke. He was expecting me to rise to his bait and ask about his inner woman. So I didn't. See? I'm learning. "Ha ha hah," I laughed. "Who was the other message from?"

"*Le Dickhead.*"

"Stephen, I'd prefer it if you don't talk like that."

"I don't talk like that unless it's appropriate. Mom, even you have to admit *dickhead* is an understatement."

I nodded agreement. *Le Dickhead* was Stephen's endearment for the Asshole Professor. I should have listened to my son. "What did he want?"

"Something about his new girlfriend having your skillet." He consulted his notes. "Barbaretta loves your skillet and doesn't know it's yours. It'll take a few days to pry it loose from her. Call next week to arrange a time to reclaim custody."

"What a dickhead." I couldn't believe he'd given *my* skillet to his bimbette. My neck muscles tensed. Blood rushed to my face. Fury coursed through my arteries. My hands fisted. *Calm down, calm down*, I told myself, not wanting to go postal in front of my son. Besides, I needed to save the fury, bottle it up, so I could unleash it on the Asshole.

"You said *dickhead*." Stephen tossed the pad on his bed.

Once I controlled my spiraling anger, I managed to calmly, very calmly, placidly, in fact, remark, "I really want my skillet back. Why does this have to be so hard?

Do you know any thugs or Mafia types?"

"No thugs." Stephen laughed. "Tom's parents are in a custody battle, too—but over Tom and his little brother. At least you and Stormy didn't do that to me."

"I'm glad you appreciate that fact." I moved in for the kiss, but he dodged it. That's the problem with kids: they quickly catch on to your tricks.

"Don't get mushy on me, *Maman*."

Perhaps our relationship wasn't too bad? Maybe it was normal to have moments of intimacy mixed with days of noncommunication? I'm not sure, but I embrace every morsel of intimacy he tosses my way and suspect I always will. My son. My world. The ganache on top of the 2,310 identical petit fours of my life.

CHAPTER SEVEN

Dear Jill,

The advice I'm about to share with you wasn't covered in your survey, but I'm a proponent of paying it forward, and feel it's my obligation to share the secret of a happy marriage with you. I hope you'll share this advice with other young women down the line.

On my wedding day, over fifty years ago, my mother-in-law sat me down before the ceremony to have a little chat about the birds and the bees—or so I thought.

What she told me has since been the theme of several best-selling books and numerous romantic comedy movies. Yes, I'm talking about manipulating the man you love.

Whether it involves husband training along the lines of a dog manual, using sexuality and answering the door in the nude to make your man obey your bidding, or whatever new spin on this age-old standby, the bottom line remains the same.

The way my mother-in-law explained it to me is that it's a woman's job to make the decisions. It's also her responsibility to make her husband believe he is the one making the decisions.

Thanks to my dear mother-in-law, whose advice I took to heart, my marriage has been immensely successful. Henry, God bless him, has never had an inkling who truly wears the pants in this family.

It's worked perfectly for me and I do hope you find it works for you, as well.

Sincerely,

Prissy Jones

Every midafternoon, I seem to hit a sugar low. Or maybe that's when my self-control is at its weakest. All I'm certain of is that three o'clock usually finds me searching for Big E. Not that he's exactly hard to find. But he knows it's time to cough up something high in fat and even higher in carbs.

My chef's whites were even more decorated with the day's menu than usual because the Future Vampires of America had their convention at La Papillon that week. I'd been having difficulty with the faux blood and desperately needed a shower. En route to the pastry chef's domain, Mandy snagged me.

"You gotta come now."

Intent on my upcoming sugar fix, it wasn't easy to change my course. "Where?"

"The Classical Cookware is having its reception right now. I want to introduce you to Aiden Campbell."

"Give me fifteen minutes to change."

She shook her head and crossed her arms. "There's no time to spare. He might leave."

"I can't go looking like this. I'm covered in faux blood!"

Mandy grabbed my arm and yanked me toward the elevators. "You look great."

I so did not, but I patted down my hair and hoped it didn't look as awful as I feared, because Mandy on a mission was impossible to stop.

Once we arrived and acclimated ourselves to the crowded ballroom, Mandy pointed toward a man at the far end of the room. "There he is."

Okay. She likes nerds, but her taste can't be this awful? "The man by the lectern?"

"Yeah. Isn't he great?"

I bit back a request for her to define *great*. The man she indicated was about five feet, five inches tall, assuming he wasn't wearing lifts, three -hundred pounds, and wore a squirrel on his head. Honest. It was either alive or had to be the worst toupee ever created. "I thought you said he looks like Harrison Ford."

"His eyes look like Harrison's."

Since the little man's back was to me, I couldn't check out his eyes. But my gaze was transfixed by the squirrel. Was it hoarding cocktail peanuts? I kept expecting it to move.

The man chose that moment to do a little moving of his own. He turned, giving me a view of him from the front.

But my gaze wasn't drawn to his eyes. He wasn't wearing a tie and his shirt collar was open, revealing enough hair to reforest Somalia. Either that, or the squirrel had lost his tail. All in all, he reminded me of a Mini-Me version of the abominable snowman—without the snow.

After a sustained shocked silence, I finally moved my gaze up to take in the little man's eyes. They looked more like Igor in Gene Wilder's *Frankenstein*. "When was your last eye exam, Mandy?"

"Last month." Then she realized I was giving her a hard time. "What's your problem? Come on, let's go meet Aiden."

She began making her way toward him. I trailed her, wondering if she'd forgive me if I slipped out the service door. "Don't you think he's kind of short?"

"Short? He's over six feet tall— Oh. Not the short guy. Behind him. That's Aiden."

Whoa. The man in question was tall, fully muscled in all the right places. Better yet, no animal headgear. Mandy was right. Aiden did resemble Harrison Ford, back in his early Indiana Jones days. Wowwie.

Best of all, his eyes met mine as we approached and he looked at me like he thought I was as hot as he was.

"Hey, Aiden. This is Jill, the one I told you about," said Mandy, with a flourish of her hand in my direction.

"You didn't say nearly enough." He gave me the kind of look every woman recognizes as *interested*. *Very interested*.

Cute, sexy, and interested? What more could a woman ask for in a traveling salesman? I wanted to fall to the floor and grab him by the knees in gratitude. Instead I shot him a similar leer. "It's a pleasure to meet you."

"The pleasure is all mine." He addressed Mandy,

"Why didn't you tell me about Jill's dazzling smile?"

So what if it was a line? It was a great one! Probably the best I'd ever heard and light-years ahead of the clichés most men toss around like dirty underwear.

I'm not even going to mention the women who fell for the lines in order for them to become clichés. Aiden was *refreshing* in that he didn't talk about my eyes, how sexy I was, or my legs. A dazzling smile implies more than good looks. It suggests personality.

"What kind of cookware do you use?" he asked.

"Classical, of course." It was true. The hotel used Classical and I had a number of their products at home.

"Beauty and brains!"

His smile did something to my knees, making them wobble.

"I hear you're talented, too," he said.

"Very." I grinned wickedly. "Want to— " I was interrupted mid-flirt by Big E, the pastry chef, who seemed to interrupt me quite often lately.

"Jill, thank God I found you. You're needed in the kitchen." Big E twisted his hands with worry.

"I'm off the clock." Dammit, I finally found a guy who might be Mr. Right and couldn't bear an *interlude interruptus.*

Big E lowered his head to my ear level and whispered, "We need you."

"I'm busy." I turned back to Aiden. "What's your

favorite Classical product?"

As Aiden started to answer, Big E shifted around. "You gotta come now."

I waved my hands for him to go away.

"SOS. 9-1-1! Emergency!," hollered Big E.

"Is there fire, blood, or broken bones?"

"All three."

He grabbed my arm and began pulling me away from Aiden and Mandy. I wasn't about to let Aiden get away, though. As Big E dragged me bodily away, I called to Aiden, "Come to my house for dinner Saturday night? I'll cook."

"Love to." He ran to catch up with us and handed me his business card. "Call me and we'll arrange."

"Great," I called over my shoulder as Big E continued his caveman antics, removing me from the Cocoon Ballroom and my dream salesman.

"This had better be serious, Big E."

"It is. A Fed is here. Chef Radkin is holding him at bay."

"A Fed?"

"An INS agent. Spooking the staff."

Shit.

We neared the kitchen and I heard Radkin calling out, "You'll soon be walking the plank, you skullduggerous blackguard."

Double shit. What the hell was Radkin up to? He sounded like he'd been hitting the bottle again, like that was new. My stomach clenched.

We came to a screeching halt behind the INS agent, who stood in the kitchen doorway. I leaned forward to see what the hell was going on.

Radkin was holding the agent at bay, all right. With a butcher knife that Miguel had sharpened earlier. In his other hand, Radkin was holding a large stockpot lid like a shield.

He directed the line cooks, "Men, toss the booty overboard!" He shouted at the INS agent, "You'll not get my pirate's treasure!" Then, like a movie swashbuckler, Radkin brandished his butcher knife. Overhead fluorescent lighting sent a chilling gleam down the knife's steel tip.

I tapped the INS agent's shoulder to get him to step aside, then slipped between him and Radkin. The chef smiled when he caught sight of me. The kitchen staff behind him looked extremely relieved.

"What's going on?" I asked.

"'Lo, Ms. Morganstern."

I sighed since there was little point in correcting him about my name right at the moment. The knife in his hand caught the light from overhead and gleamed dangerously.

His smile turned into a pout. His lower lip trembled. "The men are mutinying."

I scanned the kitchen and while I saw signs of fear, I didn't see anything to indicate mutiny. "What makes you think that?"

"They want him"—he gestured toward the agent—
"to lead them. The plank's too good for him!"

I caught the agent's eye, and it appeared he was
about to leap at Radkin. I shook my head for him not
to, letting him know I could handle Radkin. The agent
seemed to get the message. That was when I noticed
Mandy and Aiden had come up behind the agent and
Big E, having followed me from the ballroom.

Perfect. Just perfect. I made a shooing motion at
Mandy, thinking she'd get the hint to get out of there,
but she ignored me and instead sent me an okay gesture
with her right hand. Aiden smiled *his* dazzling smile
and I wanted to curl up in a fetal position. The last
thing I needed was an audience to Radkin's insanity.

I spun and glared at the kitchen staff. None of
them would meet my eye. "Which one of you failed to
lock up the sherry?"

Miguel looked sheepish and I knew it was him. I
schooled my expression to something more placid and
faced Radkin, wishing Davin Wesley was here because
he was welcome to fix *this* mess. Everyone appeared to
be waiting for me to do something, so I thought fast.
"Your men aren't mutinying, they're merely stunned by
your leadership."

I didn't know what else to say, but wanted to calm
him and get him to give me the knife. Maybe if I played
along with his delusion something would occur to me.

"The men are extremely loyal to you. Did you ask this gentleman for his papers or documentation?"

Radkin looked confused. "No. He's a scoundrel. A cur. A miscreant. Probably on Napoleon's payroll. His papers are likely forged."

I gestured to the INS agent. "Give me your badge."

He slipped it from his coat and handed it to me.

"As I thought," I cried melodramatically. Would Radkin go along with this, I wondered and figured it depended on exactly how much sherry he'd imbibed. "Our boss, the king of Estovennia, personally vouched for this man."

I showed Radkin the badge. Hell if I knew whether his fantasy ran to kings or queens. If he was stuck in the Napoleonic era and knew a lot of historical facts, there wasn't much chance my plan would work since I'd slept through that week of world history class. But it was the only shot I had at calming him without calling in Security. "Look, this is his royal seal of approval!"

"Oh! I see! I see! Why didn't you tell me?" he chided the agent. "If you'd mentioned the king, why, I'd have welcomed you with open arms!"

Since he still had the knife in his hands and was waving it drunkenly, being welcomed by his open arms didn't hold much appeal.

The INS agent hung back and I wondered if he packed heat. For an instant I felt like an actress on a cheesy TV program talking about someone carrying a gun. But there was nothing about this situation that reeked of camembert.

"Men," Radkin bellowed. "Prepare a feast to welcome the king's own man!"

Once it became clear the INS agent was about to get past the chef, the entire kitchen staff, Miguel, Juan, Jose, and all the others skedaddled out the back door.

The agent attempted to chase after them, but Radkin blocked his path, yelling, "Lily-livered, yellow-bellied vermin!"

"Don't worry, Radkin. They've probably gone to get feast supplies. And speaking of feasts . . ."

"Yes, Ms. Morganstern?"

"I need that knife to slice the royal majestic beef in preparation for the feast."

"S'right."

He handed me the blade, which I carefully put away, out of his reach. I hoped he wouldn't search out another weapon; the kitchen was filled with sharp objects. "If you'll come with me to your office, maybe we can discuss the menu?"

"Very well."

Careful to protect my boobature, I gestured toward his office and he scampered past me, then stopped near the office doorway.

"I'll be there in a sec, Radkin. Let me instruct Big E on the pastries we'll need."

He nodded happily and toddled off.

"I'm sorry," I said as I returned the badge to the agent. "Big E, please take care of him while I handle Radkin."

The agent did not look happy, but considering what had transpired, I didn't expect any better. He said, "Your chef is insane. Perhaps a call to the police would be in order?"

I looked at Big E. "Call Security and have them alert detox."

Mandy stepped from behind the agent. "I'm the catering manager. Why don't you come with me to my office where we can wait for Jill to join us after she's finished here?"

Thankfully, he appeared to be appeased as they headed off together. Mandy has that effect on most men.

"Well done." Aiden patted me on the back. "You were magnificent."

I opened my mouth to deny his compliment, but Radkin popped out of his office door with the stockpot lid still in his hand.

"Ms. Morganstern. Are you ready to get started making babies?"

CHAPTER EIGHT

Dear Jill,

I've enclosed my answers to your survey and I'm glad I completed it. It really got me thinking about life, marriage, men, and families.

Frederick is my second husband. I had a very short and very passionate first marriage. Here's what I learned: having *no* man is much better than having a bad man. I'm not saying my first husband was a criminal or anything. He was simply bad news for me. On the surface a man may seem perfect, but that doesn't mean he'll be the perfect mate for you.

Life with my second husband is peaceful, makes me feel good about myself, and he truly loves me as I am. My wings have been free to spread in our relationship and I think that's what every woman needs more than the passion and more than a perfect man.

No matter how suitable he seems, don't be so anxious to find a man that you make a poor choice for yourself.

Happy man hunting,

Virginia Banks

A short time later, the INS agent had departed, Chef Radkin had been carted off, and I'd thrown four roasts into the oven.

I was too busy to allow myself the time to worry about Radkin. While I was genuinely concerned about his alcoholism, nothing seemed to help for any period of time.

We had a like/annoyed relationship rather than love/hate. He was extremely talented when sober. As his disease progressed, my annoyance with him seemed to increase, as well. Since he was in a stupor half the time, I had to handle not only my job responsibilities but his, as well, and I had been doing so for some time—without the benefits of money or promotion.

I'd tried cajoling him and guilting him, but an addict of any type simply isn't going to change until he's ready. Radkin had hit bottom, and it scared me, but maybe it was a good thing. Hitting bottom might provide his best chance at conquering his fondness for the bottle.

Addiction to both drugs and booze is common in the food service industry. I think it's because we get our highs by operating on an emergency level during working hours. We work our asses off, as quickly as possible, to get well prepared meals to customers, despite inevitable problems. Our bodies crave the adrenaline high, and some crave it 24/7. Radkin was like that.

No matter how concerned I was about him, there were still three more banquets to be served without any kitchen staff to prepare them.

Did I mention operating at an emergency level?

The good news was that Aiden hadn't yet bailed and seemed inclined to assist me. The bad news was that while he knew the names of the cookware, he had no clue how to use it.

I couldn't very well serve only bread, raw meat (sushi, anyone?), faux blood (if there was any left), or pastries to the four--hundred--plus people waiting for food. I had to feed them something and I needed help. Since my choice seemed to be begging for assistance from Housekeeping or Security, and neither was a great choice, instead I called Kurt at Patisserie. Having worked with me at the hotel, he was familiar with the kitchen and besides, when he left, he took half the staff with him. "Help."

"Have you forgiven me yet for kicking you and your date out?"

"No. You owe me." I quickly filled him in on the situation and begged for help.

"I don't owe you that bad," he said dryly.

"I'm desperate here."

He made an exasperated grunt that I knew was the sound of capitulation.

"You're going to help me, aren't you?"

"I can probably spare a couple of guys and Nikolai has a brother looking for work."

"Thank you. Thank you."

Twenty minutes later, two cooks and Kurt himself arrived, along with Carlos, who, while a maître d', knew his way around the salamander.

I grabbed Kurt and hugged him fiercely. "You're a lifesaver."

"Shut up and lead me to Fang." Kurt never was comfortable with anything the least bit touchy-feely.

By the time we finished dishing up, I turned to check on Aiden, but he'd disappeared. "Where is Aiden?"

"The cookware salesman?" asked Carlos.

"Yeah?"

"He left about an hour ago."

Damn.

"You dating him, too?"

"Instead." I could only hope Aiden still wanted to go out on a date with me after everything he'd witnessed. "Or hoping to."

"Just don't bring him to Patisserie, *capisce*?"

ↄ ↄ ↄ

There are times in a woman's life when she's obligated to do things she doesn't want to do. A few days later found me in that exact situation.

Attending a baby shower.

Want to strike fear in the heart of a woman over forty who's a) not pregnant, or b) not expecting a grandchild? Mention a baby shower and excuses will start flying.

When Susan's thirteen-year-old daughter, Jordan, insisted on throwing her mother a baby shower, we all tried to get out of it. But Susan begged nicely and promised booze. Lots of booze.

Susan kept her word about the booze. About a dozen very ladylike, nicely dressed women were seated in her stylishly decorated family room, daintily eating cake from colorful paper plates, pretending to enjoy themselves, and gulping down the punch. When I tried a sip, I wasn't quite sure what was in it, but I guarantee it packed a wallop.

However, Susan did *not* keep her word when it came to our demand for "No games!" It wasn't entirely her fault, because a teenage girl on a mission to throw "the best shower ever" can't easily be deterred.

Sadly for me, I was the designated driver and couldn't drown my misery in the kick-butt punch. Other than Susan and Jordan, I was the only sober woman in the room when Jordan first suggested some game about naming baby parts, and it probably sealed her fate as far as Connie was concerned. She quickly nixed the idea.

Jordan began guiding the group through a drunken update to Pin the Tail on the Donkey called, brilliantly, Pin the Diaper on the Baby. Unfortunately, the party revelers were *not* behaving themselves; they were attempting to one-up each other on the funniest placement of the diaper.

"Mom," said Jordan between giggles. "Your friends are *sooo* weird."

She was laughing *at* us, not with us, and I didn't blame her. It's not a pretty picture being one of the few sober people in a room filled with drunks. I suspected I'd have nightmares for years to come about women trying to pin diapers to baby heads.

When it was Connie's turn for diaper pinning, she was blindfolded as expected. However, after Jordan spun her around, I feared Connie would get sick because she staggered, ahem, drunkenly. Rather than going after the baby poster with her thumbtacked diaper, her orientation was off. Either that or she could see through the blindfold.

With her hand stuck out, pointy thumbtack foremost, she homed in on Jordan.

The teenager screeched and jumped back before Connie's thumbtack hit its target. Connie lunged at her again. Then all hell broke loose, with lots of giggling and screaming, as Jordan fled and Connie began chasing her through the family room, into the kitchen, into the formal dining room, and back into the family room.

Next Connie went after MaryEllen and a woman from Susan's husband's office. Paper cups and plates, napkins, and bits of cake went flying. Women who had previously been on their best behavior amazingly turned into hollering hoydens. They were hopping, leaping from chairs, and running for cover. I tried to escape to the bathroom, but three women had barricaded themselves inside, beating me to safety.

When I turned back to the family room, it looked as if the contents had been tossed into a mixer—puree de furnishings. How had things so quickly gone from exceptionally polite and well mannered to soooo very wrong?

Baby shower gone bad.

Connie's attention had returned to Jordan. Connie managed, legs akimbo, to corner the teen near the TV in a corner of the family room. Jordan escaped by ducking down and crawling between Connie's legs.

As Connie spun to find her next victim, Susan grabbed the thumbtacked diaper from Connie's outstretched arm, ending the inebriated version of semi-musical chairs and squealing guests. Susan announced, "It's time for me to open presents!"

Everyone sighed with relief and took up positions around her for gift unwrapping. After all the packages were opened, Jordan's need for a baby shower was appeased, and the other party revelers departed.

The Baby Swimming Group was seated in Susan's kitchen while Connie and MaryEllen polished off the last of the punch.

Susan handed me her list of gifts with the names of the givers on it and asked me to check it to see if it was fairly accurate since MaryEllen had written it while under the influence.

I couldn't read it. I pulled it closer, and it was still blurry. I held it farther out and it became more clear. In, out, like a trombone.

"Looks like you're a candidate for reading glasses," said Susan.

"Welcome to age forty, when your body parts start to wear out," said Connie.

"Here," said MaryEllen, pulling a gadget out of her bag.

She handed me a lighted pop-out magnifying lens. It worked and MaryEllen's list only needed a few clarifying notes, but I was not thrilled.

Being forty flipping years old pretty much sucks, except the alternative sucks even more.

"One of Jordan's games sounded interesting," said Susan.

"You're kidding, right?" Connie gulped more punch.

"It's where each person writes down one piece of advice for the mother-to-be."

"I know what advice I'd give," said Connie. "Next time don't forget the birth control."

"I know what I'd zay." MaryEllen, who'd misplaced her esses again, chipped in, "Epidural. Itz the only way to go."

My mind, however, had fixated on the telephone

conversation I had with the prison warden before the shower, the call my mom made me make. "My advice is to avoid phones."

"Good heavenz, why?" asked MaryEllen as I handed her the magnifier.

"Okay. Make it avoid calls from my mother. Hell, just avoid my mother entirely."

"What's she done this time?" asked Susan.

"She nagged me until I called the warden about her insane plan for fiftieth wedding anniversary photos."

"I think it'z zweet." MaryEllen carefully folded up the magnifier and slipped it back in her bag.

"Do you think it was sweet of the warden to coerce Mom into using his son-in-law as the photographer? Evidently he's tired of supporting his daughter and son-in-law while he struggles to get a photography business off the ground. The warden feels a society sponsor would make his son-in-law's business blossom."

"So he's going to allow the photographs? That'll make your mom happy."

"Yeah. He's even going to allow Dad to be fitted for a tux—kind of. The guard will do the measure-ments while the tuxedo tailor looks on and gives him directions from the other side of the window."

Connie cracked up. "I'm picturing what'll happen when your father's inseam is measured."

"Oh, Gawd." I noticed the kitchen clock behind MaryEllen's head. "It's getting late and I have to get to work early tomorrow. I'm dreading it."

"Why?" asked MaryEllen.

"Radkin went off the deep end. It's going to be really hard, but for once I have a great opportunity for advancement. I seriously want his job."

"It would be perfect."

"Yeah," said Connie. "You've been doing his job for a long time."

"Kurt's going to be jealous. He left and started his own restaurant because there wasn't room for advancement. His loss, my gain. So I've got to work my tush off to show my boss that I'm ripe for advancement."

"I don't get why you haven't left, too," said Mary-Ellen.

"The shorter hours and big staff make it easier to be a single mom. Plus the health benefits."

"You couldn't start your own restaurant like Kurt?"

"You know how broke I am. It's just not doable, even if I only kept the place open the hours I'm available. I still need to be there for Stephen." I liked working in a huge hotel with a lot of staff. The predictability of a shift, and the shorter hours, made it possible for me to juggle parenthood with working for all these years. "It's my chance to let hotel management see that I'm up for the job. It's the opportunity I've dreamed about."

"With the way you've been doing Radkin's job anyway," said Susan, "they'll finally know it's you who's been keeping things running smoothly."

"Good luck," added Connie, grabbing her purse. She headed toward the exit and we all followed. "We're all rooting for you."

We walked out the door and Connie added, "Knock their socks off, babe."

Susan had come in her own car, but I'd driven MaryEllen and Connie. I dropped MaryEllen off first since she lived nearby, then headed for Connie's place.

As I pulled up in front of her home, the fixture at the door cast enough light to reveal someone sitting on the porch step.

"Oh, God. Oh, God! It's Mike. Keep driving," said Connie, sounding as if she was hyperventilating.

I did as she asked and pulled to a stop a block down the street, wondering if there was a paper sack in my trunk if Connie needed it.

"I can't believe Mike is here. What am I going to do?" Her breathing slowed somewhat, although even in the dim light I could see her hands shaking.

"That was Mike? Are you sure it's not some home-less person?"

"He *is* a homeless person. Did you see the huge backpack beside him? He's brought all his worldly goods! Shit."

This was serious bad news for Connie. "Here's what you're going to do. You'll spend the night at my place. You can have the bed and I'll sleep on the sofa."

"I'm not going to put you out that way. I'm a grown woman. I should be able to handle this."

"But can you? It's asking an awful lot, no matter how mature you are."

"I can't believe the jerk showed up without calling first."

"He should have known when you didn't call him back that he wasn't welcome."

"How the hell did he find my place, anyway?"

"Maybe the Internet?"

Connie babbled as she angrily straightened her clothes. "Okay. I'm ready to tell him he's not welcome anymore. Drive back around."

"Are you sure?" This couldn't be a good idea.

"Absolutely. Until I tell him to get lost, he's going to keep coming back. I'm not going to allow him to keep me out of my own home."

I wasn't sure she was ready, though. He'd done a number on her twice before. Was she prepared to confront him again? "Let's practice what you're going to say."

"I'll say: *Get lost. Go away.*"

"That's good for a start. But he's always been able to talk you around."

"There's nothing he can say that'll change my mind." Her jaw was squared and her lips tightened with resolution.

"If you're sure."

"Positive."

A few minutes later I parked in front of her place. The engine noise from the Animal woke Mike, who stood up, waiting for us.

I didn't like the smarmy expression on his face. She needed me there as backup. "I'm coming with you."

Connie shot me a worried smile. "Thanks."

She hitched her handbag over her shoulder as she stalked up the walkway to her home. I quickly scrambled out of the Animal and sped to catch up with her.

"Remember," I said. "Start with *get lost*."

Nodding, and with a serious expression on her face, Connie reached the landing where Mike stood waiting.

He grinned hugely, making the hair stand up on my spine. Yuck.

Connie opened her mouth to tell him to go away, when Mike made his move. He grabbed her, bent her over slightly backward, and laid one hell of a kiss on her.

I have to tell you that, as I watched them, I wondered what the hell I'd been missing in the bedroom if the front porch could be this steamy. No wonder it was difficult for Connie to deal with him. I honestly don't think I've ever personally experienced that much animal magnetism and, if I'm totally honest, passion.

It was depressing. That damn kiss went on and on, too.

I rubbed my shoe toe against the back of my leg, wondering what to do and whether I should interrupt

Connie and remind her she was supposed to be getting rid of Mike, not welcoming him with open arms and tongue lock.

I stepped closer and that was when Connie made her move. She opened her front door, pulled Mike inside with her, mouthed, "Sorry," at me, and slammed the door in my face.

Geez.

This was not on the program.

I banged on her door. "Open up!"

The door didn't open, but I heard Mike yell, "Get lost."

That was what Connie was supposed to tell *him*! Unsure what to do next, I stood there for a few seconds gathering my wits. There was no next action on my part. Stomping back to the car, I couldn't see what I could do to help Connie other than calling the police and reporting a prowler. Somehow, I didn't think she'd appreciate that.

Instead, I headed toward home. When I stopped at a traffic light, I realized the red light and my mood were in accord. Thinking about Mike hurting Connie made me see red. Sometimes men can be such jerks.

It seemed a pity to waste all this pent up anger at men, and at two men in particular: Mike and the Asshole Professor.

I wanted my skillet back. I wanted it now. I headed to his townhouse. It wasn't that late, only just past ten o'clock, and with any luck, I'd disturb him right after he'd gone to bed. I admit I was in a mood.

When I pulled into the parking lot, I elected to leave the Animal running as I pursued skillet collection. I knocked on the door.

Yeah, yeah, yeah. I didn't knock. I banged.

I yelled, too. "Open up and give me my skillet!"

He opened the door seconds later. "Shush. You'll wake the neighbors."

I just hate it when people use that shushing tone of voice with me, and it didn't help that it was the Asshole Professor. "Screw the neighbors. Just give me my frying pan and I'll be on my way."

"I told you, I don't have it."

Why was he giving me such a runaround? The skillet was mine. He had it. He should give it back. "How can you not have it? I left it here."

"My girlfriend took it."

That's not the only thing of mine she'd taken, but it certainly was the most important. She could have the Asshole P, but I wanted my skillet. "What's her address? I'll go get it from her."

"You'll wake her up."

Wrong answer. I pulled out my cell phone from my pocket and flipped it open. "What's her number?"

He eyed my phone. "I thought you cancelled your cell phone."

"I changed the number."

"What's your new number?"

"Get real. Why do you think I changed the number?"

"Why do you have to make everything so difficult?"

I started to argue back, but shut my mouth. This was just what he needed to justify having dumped me for Betwitna.

After controlling my temper, I asked, very nicely and politely I might add, "May I please have your girlfriend's phone number?"

"No."

"Her address?"

He slammed the door in my face. I was really and truly getting tired of this slamming-doors-in-my-face thing. I settled for heading back to my car and phoning the Asshole Professor from behind a locked car door. Naturally, I used call blocking to protect my new number. He answered on the first ring.

"Please. I need my skillet."

"I'll get it by next week. When and where do you want to meet?"

My mind worked fast because I didn't want to see him ever again. "My schedule is chaotic right now. Radkin's out and I'm filling in. Can you drop it off with the bellhop at the hotel? By Tuesday?"

"Make it Thursday."

"Now look who's being difficult. Fine. By Thursday.

Noon." Why hadn't I noticed what an ineffectual jerk he was before he dumped me? I snapped the phone closed, put the Animal in gear, and headed toward home, with only three goals in mind: a) My skillet, b) college tuition, and c) taking off my shoes. Was that too much to ask?

CHAPTER NINE

Dear Jill,

It was a pleasure to meet you yesterday and to see your cute smile firsthand. I'm looking forward to dinner with you on Saturday. After watching you in action at the hotel, I'm certain to be impressed by your culinary talents.

Not wanting to be trite and send you dead flowers, I decided this cookie bouquet is more fitting. The fact they are baked on Classical products is an added benefit.

Fondly,

Aiden Campbell

Running errands is a necessary, and usually dull, part of a woman's life. While not always possible, having company during the running here and yonder makes it more enjoyable. I came up with what I think is the perfect solution: cell phones.

As I ran my errands, including a necessary visit to the grocery store to pick up items for my dinner with Aiden, I chatted with Susan, who had *come with me*, digitally speaking, on my cell phone. "I think I'm in love."

"You've barely met him," Susan said.

"So?" I grabbed a head of cauliflower and tossed it in my shopping cart. "What other guy would send cookies spelling out *Looking forward to dinner with you*? One word on each cookie!"

"Sounds desperate to me."

"That's your pregnancy hormones talking. You should see Aiden. No way this guy is desperate."

"I wasn't talking about him."

"Very funny." I grabbed a box from a nearby display. "What's the fat content of dessert crackers?"

"How would I know? I'm eating as much fat as this pregnant body can hold. Read the nutrition information."

"Ha. I tried. The print's way too small."

Susan made a humph noise. "You need reading glasses."

"Well, I'm fresh out of 'em."

"Go to the pharmacy department and get a pair."

"Ah. Good idea." I pushed my cart to the in-store pharmacy and deliberately avoided the leg wax display on an end cap. I'd barely healed since my last encounter with the stuff. Faux leg wax ought to come with a warning: *Apply at risk of life and limb.*

It didn't take long to find a spinner rack with all sorts of reading glasses. After checking out the selection, I was a bit disappointed. "Most of these look like something my mother would say was too old for *her.*"

"Keep looking. I'm sure you'll find a pair that isn't too awful."

"Oh, this pair looks cute. It folds up to the size of a pencil stub."

"Try them on," said Susan. "I adore those collapsible glasses. Do they come with a little tube to put them in?"

"No, but there's a little case thingy." There was a tiny slanted mirror at the top of the rack. When I stood on my toes I could see my reflection. I stuck the phone between my ear and shoulder, tilted my head to keep it in place, then slipped on the glasses. It was hard to assess how they looked from my odd angle in the mirror, but they seemed small, almost unnoticeable if you were as blind as I was becoming.

I glanced at the nutrition guide on the dessert cracker box in my cart. "Perfect. I can see again."

"One problem solved."

"Only two-hundred thirty-seven more to go!" Which reminded me. "Did you ever reach Connie?"

"No. Voice mail."

"Me, too." That was the moment I saw Davin Wesley squeezing the Charmin. Wanting to avoid him, I immediately about-faced my shopping cart. "Ack," I whispered. "Stephen's nutso teacher is here."

"Go hide in the feminine products and he'll never see you."

"Good thinking." I headed in that direction. "Are you as worried about Connie as I am?"

"Well, I called her office and learned she called in sick today. I hope she's okay. I can't believe she let Mike in the door."

"I'm pretty sure she's okay for now. Considering the intensity of their kiss, I'm surprised she was able to stop long enough to call in to work." Perspiration broke out on my brow and I wondered if it was sympathy sweat.

"Mike's going to break her heart."

I hoped Aiden wouldn't break mine as I picked up a box of tampons and read the label. The reading glasses were awesome. I then grabbed a box of condoms. Just in case.

I was feeling more and more uncomfortable. The grocery store was unnaturally warm. By this time I was reasonably certain that I'd hidden from Wesley long enough not to meet up with him, so I removed my sweater as I wheeled my cart toward the frozen food aisle. Since I generally freeze along with the food items in the freezer aisle, I was sure I'd feel better soon.

"You're probably right about Mike breaking Connie's heart," I said. "But we can't be sure he hasn't changed. Maybe he meant what he said about leaving her being a mistake?"

"We're talking Mike here, Jill. Lowlifes like him never reform."

"Good point." I was so hot I began fanning my collar, hoping for a breeze as I approached the dairy section. Frozen food was just up ahead and I felt desperate to reach it. Was I coming down with something? Had the air-conditioning in the store gone on the fritz? "I'm just hoping I'll have as much fun with Aiden as Connie is probably having with Mike right now. Geesh. It's hot in here."

"Maybe you're getting all worked up over the idea of s-e-x?"

"I wish. No, I'm perspiring. It started at my hairline and worked its way down my face. I feel like I'm experiencing a nuclear meltdown. I'm even sweating under my new boobs!"

"Hmm. Could be premenopause. Have your periods been regular?"

"No," I grunted as I bent down to snag a carton of Häagen-Dazs Dulce de Leche ice cream (my idea of pure heaven) from the freezer bin. Although my reading glasses worked perfectly on the ingredient list, I deliberately chose not to read the calorie count.

"Have you been irritable?"

"What do you think?"

"Are you sleeping well at night?"

"I get up a lot."

"When did your mom go through menopause?"

"Hell if I know. Is that what you think this is?"

"Jill, it sounds like a hot flash to me."

"I'm too young!"

"I've heard of women going through the change as early as their mid thirties. You're not too young. It runs in families."

"All I know, Susan, is, if this is a hot flash, I might spontaneously combust!"

"Ask your mom and maybe call your—"

I didn't hear what Susan had to say next because that was when I heard Wesley's voice. "Hot flash? I know what to do about it!"

I caught a glimpse of him from the corner of my eye. The next thing I saw was a frozen okra label smashed against my nose. My head had been dunked into the frozen food bin.

I came up sputtering. "You jerk! What the hell do you think you're doing?"

"I thought I was helping. If you bend back in there-—"

"What are you, some mad Mr. Fixer of My Universe?"

My hand searched my face and I cut him off. "I lost the reading glasses!" I bent back to look for them and found them squeezed in between the boxes of broccoli and the bags of rutabaga. When I grabbed them, one of the arms dangled drunkenly. "You broke them."

"I'm sorry. I was trying to help you."

"You're going to help all right. These aren't my glasses. They belong to the store. And now you get to help by paying for them!"

"I'll pay for them and for a new pair, too."

"You bet you will."

"Jill? Jill?" I realized Susan was still on the phone, which was also in the freezer bin.

I snatched up the phone. "Sorry, Susan. I'll call you back."

"Everything okay?"

"Fine. Mr. Wesley was just showing me how to overcome hot flashes by wading through frozen food bins." I snapped the phone closed and stuck it in my pocket.

Wesley pulled something from my hair. "The temperature setting must be off."

"I *knew* it was hot in here."

"I didn't mean in the store, I meant in the frozen food bin. The food isn't as frozen as it should be." His expression was guarded, as if he expected me to snap at him. I was wondering why he expected me to do that, when he pulled something else from my hair.

"What *are* you doing?" I felt all trembly as I pulled away from him. Had to be another menopause symptom. It could *not* be because of Wesley.

"If you hold still, I can get all the corn out."

"Corn?!"

He reached for me again, and I retreated behind my shopping cart.

"Corn's stuck in your hair." He pointed at the bin and I saw there was corn scattered around where a box had come open.

"I can't believe this. First you try to freeze me and now you make sure I have to shampoo my hair again before my date."

"You have a date?"

"Does that surprise you? You're the one always accusing me of being a party girl. I have a date. Sue me. I'm cooking dinner for him, so don't come over tonight. Stephen is at his dad-- Stephen is with Stormy."

A muscle clenched in his jaw. "I never said you were a party girl, but I do owe you an apology."

I agreed that he did, but it seemed churlish to say so. Besides, even I was thinking my attitude was somewhat bitchy. Did Susan mention irritable?

Maybe it was menopause. Maybe it was Wesley. Maybe I'm just a bitch.

"I didn't mean to imply that you're neglecting Stephen. He explained the other night that you've rarely dated. That's why I was surprised you had another date so soon."

"Like, who would ask me out?"

"No. Like, I'm making a mess of this." He looked down for a moment and seemed to gather his thoughts. Or maybe he was looking at the box of condoms I was self-consciously aware of in my shopping cart?

"You're very attractive. I just thought maybe you weren't much into men because of the number your ex did on you."

"Oh." He thought I was attractive? At least he didn't mention the condoms. "Well." I cleared my throat while shifting the Häagen-Dazs carton in my cart to cover the condoms. But just in case— "I *am* into men. Or at least salesmen. The ones who travel."

"You're kidding, right? Salesmen?"

I should have known we couldn't have a real conversation without him making fun of me. "Just forget I said anything."

I began wheeling my cart away, but he grabbed the cart and held out his hand. "Your glasses?"

I tossed them back into the freezer bin. "Forget about them."

"I said something wrong again, didn't I?" He pulled the glasses from the freezer bin, then looked at me with an unreadable expression. Almost like he really wanted to know what I had to say.

"Either you think I'm a loser or you feel sorry for me. Neither is good."

"I don't think either of those things." He brushed more corn from my hair. "I admire your strength. You don't let anything or anyone get you down. And it doesn't hurt that you're also sexy."

My jaw dropped.

"I always seem to say the wrong thing when I'm around you." This time I had no trouble reading his expression. He looked confused. "I'm not usually this way. Usually people like me. Think I'm a nice guy."

"Well." I wasn't sure what to say, but he appeared to be waiting for me to comment. "We don't know each other very well."

"Maybe that's a mistake."

I thought about him dunking me in the freezer bin. I thought about Aiden and how right he seemed for me. "Maybe it's not."

"Why? Afraid I'll break more glasses?"

I was afraid of lots of things, but broken glasses weren't one of them.

Every instinct in my body warned me not to let that on to him.

What made it difficult for me is that Davin was actually a very nice guy when he wasn't behaving like a member of the Spanish Inquisition. He was thoughtful and very sweet.

But sweet doesn't pay the bills. Sweet doesn't cover college tuition. And while sweet is fun to play with, it tends to cloy if it sticks around too long.

"I'd better run," I said, hoping to make my getaway at last.

He reached forward, smoothed my hair, and tucked a curl behind my ear.

Oh, Gawd. He *was* nice. I quickly headed my cart away from him. Broken glasses were so the least of my worries.

CHAPTER TEN

Dear Jill,

I don't imagine your survey respondents will be frank enough to tell you the true secret to a successful marriage.

One word.

Viagra.

Yours truly,

Gracie Pine,

DDS

P.S. Good dental hygiene doesn't hurt, either.

Preparing food is one of the delights in my life. I love cooking. I love the feeling I get, as if I'm nurturing through nutrition.

Aiden seemed like a meat-and-potatoes kind of guy, so I decided to make one of my standbys for dinner, prime rib.

My recipe is incredibly simple. I smear the roast on all sides with margarita salt, freshly ground coarse pepper, and dried cilantro, then stick it in the oven with a little foil over the top. The salt melts into the roast and takes the pepper and cilantro flavoring along with it.

To add a little Southwestern flair, I made my own version of Yorkshire pudding, which I call Vegas Pudding. I substituted one-quarter of the required flour with cornmeal. I like the texture, it doesn't rise as much as the Yorkshire version, and when I add drippings from the prime rib, the cilantro gives it zing.

A fresh salad and Chocolate Pots de Crème completed the menu. All are easily prepared in advance and very impressive when served.

I was excited while waiting for Aiden to arrive. I'd prepared so much ahead of time that I wasn't quite sure what to do with myself until he arrived. Stephen was at Stormy's, I had gotten all the corn out of my hair, dinner was ready to be served whenever I wanted, and my apartment was as clean as it had ever been.

I set the table with my best stemware, dishes, and candles, which I'd light just before serving our meal.

All I needed was my date.

I checked the clock. Aiden was four minutes late and I hoped he wasn't the fashionably late type. As far as I'm concerned, parties are time-optional, but not dinner dates. Even dinners with built-in holding patterns don't keep forever. The phone rang and I jumped to the conclusion it was probably him, calling to cancel.

Wrong.

"Hello," I said in my best sexy-throaty-voice.

"Are you coming down with a cold, dear?" said Aiden, with my mother's voice? I held the phone away from my ear, wondering what had gone wrong, then realized it actually *was* my mother.

Damn. Why was I paying for caller ID when I always forgot to check it? "I'm not sick, Mom. I'm just busy."

"It's Saturday night. What are you busy doing?"

I didn't want to mention my date because she'd start planning my wedding, which is why, thank God, I had the foresight never to introduce her to the Asshole P. "I've been cooking dinner."

"That's nice. You've got time then, to discuss my anniversary photos." My mind wandered as she rattled on about how brilliant I was for talking the warden into doing my evil bidding and, "Blah, blah, blah . . ."

I wondered if I should have mentioned I had a date, after all, because then perhaps she wouldn't have launched into one of her monologues. I concentrated on making "Uh-huh" noises periodically, while I went to check on the prime rib to make sure it was still warm and not blackened.

Mom was in midyammer, and I was getting ready to ask her about menopause, when the doorbell rang.

"Mom, someone's at the door, and I have to go."

"What? I thought you were alone."

"Not anymore. Dinner plans." I started to hang up, but remembered. "Oh, Mom, how old were you when you went through menopause?"

"Um . . ."

By this point, Aiden had progressed to knocking on my door.

"I think around forty," continued my mother. "The doctor said it was unusual to start so early, but not abnormal. Why do you ask?"

"Hang on, Mom." Shifting the phone to my shoulder, I unlocked the door and opened it.

Aiden was sooo cute, wearing jeans, a snug, dressy T-shirt, and carrying a stuffed teddy bear and a bottle of wine.

"Hi!" he said as I signaled for him to come in.

"Is that a man's voice?" asked my mother in a scandalized tone, although why she felt there was anything more than mildly titillating about her forty-flipping-year-old daughter having a dinner date was beyond me. Did she believe I was unable to find a date without her help? "Gotta go, Mom."

I clicked off the phone and closed the door behind Aiden.

"You look great," I said.

"So do you, and something smells just as good."

Time to 'fess up. After my mom confirmed my worst menopausal fears, and after the way my body had begun falling apart, I was relieved that Aiden thought I looked okay, and there wasn't some huge neon *M* (for *menopause*) flashing on my forehead.

We headed to the kitchen where he placed the bottle of red wine he'd brought on the counter, then handed me the stuffed bear. "It made me think of you."

It was really cute.

"Press the button," he instructed.

I did as he asked and the bear jiggled while playing "Wild Thing." "Too cute."

Things were going swimmingly and I was starting to calculate all his assets.

A) He looks *really* good.

B) He likes my dazzling smile. (I shot him another dazzling smile for good measure.)

C) He's got great taste in wine—I knew because I'd peeked and checked the label.

D) He gives cute gifts.

All he had to do was pass the audition and I'd have a winner, assuming I passed whatever tests he had in mind for me.

"What's for dinner?" he asked, while doing an air

putt—like a golfer's swing—in the middle of my kitchen.

My brow furrowed. "You're into golf?"

"Yeah. There's something about yelling, 'Fore!' that gets my juices flowing. Do you play?"

"I never had the opportunity," I said, then explained the menu. He grinned with pleasure.

"Why don't you have a seat at the table while I open the wine?" I indicated the dining room.

He nodded and proceeded to the table. When I stuck the corkscrew in the wine bottle, I noticed he'd stopped in front of the decorative mirror that ran along one wall of the dining room.

I continued opening the wine, but as I poured it into goblets, I realized he was still at the mirror.

He was making different faces at his mirror image—surprise, sexy, intrigued, sad.

Ah, hum. How cute.

As I carried our wine into the room, I saw him making an exaggerated scared expression.

Odd. Very odd.

He saw me in the mirror reflection and smiled, then turned around. "I do impressions."

"Cool. Who do you do?" I asked as he took another air putt.

He stopped midswing and looked at me as if I was a total ditz. "Harrison Ford, of course."

"Oh." Since he resembled him, that wasn't too surprising. "Who else?"

"Just Harrison Ford."

I swear he said that in all seriousness.

"Oh. How nice." I handed him his glass and hoped my incredulity didn't show on my very not-a-poker face. "Here's the wine."

"Let's have a toast."

I held up my glass to clink against his.

"To new relationships."

That was a nice thing for him to say. I added, "To new friends."

We each took a sip. So I'm thinking that maybe Aiden's a little different, but none of his foibles were enough to take away from his assets, either. I lit the candles on the table. "Have a seat while I bring in the salad."

It was while I was bringing in the second course that I realized he could still see himself in the mirror and was continuing with his Harrison Ford impressions every time I left the room. This was getting past the foibles stage and heading directly into eccentric territory.

As he bit into the prime rib, he looked like he'd found heaven. "This is incredibly wonderful."

"I'm glad you like it." Actually, I love it when someone praises my cooking, so I sort of glowed under his attention.

"I'll get dessert," I said as we finished our main course. Taking both plates to the kitchen, I paused, wondering if it was me or if Aiden was decidedly nuts.

Surely these were just little flaws, the kind of thing that annoys you a bit, but not the type that drives you away entirely? Sort of like squeezing the toothpaste at the wrong end or leaving the toilet seat up?

I was still very attracted to Aiden, and he was very successful according to Mandy, so he couldn't be *that* nuts. I added a few toasted almonds to top off the Chocolate Pots de Crème, then returned to the dining room.

He took one bite of dessert, then said the exactly perfect words to redeem himself. "This has got to be the best meal I've ever had in my entire life. You're brilliant."

I love praise, so sue me. Nothing can butter me up more than flattery. And Aiden's kind words got me in the mood to get started with his audition.

I stood and began gathering dishes to take to the kitchen and Aiden pitched in to help, too.

"I'll dry if you'll wash," he said.

I filled the sink with hot water and bubbles, then Aiden grabbed the dishwashing liquid and added a little more.

"I like bubbles, don't you?" he asked in a bedroom voice and my knees nearly buckled with longing. How could he seem so weird one moment and the next seem so incredibly sexy?

The kitchen felt very homey and cozy while we worked our way through the dishes. As we finished, Aiden leaned over the sink, gathered a dollop of suds on his finger, and dabbed it on my nose. "That's more like it."

I removed it with his towel. He leaned forward and kissed me.

You can tell a lot from a man's kiss. Some kisses tell you that you're just friends, some say the guy's not certain about you, other kisses say they want to be much more than friends.

Aiden's kiss said: *Wow! I'm totally into you.*

My arm wound itself around his neck and we smooched some more. Then he gentled his kiss and stepped back.

He was a skilled kisser and I wasn't ready to stop. "Something wrong?"

"No. Very right."

"But?"

"The kitchen counter is digging into my right hip," Aiden groused.

"Want to go in the living room?"

He nodded. As we left the kitchen, he wrapped his arm around my shoulders. "Your kissing is as good as your cooking. Are you sure you're available?"

"I'm positive." I laughed. "Guys aren't exactly banging down my door."

"Stupid guys." We took a seat on the sofa and he gazed into my eyes. It was one of those soulful gazes. You know the kind I mean, where you feel like you're looking directly into his heart?

However, that was when Aiden noticed the mirror over the TV set. Then he started with the damn impressions again.

"Check this out." He pointed to the mirror. "Don't I look just like Harrison Ford when he's angry?"

"Spittin' image." Wanting to get his attention back on the subject of us and off Harrison Ford I said, "I never knew salesmen could kiss like you."

He continued his facial antics, but commented, "Oh, I'm not a salesman." He made a brooding face at his reflection. "Nope, left those days long behind me."

He wasn't a salesman? Shit. "But I met you at the Classical Cookware sales convention!"

"True." He turned back to gaze into my eyes and I was wondering what his job now was, when he gave me a bedroom look.

Even if he wasn't a salesman, maybe he'd be gone a lot? A girl could hope. Visions of being a golf widow danced in my head. The only problem was that golf wouldn't take him away from home for three weeks at a time. "So, do you travel a lot?"

"Not as much as I used to. I've finally gotten to the place where I choose when, where, and with whom I travel. I've reached my business goals and realized I'd been neglecting my personal goals. Right now I'm looking to settle down, find the right woman, and . . ." He kissed my nose when he said that, but I didn't find it nearly as admirable as I'd found his caresses earlier. "Plant roots, you know?"

Plant roots? What did he mean by that? "Are you

planning to buy a house?"

"I already own a great place. You'll love it."

By planting roots, he couldn't mean . . . "You mean, have kids?"

"Yeah. You've got a toddler, right?"

"I have a son. Stephen's seventeen, not a really a child anymore."

"Where is he? I'd like to meet him."

"He's with his other mother," I said, still trying to process the fact that Aiden was not a salesman, didn't travel a lot, and wanted to start a family. I was way past the point of wanting babies!

It might seem shallow, but I'm ripe, not desperate. Don't get me wrong, I wouldn't want to live life without my son, but just as assuredly, I didn't want to start playing Mommy again at my age. I needed college tuition, not day care expenses. I was ready for fun and a little freedom from the responsibilities of parenthood. Dammit, I wanted three weeks off, followed by a week of sex so hot it melted asphalt. That and my son's education financed.

"Steps can be a pain, can't they?"

I must have looked at him with confusion, because at first I didn't know what he meant, then realized he thought Stephen was with a stepmother because I'd mentioned him being with his other mother.

Aiden evidently misinterpreted my look to mean I was asking if he'd ever been married. "Not that I know from personal experience, but my sister has to deal with her ex-husband's new wife all the time."

He made another face at the mirror and I slowly pulled away from him. This wasn't the time to explain about Stormy. Talk about splashing cold water on any lurking libido I might still retain. If there was any chance of a future between us, I'd have taken the time to explain about Stormy. Without a reason, though, it would merely be a waste of words. It wasn't likely there would ever be a time, either.

The good news was I didn't have to get kicked out of a restaurant to figure this out.

The bad news was I wasn't sure how to get rid of Aiden.

"My sister's children are great," he added. "Most kids are really cool."

"They are." Let me digress for a moment. Sometimes little white lies aren't so bad. Sometimes lying is the most polite way of getting out of awkward situations. Actually, I'm always guilt ridden over the tiniest of lies. It's not something I do often or ever do well. Between the golf swings and impressions, I wasn't sure this guy's pilot lights were all burning. A little white lie suddenly seemed the right choice—and the only sane one. And so it was that I lied through my teeth. "I'm sorry, Aiden. I really like you, but I can't have more kids."

"We could adopt?" He looked at me hopefully.

I shook my head. Sometimes white lies work, and this one did.

We chatted for a bit, but he seemed uncomfortable. At last he said, "Sorry, but I should be heading out now. Got an early morning."

He gave me another kiss, but this one didn't jingle my nerve endings as the first one had.

"You sure about the kids?" he asked, rising from the sofa.

"Certain."

He nodded. "Want to have sex anyway?"

"No, thanks." I led him to the door and opened it for him.

"Thanks for the incredible dinner."

The nice thing was Aiden didn't tell me that he'd call, because we both knew he wouldn't. We parted amicably because neither of us had expectations the other didn't. He took another air putt and I felt genuinely relieved that I'd never have to go out with him again, not even on a mercy date.

And I did a little air putt of my own.

CHAPTER ELEVEN

Re: Marriage Survey

Dear Ms. Storm,

Who put you up to this practical joke? One of the inmates at the state pen? If my ex-husband had anything to do with this, then you're an accomplice in violating his restraining order.

Do not communicate with me again.

Lucy Baker

When you have children, there are certain things you know you're signing on for, such as middle-of-the-night feedings, potty training, and the terrible twos. However, there are some things other parents never mention, probably because misery loves company and they don't want to scare potential parents off.

These items include the impossibility of communicating with a teenager, functioning as a prison guard when it comes to homework, and the item that most bothers me as a single mother, the fact that I no longer have possessions. My teenage son thinks what's mine is his and what's his is his.

It's not hard to understand why I wandered around that morning, with my hair in a towel, aimlessly searching my apartment for my missing blow-dryer. What had Stephen done with it?

I was looking beneath the sofa cushions when the phone rang.

Connie's name came up on the caller ID. I yanked up the receiver. "Have you been avoiding my calls? Are you mad at me?"

"I'm not mad at you."

"So you're merely avoiding me."

Connie sighed. "Do you want to do brunch or not?"

As far as invitations go, it was particularly ungracious, but Connie wouldn't do better so there was no point in razzing her. "Brunch it is."

We agreed on a time and I hung up the call to the sound of my front door opening.

"Hey, kiddo. You're home early from Stormy's," I said to Stephen. His friend Tom, a gangly computer geek, came in, then headed straight to the kitchen and began looking through the cupboards.

Following, I asked, "Busy with something?"

"*Oui.* Tom and I are working on a project."

"Stormy doing okay?"

"*Bien.*" He rolled his eyes and opened the door to the pantry. "Are we out of olive oil?"

"Is that what you're looking for?"

"*Oui.*"

I went to the spice rack and pulled out the olive oil, noting the items they'd piled on the counter: two eggs, a cup of milk, some leftover Vegas Pudding from my date the night before—and a potato???

"*Merci beaucoup.*"

"What are you cooking?" I asked Tom.

"We're not cooking," he said. "This is for our project."

"Science project?" I couldn't think of any other type that would require food because I knew he wasn't taking any home ec or cooking classes.

"Sorta," replied Stephen as he and Tom headed to Stephen's room.

Tom snickered as if Stephen's reply to me was funny, raising my maternal antenna. "You're not making drugs with that stuff, are you?"

Stephen stopped and turned back. *"Non."* He didn't look guilty.

"You're not using drugs?"

"Only if you consider lead paint pigment a drug."

I eyed the blue spikes on his head. "You're not using it on your hair, are you?"

"Non."

"Then I guess the lead paint is safe?" I glanced in the refrigerator, wondering if I'd been distracted enough by dinner preparations yesterday that I'd accidentally put the blow-dryer in there.

"I'm careful."

"Good." The dryer wasn't in the fridge or the pantry or the bathroom. "Do you know what happened to my blow-dryer?"

"I borrowed it. Sorry."

Stephen ran to get it. I met him halfway as he came out of his room. When he gave me the blow-dryer, his guarded expression puzzled me. He and Tom were obviously up to something.

I tried to see past him into his bedroom, but he was tall enough to block my view. All I could make out was Tom looking at something on an easel. Obviously whatever they were doing involved "art," so they couldn't be up to much trouble. "Connie and I are going out for brunch. Do you and Tom want to come with?"

"No time. Tom's only got a couple of hours to help me before he has to go home."

"Too bad. By the way, I also couldn't find my pumice stone . . ."

"Um, I used it. Just a sec."

He came back a second later with the pumice. It had been ground down to a mere shadow of its former stonely shape. "What did you use it for, sanding furniture?"

"I needed it to smooth out a canvas. *J'ai regret.*" His eyes darted furtively.

"What is going on, kiddo? Did something happen at Stormy's last night?"

"Nothing's going on and nothing happened at Stormy's. And before you ask, I don't have an inner woman aching to break out."

"Fine."

He went back to his bedroom, closing the door loudly enough to be heard, but softly enough not to qualify as a slam.

Unsure what I'd done wrong, I returned to the bathroom with my unpurloined items and finished getting ready.

A short time later, Connie rang the bell and I let her in. I checked her face for signs of stress or tears thanks to Mike, but she looked great. Better than great. She was glowingly happy. It didn't take an advanced degree to figure out that she'd given up abstinence since Mike's return.

She jiggled a tote bag filled with flyers and

booklets. "This is for Stephen."

"What is it?"

"He asked for information on France and some French museums."

"He never mentioned it to me." Since Connie's a travel agent, it made sense that he'd go to her.

"Well, he called my office a couple of days ago and it was no bother."

"That's really nice of you." While I was pleased he'd had the gumption to ask Connie for help, to say I was surprised that he'd done so without telling me about it was a vast understatement.

I tapped on Stephen's door and told him Connie was here. He came out, saw the bag in her hand, and his eyes lit up.

"Here you go," she said.

"*Merci*." He took the bag and looked inside, grinning at what he found.

"I threw in some stuff on Italian art museums, too. Just in case it might interest you."

"*Merci, merci*."

"You're welcome. Any time."

"You ready to go?" I asked her.

She nodded.

"Okay. We're off." I told Stephen where we'd be, then Connie and I headed out.

As we walked to the car, I said, "You look great."

"I feel great, too." Connie did a little spin. "I'm

so happy."

"Mike?"

"I think he really means it this time, Jill. He's out right now, looking for a job."

"What's he looking for?"

"I suggested something in sales, but he thinks it would be fun to do retail. He's over at the mall, going store to store and putting in applications."

Mike had never been much of a go-getter, except when it came to separating Connie from her money. He'd get it, then go. So this was a huge departure from his past behavior. "I hope he finds something quickly."

"He's so good with people, I wouldn't be surprised if he's hired on the spot." Connie's voice lowered. "He said that without me in his life, there just wasn't anything to live for, anyone to aspire for."

Now that sounded more like the Mike I knew and detested. How anyone as smart as Connie could fall for his sweet-talking, smarmy lines was beyond me. I kept my lips zipped.

"I know what you're thinking," Connie said as she punched the button on her key ring that unlocked her car doors.

"You do?"

"You're thinking that Mike's just going to hurt me. Maybe you're right. But I'm being very careful this time."

We climbed into the car and she added, before

starting the engine, "I told him he wasn't getting a red cent out of me. Not a penny. If he wasn't sincere, don't you think he'd have left?"

"Maybe." I kept my opinion to myself, but I seemed to recall her having told him that in the past and then coughing up the cash when push came to shove.

"Instead of leaving, he said he deserved my insults. That money wasn't why he was with me." She looked straight into my eyes. "I believed him. I believe him."

Maybe we all believe what we want to believe. Maybe we hear what we need to hear? I just couldn't imagine a snake shedding his skin and turning into a lamb.

"I love seeing you this happy." It was the total truth. What I didn't love was the sick feeling at the pit of my stomach. Helping Connie through Mike's next desertion would be even more difficult than the first two times.

c⅃ c⅃ c⅃

La Papillon Casino and Hotel is controlled by a respected Japanese conglomerate. As a result, upper management at my place of employment is all Japanese.

It was Thursday and I had a meeting scheduled with management between breakfast and lunch. I'd brought a fresh set of whites to wear to the meeting since I can never seem to leave the kitchen without wearing the day's menu.

I quickly changed clothes and headed upstairs, stopping in at Mandy's office on my way.

"I'm meeting with Mr. Nagasaki in fifteen minutes," I said as I took a seat in her office.

"Do you think it's about Chef Radkin?"

"Yeah."

Mandy looked at me consideringly. "How long have you been sous chef?"

"Over five years."

She grinned. "It's past time, then, for them to promote you."

"That's what I'm hoping." I inhaled deeply, almost as if by drawing in the breath I'd bring some good luck along with it. "I've been doing Radkin's job for four of those five years, along with my own. It's about damn time I'm made chef."

"You deserve the recognition."

"The extra money wouldn't hurt, either." Any kind of raise would help cover Stephen's tuition, no matter how miniscule. I checked my watch. "I'd better run."

Mandy came around her desk and gave me a big hug. "Good luck! I'll say a mantra for you."

"Thanks." I quickly headed down the corridor to let Nagasaki's assistant know I was there.

Within a few minutes, Nagasaki sprang out of his office (and I don't say that casually; Nagasaki always seemed to spring whenever I saw him—he was a definite candidate for ADD medication), then came to an abrupt halt in front of the chair where I was sitting.

I stood.

He bowed.

I bowed.

He bowed again then gestured toward his office. "Come in, come in."

He frowned as I passed him, I think probably because he's not very tall and I'm not exactly short. He always tended to frown whenever we were standing.

As I entered the office, he said, "Take seat."

I did as instructed, figuring he'd be more comfortable if I was off my feet.

While he circled his desk to his own chair, I casually glanced around his office. There wasn't much reason for the hotel sous chef to spend time with management, and so I hadn't been in his office more than a handful of times—and I loved it here.

The room was decorated with a mix of American modern and traditional Japanese. Even Nagasaki's desk was a work of art. It was formed from a wide expanse of cherry mahogany, with only a few odds and ends scattered on it, all black.

There were no papers—there never were—except a small piece of origami.

Cool.

"Did you make this?" I asked.

"My son did," he said proudly, lifting it to show me the shape of a bird and how a twist of one corner made the bird move its neck.

"Very nice. Origami is one of my hobbies."

"Very nice," he said, except of course, his "r" was pronounced as an "l." "What medium do you prefer?"

I gulped, not wanting to admit that most of mine was made of toilet paper, and not wanting to lie because I always feel guilty if I try. "Tissue paper," I replied, thinking that tissue and toilet paper were pretty much the same thing.

He nodded and I nodded back.

"Ms. Morgan Storm, you're a very good sous chef."

"Thank you." *Here it comes*, I was thinking. The promotion I was dreaming of.

"You're doing a good job of covering for the chef."

I swallowed, framing what I wanted to say without sounding too pushy. "Well, Chef Radkin has been . . . shall we say, indisposed . . . for some time. I've been covering for him for quite a while."

"You've been doing his job along with your own?" He looked surprised, maybe even a little disbelieving. That wasn't exactly the reaction I wanted.

Not wanting to sound like the job was too difficult or too easy, either, I shrugged. "I come in early and leave a little later than usual."

"You've done this for how long?"

"Four years."

He opened a drawer, riffled in it for a moment,

then pulled out a file. After turning a few pages and scanning them, he looked back up at me. "You like working at La Papillon?"

I nodded eagerly. It was about to come, I could feel it all the way to my toes which were beginning to wriggle in my shoes. The promotion was right around the corner.

Someone once said, "Savor the moment just before."

This was the moment just before and I took a second to enjoy it to the maximum. My stomach did excited flip-flops like when you're on a roller coaster and approaching the big plummet.

Nagasaki again nodded at me, turned a couple more pages in the file, then seemed to come to a decision. "You will be happy to know, Ms. Morgan Storm, that things will be changing to the better."

"Yes?" Oh, Gawd, I wasn't sure if I could breathe properly. I almost felt as if I'd been running.

"Human Resources is in the process of interviewing several candidates to replace Chef Radkin. We should select someone within a few weeks. Until then, if you will continue running the kitchen—"

"What?" I cut him off. I knew disappointment was written all over my face, but, dammit, I was disappointed. This was supposed to be my chance! I couldn't believe it. I had to have misunderstood him. "Can you please repeat that?"

"You'll continue running the kitchen?"

"No, the other part."

"Human Resources will replace Chef Radkin within a few weeks."

"Do I get to interview for his job?"

"I'm sorry, but you're not one of the candidates under consideration."

"Aren't I doing a good job?"

"You're doing an excellent job. Exemplary. I made a note in your employment file."

So that's what his file was. I tried to read upside down whatever the page was he was looking at, but half the scrawls were in Japanese scriggles, not something I could read even if it was right side up. "Since I'm doing such a good job, why aren't you considering promoting from within?"

His lips narrowed and he closed his eyes for a moment, as if he were praying I would hurry up and commit hari-kari and get out of his perfect office.

I added, "There was a memo about promoting from within just last month."

"Whenever feasible we try to promote from within. In this case, it's not possible." He opened his eyes. "I can promote you to Chef if you'll take the second shift?"

"You know I can't do that. I'm a single parent."

He scooted back his chair and came around his desk to take a seat in the chair beside me. "Can we talk plain?"

"Yes, please." I plainly wanted to know why I was being skipped over.

"You don't have the name to be a draw. The Chef at La Papillon must be well known."

I bit my lip, regretting that I'd set myself up for this. I should have known better than to hope for Radkin's job.

"Write a cookbook, get it published, become famous, then we'll talk again."

"I don't think I can write a cookbook." I had actually tried once, but MaryEllen said it was like reading recipes written by Alzheimer's patients.

"I'll give you advice, then." Nagasaki looked genuinely upset over having to tell me the straight facts.

"Please."

"If you tell anyone I said this, I will deny it."

"I promise not to tell."

"Start your own restaurant, like Kurt."

"I can't. No money."

"Investors?"

I shook my head.

He smiled then, as if he'd come up with the perfect idea. "Go to work somewhere else." He waved his hand toward the hotel across the strip from La Papillon. "Then maybe I can hire you back as Chef. Later. When you have a following."

He patted my knee, then rose.

I signaled for him to take a seat again. "Mr. Nagasaki, I've got a kid to support. I can't leave La Papillon. Even with the extra time I'm putting in, no other kitchen would allow me to work such reasonable hours."

"Ms. Morgan Storm, you will always have job as sous chef at La Papillon. I'm sorry I can't offer more than that."

"I understand. I'm sorry I can't take the night chef job. Right now I'm trying to find the money to pay my son's college tuition."

"Have you applied for the hotel scholarship?"

"There's a scholarship offered through La Papillon?"

"Yes. All children of employees who have a 3.0 or higher can apply."

"That rules out my kid. He's got a solid 2.3."

"Does he play sports?"

"No. He's into art."

"Sorry. I can't think of anything to help, but tell you what, I'll keep thinking." He tapped his forehead, then walked to his office door and opened it for me to leave.

Obviously our interview was over. As I left, he said, "You'll think over my suggestions?"

I nodded. "I will."

He bowed.

I bowed.

He nodded.

I nodded.

I could tell he wanted me to leave first. Maybe it was a Japanese form of politeness? So I bowed and again, then headed down the corridor. Once I was no longer in his field of vision, I slumped against the hallway wall.

Damn, damn, and double damn.

CHAPTER TWELVE

Dear Jill,

There's nowhere on this survey to tell about how thoughtful your spouse is. Gifts are material objects and can't replace kindness, thoughtfulness, and courtesy.

We've been married forty years. He travels with a rock band (he's a sound technician), but he's always thinking about me. He tucks notes in the refrigerator, beneath living room pillows, even in my underwear drawer. His notes say he's thinking of me. I never know where I'll find one!

He brings me souvenirs from his trips, but mainly he lets me know he's missed me. He takes me to dinner frequently. Back when our children were small, he used to arrange for babysitters so we could have a night out alone together. He even insisted that I have a housekeeper once a week to do the heavier cleaning, so I wouldn't feel like a household drudge.

Jill, when you find a man who values you and treats you good, keep him. I've never regretted marrying my sweetheart, John.

Sincerely,

Althea Nelson

Shortly after my meeting with Nagasaki, Mandy found me in the corridor, still using the wall for support.

"How'd it go? Did you get the promotion?"

"Not so well. No promotion." Hell, I felt lucky that I still had a job at all, which was not the way it was supposed to go.

"I'm sorry." Mandy pulled me away from the wall and hugged me, then gestured toward her office. "I've got even more bad news."

I straightened my shoulders. "Today seems the day for it. What's up?"

"Your ex-boyfriend is in my office. Something about a skillet?"

"The Asshole Professor?"

"The one and only."

"How'd that happen? I told him to leave my skillet with the bellman."

"Your ex demanded to see you and present the skillet personally. I told the bellman to bring him to my office since you were tied up."

"Thanks." I took a step toward her office. "It shouldn't take long."

"Good luck."

I nodded, needing all the luck I could gather since my luck gauge was running on empty. I was not in the mood to deal with the Asshole Professor, but on the upside, I was finally getting my skillet back. At least there was *something* good about today.

"Hi," I said as I entered Mandy's office. The cradle robber stood awkwardly beside Mandy's desk as if he'd been about to riffle through her drawers. In his left hand was a department store bag. I had hoped he'd look haggard and drawn, but he appeared to be chipper and in good physical condition. Darn it.

"Hi. I brought your skillet."

"Great." I held out my hand.

"There's a small problem."

"What's that?" Surely he hadn't washed my perfectly cured frying pan in the dishwasher? I started to take the bag, but he tightened his grip.

"I told Barbaretta that it was your pan and you wanted it back."

That *really* was her name? He had dumped me for a child whose name sounded like a stuttering hair clip?

He continued, "When she learned it was your skillet, it would be an understatement to say she went into a tizzy. She's extremely jealous, particularly of you."

"How peachy." She was jealous of me? Weird, since she was the relationship wrecker. I couldn't care less what she thought of me. Despite his attempts to stay my hand, I grabbed the bag, opened it, and pulled out the pan. "This isn't my skillet!"

"Barbaretta donated yours to charity." He shook his head.

"What?"

"The saleswoman assured me that this one is

excellent."

I bit back a snort. Like I'd ever use Teflon? He'd probably bought the cheapest pan he could find and then put it in a department store bag.

I pushed the pan at him, bag and all. "I want *my* skillet."

"Barbaretta gave it away."

"Get it back."

He looked at me as if *I* were the crazy person in the room. "It's gone."

"Which charity did she donate it to?"

"Goodwill." He held out the skillet. "This one will have to do."

I pushed it away. "Just leave."

I was pissed and wanted to go for his jugular. He must have caught on because he began backing from the room.

When he reached the door, he said, "I'm sorry."

Yeah, yeah, yeah, yeah. I'd heard it all when he'd dumped me for a child. I didn't want to hear it all again.

❧ ❧ ❧

I arrived home that evening, ready to bury my head under the covers. As I let myself into the apartment, I was met by the odor of cooking food—or maybe it was the odor of third-grade teacher. Stephen had company. You got it, the guy I didn't want to see again, Davin Wesley.

They were seated in the living room with their heads bent over a picture book of some type. They appeared very intimate—almost like father and son.

My stomach clenched.

Davin glanced up at me, then stood. "Hi, Jill."

"Hi. How was school today, Stephen?"

"Good."

"Have you given any thought to Ping-Pong?" There had to be some sport he was good enough at to qualify for a scholarship.

Stephen snorted and I could have sworn it was a French snort.

As I began making my way through to my bedroom, Davin stopped me.

"This is for you." He handed me a small grocery bag.

I only hoped it wasn't another wrong skillet. "What is it?"

"You left the store the other night before I had a chance to give you your glasses."

"You didn't have to do that."

"I did it for selfish reasons."

"What selfish reasons?"

Davin turned to Stephen and they exchanged a look. "Don't you have some homework to do?"

"Yes, sir. I'll go do it now." Stephen grabbed the picture book and headed to his bedroom.

Without grousing.

Without argument.

He even said, "Sir."

Shit. Davin was a better part-time parent than I was full-time, and he wasn't even related to Stephen.

Davin turned his attention back to me and I unconsciously straightened, half-expecting him to remind me I had dinner to cook or an apartment to clean.

"I had to buy the glasses because you look so darn cute in them. Why don't you put them on now and read something?"

I admit it. I snorted at that comment. I don't know why some people have such a problem with snorting. Sometimes it's the perfect expression of how you're feeling, you know? So I snorted. "What happened, did the manager catch you breaking the glasses on videotape and demand you buy them?"

"Honest. I had no other reason, except maybe currying your favor."

"And why would you want to do that?"

A smile slowly appeared on his face and crept into his eyes, which were gazing into mine. "I like you."

If he liked me, he sure had a fine way of showing it, always pointing out my flaws and generally annoying the hell out of me. I didn't know how to respond, so I took a step back, toward the kitchen. "Well, thanks. I have to get dinner started now."

He shook his head. "No, you don't."

"I don't?"

"You don't if you don't want to. I imagine you get tired of cooking all day and then coming home to do it some more. I made dinner tonight."

He was totally right about sometimes getting tired of cooking. But I couldn't believe he was perceptive enough to know that. So that's what I smelled when I came in. I probably looked a bit like a fish, what with the way I kept opening and closing my mouth. Finally I smiled and found my words again. "What's for dinner?"

"Baked pork chops, homemade mac and cheese, and a bag of mixed greens for a salad."

He looked kind of cute. A worry line creased his forehead as if he were concerned I'd be unenthusiastic about his menu. Little did he know that I'd be happy to eat a TV dinner if it meant I didn't have to cook. "It sounds delicious! I'm so impressed."

"Great." He headed toward the kitchen, stopping long enough to place his hands on my shoulders and gently spin me to face my bedroom. "Go get changed, then read a book while I get it ready to serve."

"Wow. Okay." My opinion of Davin Wesley went up about three-thousand fold. "Do I have time for a shower?"

"A quick one."

"Perfect." I tapped on Stephen's door on my way to the bathroom.

"Did you know about dinner?"

"*Oui.*" Stephen grinned conspiratorially. "I told

him it was a great idea. I hope that's okay?"

"Oh, yeah. It's terrific not to have to cook."

"I thought you'd say that."

"Thanks," I said, as I left his bedroom and head-ed to the shower. Afterward, I quickly changed into a clean pair of jeans and a comfy T-shirt. And in case you're wondering, no, I didn't put on my "COOKS DO IT" T-shirt. I have more class than that. I put on my "TALK TO THE HAND" T-shirt.

I made my way to my desk in the dining room, with my new reading glasses perched on the tip of my nose, ready to look over the latest surveys I'd received.

Mr. Fix-It had purchased both pairs of glasses and I was wearing the broken pair, the one taped together with a small strip of black electrical tape.

The repair was barely noticeable and they worked perfectly well. I'd placed the extra pair in my handbag for use when I was away from home.

When I reached the dining room, I noted that the dining table was only set for two. I peeked into the kitchen. "Only two for dinner?"

"Stephen already ate."

"Ah. Okay." More like *ohhhhh*. There was defi-nitely something fishy going on. "You don't think this is a date, do you?"

"Why?"

"In my experience, if it looks like a duck and quacks like a duck . . . You bring food, you feed my kid and send him off, and the table is set romantically for two."

"It's not a date."

"Why are you being nice to me?"

"I don't have an ulterior motive, if that's what you're worried about."

"That's exactly what I'm worrying about."

"Well, don't. Go. Read. Relax."

"As long as you aren't expecting sex if I eat your pork chops." I blushed. I couldn't believe I said that, even though it was exactly what I was thinking.

"I'm planning on dinner. Sex with you, while intriguing, is not on the menu." He looked amused. "Even if you want sex, I promise to defend your honor."

"You don't want to have sex with me?"

"I didn't say that. Why can't you go relax while I get dinner on the table?"

"You've got a point." I took a seat at the desk and slit the envelope of a new survey arrival. Like the majority of surveys that had been returned, this one also featured an absentee husband.

But I couldn't concentrate. Davin was making too much racket. I poked my head back in the kitchen. "I'm sorry, but I need to know what's in it for you. Why are you feeding me and my kid? Why are you here?"

He shook his head as he put the spoon he'd been using on a paper towel. "I like your kid. Since we got off to a bad start, I thought cooking for you would give us a chance to get to know each other. Is that enough of a reason?"

It would do, I supposed, since it was all I was going to get out of him. "If you want to get to know me, wouldn't it be easier if we were in the same room?"

"It's all part of my evil plan."

I knew he had an evil plan!

"Step One—disarm you, by making you relax." He began ticking items off on his fingers. "Step Two— chat you up over dinner."

"What's Step Three?"

"That's the truly nefarious part of my plan. Step Three—leave with you wanting more."

"You plan to skimp on my dinner?"

"I forgot to mention Step Two-A." That was when he slid my reading glasses from my nose, pulled me to him, and laid one hell of a kiss on me. The kind that leaves you breathless, and yeah, wanting more.

Wow. Step Two-A was quite a doozy. He tasted of red wine vinegar, olive oil, and—I raised the tip of my tongue to my palate—"Tarragon?"

"That wasn't part of Step Two-A. I was making salad dressing."

"Are you sure this isn't a date?"

"It's not a date. Just dinner and a sneaky plan."

"Dinner and kisses—sounds like a date to me." The fact his kiss was the best I'd ever experienced made me feel exceptionally cranky.

"If that's the case, you need to get out more."

I snorted and grabbed my reading glasses. Evidently they were sort of like a chastity belt, but for the lips. "You are *so* not the right kind of guy for me."

"What's wrong with me?"

Everything about him was wrong, but I couldn't tell him that. So I settled for the obvious. "You're way too young for me."

"That's the best you've got?"

"No, but it's pretty good. Also, your job doesn't take you out of town."

"*Au contraire.* Once a year the kids and I have a field trip to the State Capitol."

"That's not what I mean. I mean travel a lot."

"I travel every day—to and from school."

"That doesn't count."

"Well, you could have fooled me and my car odometer."

"You come home every night."

"And this is a problem?"

"Yeah. Absence makes the heart grow fonder."

"What about *Out of sight, out of mind*?"

He had me on that one. But so many happily married women couldn't be wrong. "Have you ever considered changing careers?"

"Have you?"

"Why would I change careers?"

"You'd make one hell of an interrogator. Maybe you should work for the CIA."

"Ha-ha. You're so very not funny."

"Go sit down at the table and I'll bring in dinner."

"There's only one thing worrying me."

"What's that?"

"You mentioned Step 2-A. That means there's gotta be a Step 2-B."

"I'm not telling you that one until after we eat."

"Don't forget, this is *not* a date. I'm not going out with you."

"You only date old men who travel. Got it." He seemed a bit huffy, but I had to be honest, didn't I?

As directed, I took my seat at the table. The stack of surveys on my desk was in my direct line of vision. All those women had to be right. The problem was obviously me, or perhaps my taste in men.

I'd crashed and burned with two salesmen, and when I finally kissed someone and enjoyed it, he was as far from a traveling salesman as you could get. Plus, a teacher's pay barely covers necessities, not expensive colleges.

Davin's a homebody, a caretaker, a nurturer. Hell, from the happy whistles coming from the kitchen, he even enjoyed cooking. You'd think, since I'm a chef that would be a good thing. But it's not if you're looking for a guy waiting on his next flight outta town.

Davin kept whistling. How could he go from huffy to happy so quickly?

Hopefully, he didn't think there was anything

between us, or going to be anything between us. I would let him down easy; it was the least I could do since he was making dinner for me.

Next, I heard noise in the living room. Cocking my head, I saw Davin fiddling with the stereo, then the sound of classical music gently playing in the background.

Nice touch.

He brought plates into the dining room, with everything served up already, and set one in front of me. "One sec, I'll be back with our tea."

"Not wine?"

"I can't afford not to be clearheaded around you." He brought in two tall glasses of iced tea and set them on the table before taking a seat.

"It looks really good." The pork was flawlessly cooked and the mac and cheese had the perfect consistency. Even the salad looked crisp and inviting.

"Dig in," he said, waiting for me to start.

I forked a bite of salad and as I brought it to my lips, the aroma of tarragon assailed my senses, reminding me of our kiss. I dashed the thought away and took the bite. "Great dressing."

Still, he didn't eat. "Try the pork chops."

I diced off a slice and tasted it. "Tender. Good."

He seemed to relax and began eating, too, casually making periodic small talk. "Stephen said mac and cheese is his favorite food."

"He loves it. Even the microwave packet kind."

While Davin chatted amicably about his day at school, I devoured the yummy meal he'd prepared. After such a crappy day at work, it was nice being pampered.

As we completed our meal, the dining room seemed a bit too domestic, too cozy, too comfortable, so I grabbed my plate and stood. "I think I have some cheesecake if you want some?"

"That would be great." Davin allowed me to take his plate, as well. "While you get dessert, I'll check on Stephen to see how his homework is coming."

"Thanks. Maybe you can ask him if he wants some cheesecake, too?"

By the time I returned from the kitchen, I expected Davin to have returned, but he was just exiting Stephen's room and heading down the hall with a puzzled expression on his face.

"Does he want cheesecake?" I asked.

Davin shook his head. "Said he's full." He took his seat at the table again but seemed to be distracted.

"Is something wrong with Stephen?"

"No." He took a sip of tea. "Yes. Maybe."

"What's up?"

"Have you noticed what he's been painting lately?"

"*Mona Lisa*?"

"He's moved on to Matisse."

"That's a good thing, isn't it?"

"Sometimes. It's probably nothing." He looked a little concerned but didn't say anything more.

I made a mental note to check on Stephen as soon as Davin left. I took a bite of the cheesecake. Unfortunately, the slices were too small for any sustained conversational avoidance. All I could think about was Step 2-B and whether it involved more kissing.

No matter how good a kisser Davin was, it wouldn't be fair for me to encourage him to kiss me again. Would it?

And it would be silly for me to kiss someone who was totally not my type.

So why couldn't I stop thinking about it? I became increasingly nervous and increasingly more klutzy, dropping my fork, my napkin, clunking my tea glass against the side of my plate, while Davin silently watched me making a fool of myself.

I jumped up from the table. "You cooked. I get to clean."

"Is that a rule, or do you want help?"

"It's a firm rule. Your turn to relax."

He stood, stuck a hand in his jeans pocket, and withdrew a set of keys. "I've got some papers to grade, so I'd better head out now."

"What about your dishes?"

"I'll get them from Stephen later."

He meant it? This really wasn't a date? Then my eyes narrowed. What about Step 2-B? Since he was so crafty, I'd have to stay on my toes until he was safely gone. "I'll walk you to the door, then."

"Night, Stephen," Davin called to my son from the

other side of his door.

"Night," came Stephen's muffled response.

We went to the door and I opened it, wondering when Davin was going to make whatever move he had up his sleeve.

But surprisingly, he did nothing except walk outside into the hallway. "Night, Jill."

"Night." Just as I closed the door, he placed his hand in it to keep it from closing.

He asked, "Aren't you going to ask about Step 2-B?"

"I wondered when we were getting to that."

He leaned forward and gave me the sweetest, most tender kiss. It lasted only seconds, but made a lasting impression on me.

He pulled back. "Time for Step 3. Night."

As I watched him walk down the hall, I realized how totally nefarious his scheme had been and I had played right into his hands. I didn't get the chance to let him down easy, because he didn't ask for anything. And his kiss had achieved exactly his goal. It left me wanting more.

CHAPTER THIRTEEN

Dear Ms. Storm,

Your survey was great and I've enclosed my answers.

Since you're obviously searching for Mr. Right, I have a tip to offer for *after* you find him. The secret to a happy marriage is to have *separate checking accounts*. Each of you needs your own money that you don't have to account for to the other, even if it's only a tiny amount.

So many couples argue over money and I've found this to be a great way to avoid that trap.

Please let me know when you find Mr. Right. I'd love to hear back from you.

Yours truly,

Julie Neuman

After Davin's dire hints about Stephen, I almost ran to his bedroom, although I like to think my stance was more dignified than a true sprint. When I opened Stephen's bedroom door and peeked inside, everything appeared to be perfectly normal.

Stephen stood in front of his easel, painting his soul out. The room was, as usual, strewn with his various books, dirty laundry, and assorted miscellaneous dishes and discarded sneakers. It was a bedroom that even my mother would have been unable to keep clean.

Davin must have been delusional. Stephen was fine. But just in case, I asked, "You okay?"

"Fine. Just busy." He barely turned his head to acknowledge me and his paintbrush didn't seem to break stride.

There was nothing worrisome here. Nothing to create concern in even the most obsessive of parents.

Wesley had merely done it to me again.

I quietly shut the door, leaving Stephen alone with the muse that so often stole my sweet son away. I headed back to the living room, only thinking a little about Davin and about waiting. I most definitely was not going to think about his lips.

In order to get my mind off Davin and the whole wanting-more routine, I checked the time. It was only half past seven. A quick call to Goodwill ascertained they were still open. Less than fifteen minutes later, I arrived and entered the store.

Within seconds, I found myself wailing, "What do you mean you don't have my skillet?"

"We sold it," said the saleswoman.

I checked her name tag. Maybe the personal touch would help. "Meg, can you check, please, because I called ahead? I made sure you had it. The woman I spoke with said she would put it aside for me."

"I don't know who you spoke with, but the skillet sold less than an hour ago."

"Are you positive?" I felt a hot flash coming on and desperately wanted to remove every stitch of my clothing. Perspiration streamed from my forehead. I didn't care how old my mom had been when she went into menopause. I was too young for it.

My face must have become bright red, because the saleswoman added defensively, "I sold it myself."

I felt like banging my head on the counter that separated us. This could not be happening. "But it wasn't your skillet to sell. It was mine. Someone stole it from me and gave it to Goodwill. There has to be a mistake."

"I'm so sorry." Meg patted my hand to comfort me. "There's not much I can do, except, you know what? The woman who bought it comes in all the time. The next time she comes in, I can ask her to call you."

A sense of relief washed over me. Or maybe it was because the hot flash had abated. My skillet couldn't be gone forever. I had to get it back. Without it, I was like a sailboat without a sail, a target without a bull's-eye, a book without any pages.

Within a few minutes, I gave Meg my contact information. While I didn't leave the store in a perky mood, there was a chance, at least, that ultimately my skillet would be returned.

The woman who bought it would come in, get my number, call me, and readily agree to sell me back my skillet. Then everything would seem more right in my world.

Maybe I'd even find the perfect traveling salesman to fulfill my sexual fantasies and pay Stephen's tuition.

Anything could happen.

Right?

ભ ભ ભ

I'm always nervous about introducing a good friend to other good friends for the first time, especially when I introduce someone to Connie, Susan, and MaryEllen. Introducing Mandy, who's gorgeous, gorgeous, and more gorgeous, felt like a huge risk. Luckily, Mandy is not only beautiful, she has brains and a hilarious outlook on life.

On our usual night out, I asked Mandy to come with me. Connie, Susan, and MaryEllen adored her. And MaryEllen particularly loved the free booze.

"What are we going to do with all these drinks?" asked Susan as she eyed the tray of watermelon martinis the server, Samantha, was delivering to our table.

We were seated at our favorite table by the plate

glass window at our favorite neighborhood bar. Susan, of course, was drinking water because she was due to deliver in just over three weeks.

"Chug 'em." Connie tossed back one of the three martinis sitting in front of her on the table.

Mandy is a man magnet, hence all the free booze. Since our arrival, drink after drink had been delivered, all bribes from hopeful men. Hopeful-to-meet-Mandy men, I mean.

"Who are these from?" Mandy asked Sam.

Sam was our favorite server and knew us all by name. She pointed to a handsome stockbroker type by the bar.

Mandy held up her drink, mouthed, "Thank you," then turned and totally ignored him. Like she'd done with the last three guys. A couple of them had actually approached her, but she'd quickly sent them on their way. She was only interested in nerds and they weren't the type who sent drinks to women in bars. "They aren't the type to actually be *in* a bar," Mandy explained. "Unless there's some kind of computer bar?"

It seemed to be a rhetorical question. At least none of us could answer it.

MaryEllen asked, "How's the salesman hunt going?"

I shook my head. "I've been sneaking down to the ballrooms and convention area every day this week, but haven't seen one guy I'd be willing to hold hands with, much less do the horizontal boogie with."

Mandy shook her head. "There are plenty of cool guys at the hotel. I think you're feeling burned after your date with Aiden."

"What was wrong with him?" asked Connie.

Susan started humming a few bars from *Raiders of the Lost Ark*. Connie slapped her forehead. "I forgot."

"I'll never forget the faces he made in the mirror." I opened my mouth in a shocked expression. "Surprise." Then I frowned. "Sadness."

We were all giggling, probably *not* because I was so hilarious, but because we'd consumed *plenty* of gin.

And speaking of which, Sam returned with yet another round of drinks.

"'Elp, 'elp," said MaryEllen in a falsetto voice from the corner of her mouth. "This is your table. I'm drowning in watermelon martini."

"I think it's time to cut you off," I said. "Give hers to me, Sam."

"Not on your life." MaryEllen grabbed the glass Sam set in front of me. "I've still got my esses."

"Hey, I deserve extras. I went to see my dad yesterday." I tossed back more martini.

"That bad?" asked Connie.

"Visiting with Dad wasn't, but prison is sooo depressing."

"He's feeling down?" Susan looked concerned.

"Not him. I'm the depressed one. It's all the other

visitors. Lawyers, bondsmen, families without teeth . . ."

MaryEllen was taking a drink and she snorted. For a moment I thought she might be the one drowning in watermelon martini rather than the table, but she got it together again. "No teeth?"

"Not everyone, but it gives you the general motif. One woman had two toddlers. They'd never seen their father outside prison."

"That's awful."

"It is. But on the upside, I have business cards for any number of criminal attorneys, and one bondsman promised me special discount rates should I ever need his services."

Connie proposed a toast, "To discounted bond services," and we all drank to it.

Over Mandy's head, I noticed a man who appeared to be heading our way. "Don't look now, Mandy, but I think you've caught another fly in your web."

Connie glanced up and bit her lip. She cleared her throat. "So, Jill," she said hurriedly, "I've been meaning to tell you, I met the perfect salesman for you."

"You did?"

"I invited him to join us tonight. The fly is Greg Walker. He sells Purple People Movers. They're sort of like Segways."

"Only purple," piped in MaryEllen.

"Are those the things that—" I didn't have time to finish my question. Greg had arrived at our table.

Feeling a bit annoyed that Connie would invite him without asking me first, I shot her a glare. What if I'd already found the perfect salesman?

As she introduced us, she mouthed, "Trust me."

I wasn't prepared for unwarranted trust, not when I considered her own bad taste in men.

Connie sat to my left and Greg pulled a chair in to my right. He said, "Looks like it's raining martinis. You ladies celebrating something?"

"These are from Mandy's admirers." Susan glanced at Greg, then looked at the men watching us (or Mandy) from the bar. "Now that you've joined us, it'll probably encourage all of them."

"Oh, Lord," moaned Mandy. "I hope not. In this sea of men, I don't see even one techno-nerd."

"A woman with standards, I see," said Greg.

She smiled at him. I played with the wet napkin under one of my martinis.

Connie mouthed, "Say something."

I pretended not to see her.

Connie evidently doesn't like being ignored, because she kicked me under the table.

"Ouch. Why'd you do that?"

At that point, Connie pushed one of the martinis in front of Greg and said, "Have a martini," while grabbing my elbow with her other hand and dragging me under the table, then said, "Help me find my earring."

"You're not missing an earring. What the hell do

you want?"

"Shh. Whisper." Connie pulled off her earring and threw it on the carpet beneath the table. "While you look for it, you can tell me why you're not saying anything to Greg."

"Maybe because I haven't had anything to say to him?" I whispered back.

"Well, think of something." She grabbed her earring from the floor, then raised her head. "Here it is."

I sat back up and glanced at Greg and wondered what I could talk about with him.

He was cute. While he didn't resemble any of my favorite actors, he was attractive enough to hold his own. Maybe that was a good thing, especially after Aiden. "Connie said you sell Purple People Movers."

"I try to. They're catching on. You'll see them everywhere. Even the malls."

"Weren't they recalled?"

"No, that was another company."

Our conversation tapered off.

Connie threw a hand to her ear and announced, "It's gone again!" Once more she dragged me under the table, and whispered, "Why aren't you being nice to him?"

"I thought I *was* being nice," I whispered back.

"You aren't."

"Has it occurred to you that I might not know how to be nice?"

"Flirt a little."

"Now you sound like my mother," I muttered as I came back up for air.

Greg looked at me a little strangely, not that I blame him. I could only hope he believed Connie's cover. I said, "Earring," and scooted my chair a little. I needed to say something to him, but couldn't think what. There was no way I was going to use Mandy's line on him. He was a salesman, though, so I asked, "Do you travel much?"

"Yes. I enjoy it a lot. How about you?"

"I never go anywhere, but I'd like to."

He nodded, but didn't add anything to our almost-conversation. At least I was giving it a try, but then Connie started kicking me again. I threw my spoon on the floor. "Oops."

As I leaned down, I grabbed Connie and pulled her with me. "If you kick me again, you will not have a foot to walk with. Got it?"

"Sheesh. Fine."

"What do you want?"

"Tell him you're a chef."

That was the moment I realized Greg had joined us beneath the table. He seemed to be groping around for my spoon. So I said to him, as conversationally as possible under the circumstances and the table, "I'm the sous chef at La Papillon Hotel and Casino."

"Here's your spoon," he said, holding it out to me. "I bet you are a great cook."

"I like to think so. How about you?"

"Can't even make instant rice. It always ends up looking like a soccer ball."

I laughed. "Now that's bad."

"Truly."

I pointed up with my thumb. "Time to join the adults."

I sat upright, put the spoon on the table, and straightened my napkin.

He and Connie came up, as well.

Our under-table sojourn seemed to loosen Greg up and we began chatting more easily. I liked him more and more. When he asked, "Would you like to go out to dinner one night this week?" I happily agreed.

We made arrangements and he put a tip on the table. "I need to call it a night. I've got an early morning meeting. It was nice meeting all of you. Jill, Connie, hope to see you both again soon."

Connie stood and gave him a brief hug. As she took her seat again, she mumbled, "At least *he* didn't sponge off us."

Could this be some reference to the absent Mike? I *knew* something was up with her. "Trouble in paradise?"

She grabbed another martini and downed it in one swallow. "Mike asked for money."

"Not a good sign. Did you give it to him?"

"Hell, no. I reminded him of his promise not to

sponge off me."

"And?"

"He was pissed."

"What are you going to do?"

"I don't know. The only thing I'm certain about is that I'm not giving him any cash."

"Good for you," said Susan. "He's like a kid, testing you to see if you mean it."

"You think?"

"Sounds that way to me." Susan nodded. "Stick to your guns."

Connie smiled. "You know, he said something that makes me think you might be right. He said he'd asked out of habit."

"How's his job search going?" I wondered if he truly planned to get one this time. It would be a first.

"He's got a second interview scheduled at the electronic game store."

Susan looked longingly at our martinis, then took a long drink of ice water. "Once he has an income, I'm sure things will be better."

Sam approached, yet again, with another tray filled with drinks.

"I think we have enough, don't you?" asked Mandy.

"I'll clear away the old ones," replied Sam as she began scooping them up and placing new glasses in front of us. "They're warm anyway. These were sent by the blue-striped-suit at the bar."

"If he's not wearing a pocket protector, please suggest that he get lost."

"I didn't have the heart to tell him you aren't interested."

Mandy sighed. She waved at the guy, mouthed, "Thank you," then totally ignored him. Within seconds, the suit made his way to our table.

"Hi," he said. "You have a table full of drinks, so I figured you needed more."

"Thank you."

"Can I join you?"

Mandy looked him in the eye. "Do you know computer programming?"

"No."

"Do you speak Geek?"

"No."

"Sorry, then. No can do. But thanks for the drinks."

Once the suit left, Susan reached over and touched Mandy's arm. "We get that you prefer nerds. But why?"

"I'm into thumb drives, pocket protectors, and intimate discussions about computer gaming?"

I piped in, "But the suit seemed like a nice guy. He was good-looking, too."

"Mr. Armani?" Mandy shrugged. "I've had it with good-looking men. They're all about appearances, the latest hot car, and expensive designer suits."

"Sounds to me like you've got a story," said Connie.

"Same old, same old." Mandy took a sip of her martini while we waited for her to go on. Condensation dripped from her martini glass onto the table, pooling on the polished surface. She finally asked, "Are you sure you want to hear this?"

"Yeah."

"Oh, baby."

"Give it to us."

She shook her head like we'd lost our marbles. "It's not very exciting. I've just been hurt too many times by gorgeous yet shallow men who were only interested in being seen with me. Guys who didn't care who I am. They were more into how my being on their arm made them look to other people."

"Oh," said Susan. "I have to admit, with your good looks, I figured dating was the least of your problems."

"It's a problem, all right. I thought I'd found the right guy. Jed. We were engaged. But two weeks before the wedding, I overheard him talking with one of his buddies about how his career would benefit from his marriage to me. His boss thought I was hot and promised Jed a promotion after the wedding." Mandy looked down into her glass and lowered her tone. "It was after that promise that he'd proposed to me."

"Whoa." Connie grabbed another martini and took a gulp.

She looked back up at us, then continued, "Jed bragged about how he was going to trade in his Lexus for the latest Lamborghini—then he'd have the right car, the best-looking woman to make his peers jealous, and the right career move—all by marrying me."

"He wasn't just bragging to his friend?" I asked, stunned that she'd gone through such a rough time when I thought that if I looked like her all my troubles would be over.

Mandy shook her head sadly. "I called him on it and he said, 'What do you want for me to say? That I'm marrying you for your brains? It ain't true, babe. If you looked like a hag, I'd be outta here. You could have an IQ of eleven and I'd still marry you.'"

"What a total jerk," said MaryEllen. "What did you say?"

"I said it was time to move on. Ever since, I only date geeks. They're nice guys who wouldn't be interested in me if I were as dumb as a board. They listen to what I have to say, engage with me in real conversation, and if now and then I have to help them choose to pass on the checkered slacks, it's no biggie."

"You obviously know what you're doing," replied Susan. "I'm just sorry you got hurt by Jed in the process of learning your own mind."

"It was worth it. I've moved on. And speaking of which, Jill, it's time for you to move on, too." She raised her martini glass. "A toast to moving on!"

CHAPTER FOURTEEN

Dear Miss Storm,

My husband is a lingerie salesman. He travels a lot, making me ruler of my own household universe.

This is an excellent state of affairs because he brings home salesman samples! Talk about interesting role playing in the bedroom!

My best advice is to own a varied and extensive collection of lingerie. It will definitely add spice and longevity to your marriage.

Sincerely,

Donna McCall

Time to move on? I would have liked to move on,
I truly would have. But moving on is for those who
have something to move on to. While Mandy preferred
geeks, she was attractive and outgoing enough to have
any number of men ready and willing to date her. My
salesman plan wasn't going quite so well.

It seemed as if the only relationship I was building
was with the wrong man. A man who had annoyingly
left me wanting more. I wasn't sure, however, that
wanting more with Davin was such a good idea. He'd
lit a fire in my dormant libido. A fire best left banked
until I found the right person with whom to share the
balance of my life.

Selfishly, I had to resist an urge to drop hints to
him about the benefits of pursuing a career in sales—
traveling sales. It was selfish, though, because his
interests and talents were best spent with the youth of
today, developing their minds, leaving them wanting to
learn more.

That morning, I knew I needed to move on. But
it wasn't easy.

When I arrived at work, Big E met me with a message that Nagasaki wanted to see me. Was it possible
he'd changed his mind about hiring from outside? Immediately, all thoughts about my relationship problems
dissipated as I entered the elevator to go see my boss.

I'd been busting my rear trying to show how
capable I was, how ready I was to be named chef. If

hard work counted for anything, then Nagasaki would see it my way.

I waved at Mandy as I passed her office and when I reached Nagasaki's office, I smoothed my hair. For once he'd see me clean and well groomed.

His assistant was seated at her desk outside his office. "Hi, Jill."

"Hi. Mr. Nagasaki said he wants to see me?"

"Have a seat and I'll let him know you're here." She indicated the closed door to his office. "He's with someone right now."

As I took a seat, she lifted her telephone receiver, punched in a number on the base unit, then said, "Mrs. Storm is here to see you."

After disconnecting the call, she said, "He should only be a few more minutes."

A few more minutes of patience hell. I watched as she spun her in chair and began typing something on her keyboard, wondering if she knew how hard it was to sit and wait. Was it good news or bad that had Nagasaki requesting my presence? Glancing down, I saw that I already had a big black smear on the lower part of my white slacks. I shifted my legs so it wouldn't show.

Nagasaki's assistant was busy and didn't see my movements nor did she seem inclined to entertain me while I waited, so I looked around for something to occupy my attention. A glossy copy of *Hospitality News* on the table by my chair looked interesting. Picking it up, I noted that La Papillon was featured on the cover and Mr. Nagasaki stood in the foreground. Cool.

I flipped through the magazine until I found the article on Mr. Nagasaki and began to read. It talked about his opinion on how La Papillon was making great strides in the Las Vegas market, about his growth strategies, then went into some detail about his personal life, including a photo of him with his wife and family.

I scanned the article briefly, then returned to the section about his plans for growing the business. He reiterated La Papillon's policy of employee growth from within.

How could he say that and then tell me I wasn't one of those who could move up? It was blatantly unfair, unless he now meant to tell me he'd changed his mind. Finding this article had to be a good sign.

I had some moving on to do and I desperately wanted to be promoted.

Just then, Nagasaki's office door opened and a young man I recognized from Guest Services stepped out, shook Nagasaki's hand, and thanked him for his time.

Nagasaki's gaze met mine, and he waved me to come in his office as the young man departed.

I bowed.

Nagasaki bowed, then, with a sweep of his arm, indicated the chair in front of his desk.

As I approached and took a seat, I ventured, "How

are you today?"

"Well. And you?"

"The same." It wasn't a particularly good opening, but it was better than sitting there tongue-tied or shouting, "Give me the promotion!"

He took his seat behind his desk and pushed a folder aside. "I wanted to let you know that I've retained a new chef."

At least he put me out of my misery right away by thoroughly dashing any hopes I had about becoming the new chef myself. "Who is he?"

"Chef Benjamin Breck. I'm certain you've heard of him."

"I have," I said while inwardly gulping in distress. What I'd heard about him wasn't good, but I couldn't tell Nagasaki that. While I'd never personally met Breck, he was notorious. The guy wasn't a boozer like Chef Radkin. No. He was far worse.

The man was reputed to be the biggest control freak in the industry, although I did have to grudgingly admit he was also quite talented.

Mr. Nagasaki smiled. "He'll be a big draw to La Papillon."

It was certainly true that Breck was well known as a celebrity chef—something I patently wasn't. I met Nagasaki's gaze and the look he gave me was one of pure pity.

Somehow he knew I had hoped he'd changed his

mind. Somehow he knew how disappointed, and yeah, frightened I was about the future.

And he felt sorry for me.

I did, too. How on earth would I cope with Chef Breck?

Geez, I hated changes and this one was a doozy. I blinked back a couple of unexpected tears. There was no way I would allow myself to display unchecked emotion in front of Nagasaki.

"I'm certain you'll do your best to show Chef Breck the ropes and make his transition as easy as possible."

Nagasaki sure seemed certain about me, even when I wasn't so certain myself. "Yes, sir. When does he start?"

"Next week." He rose from his chair, clearly indicating our meeting was over.

I stood, bowed, and had to clear my voice before I could manage the words, "I'll do my best."

"My confidence in you is well placed." He bowed.

I bowed again and left as quickly as possible. As I headed downstairs, my stomach was in knots. I needed pastries, and I needed them immediately.

🙷 🙷 🙷

"I have no clue why I let you drag me to Barnes and Noble," I said to Mandy, later that afternoon, as she whisked me toward the self-help aisle. Mandy and

I had walked the short distance from the hotel to the store. My mood wasn't exactly kindness and light. It was more like surly and I had to fight a tendency to snarl at the other bookstore customers.

"Experts say that when you're down, the best thing to do is to get up and get moving."

I snorted. "Do they really say that?"

"Well, they probably do. We can find a book on the subject to find out for sure."

"Let's not."

"You're such a buzz kill." We reached the aisle and Mandy began to look over the selection, adding, "I'll find you a good book on career advancement. It'll make you feel much better."

"Do I have to feel better?" I had this whole negativity thing going on. Chef Benjamin Breck would start work next week. "I'm enjoying whining."

"You don't have to listen to yourself."

"Oh, yeah? Like my brain shuts off when I'm not talking?" I couldn't stop obsessing over Chef Breck. As soon as people in the industry learned he was my new boss, I had begun receiving condolence phone calls. They gossiped about him being a major control freak. I also heard whispers that he was into coke, and I don't mean the soda. Whether or not the scuttlebutt was true, everyone I spoke with ranted about his micro-management.

Not that I mind control freaks, mind you, since

I'm something of one myself. But that, you see, was the problem.

For the past four years, I'd had free reign of the kitchens at La Papillon. Becoming subordinate would take some getting used to, and I wasn't sure I could adapt. "I'm going to be miserable. I just know I am."

Mandy pulled out a book, glanced at the back cover, then replaced it on a shelf. "You haven't even met Chef Breck. Give him a chance."

"I don't have much choice, do I?"

"You could always quit if it gets too bad."

There was no way on earth I could do that. Life was evolving too fast as it was. Change was in the air, and I was clinging to the *now*, with my teeth, fingers, and toenails.

"Oh, my Gawd," said Mandy breathlessly as she pulled another book from the shelf.

"Did you find something that would help me?"

"Sorry." She read the back blurb, then waved at the book's cover. "This one is for me."

"What is it?"

"*Finding and Taming Your Techno Nerd.*"

"Huh?"

"About man hunting for geeks!" She pulled the book to her bosom, quivering with excitement. "Can you believe it?"

"I can believe anything right now, but it is hard to imagine that there are more of *your* type out there."

"We'll keep looking for a book for you. There's got to be something good on career management for chefs."

"I'm a sous chef, remember? I'm never going to amount to more than sous."

"That's not a good attitude. Look in this section." She pointed out another shelf. "There's bound to be something here."

I pretended to look, but all I could see was Nagasaki's face when he told me they'd hired Breck. He'd looked at me with pity.

"Do I seem pitiful?" I asked Mandy, pulling down a title on empty nesters and scanning the table of contents: Separation, Divorce, Children Leaving Home, Changing Jobs. Good heavens, it was like a laundry list of my life.

"You don't seem pitiful to me. Why would you think that?"

"Never mind." I slid the book back on the shelf without reading further. I was not in the mood. I had to fight an urge to hide in the nearest available restroom. Depression hit me like a wall of books. I needed to get out of there. Now. "Shoot. I just remembered. I have to pick up my uniforms from the cleaners. I gotta go."

"Are you sure? We could have some cappuccino and chat in the coffee bar."

"I need clean clothes for tomorrow. Who knows

when I'll be summoned upstairs again? The new chef might show up."

"If you're certain?"

I nodded.

She gave me a hug before I headed out, back to the hotel and where I'd parked the Animal. My thoughts kept circling the same theme over and over again. If anyone had called me a loser, I wouldn't have argued the point.

My life had pretty much reached an all-time low. While I had a date scheduled with Salesman Number Three, I didn't hold out much hope that it would be much better than Date Numbers One and Two. My luck was totally sucky, so why should Greg be any better?

ↁↁↁ

When I arrived at Evolve Dry Cleaners, my mood hadn't lightened. As the teenaged clerk moved my items to the hanger rack, the bell over the door tinkled, indicating another customer had come in.

The teenager drew in a deep breath, then smiled enormously. "Mr. Wesley! How are you doing?"

I turned and was surprised to see Davin.

He smiled at the clerk. "Hi, Gretchen."

Just what I needed, another run-in with him.

Gretchen went to the back room to get something and I noticed that he didn't have any dirty clothes in his arms. "Are you picking up clothes, too?"

"No. Stalking you." He smiled. "It's another part of my nefarious scheme, remember?"

"I'd hoped to put your scheme out of mind entirely."

I was getting pretty good at these little white lies.

Davin Wesley was *not* the kind of guy I needed or wanted. Not only was he way too young, but he didn't travel. He couldn't afford college tuition. And from everything I'd learned about him, he was a stinking homebody. Instead of staying out of my hair, allowing me to be queen of my own universe, he was the sort to call me at work to remind me to pick up toilet paper on my way home.

Not good.

But right now all I could think about was the other night—when he left me wanting more.

The good thing was that thinking about the softness of his kiss pushed all thoughts about work out of my head. I no longer felt depressed. I felt positively randy.

"It's almost dark," he said. "When I saw your car outside, I thought you might like some help."

So there I was, feeling all female. When he offered to take my clothes to my car for me, I didn't tell him no. I didn't suggest he leave me alone.

What did I do?

The stupidest thing.

I blushed.

He grabbed my dry cleaning bags, then held the door open for me. Within minutes, the bags were safely stowed in the back of the Animal.

His car, a Mustang—late model, not vintage—was parked beside mine and he leaned against it. "How's Stephen?"

"Just fine. I can't figure out why you were worried about him."

"I'm sure it was nothing. Just teacher antenna in overdrive." His expression showed concern, his brows gently drawn together. "You're tired."

I wasn't sure what gave me away. "It's been a long day."

He opened his car door and pulled the front seat forward, revealing the back seat. "Get in and we'll talk."

I hesitated. He gave a sympathetic nod toward the seat and it did me in. I was tired and it had been hell week. I needed some sympathy and someone willing to listen. Davin filled the bill. I ignored the little voice in my head making some smart-ass comment about wanting more. And I deliberately didn't look at his lips as I climbed into the car.

We'd just talk. Nothing more.

I chose to dismiss the idea that somehow, using his ample male wiles, he had maneuvered me into a) getting into his car, b) deciding to talk, and c) allowing him to choose the back seat for the discussion.

Now, I spent a lot of high school hours in the back of a car talking with various boys. As I climbed into the back of Davin's car, noting the darkly tinted windows, I couldn't plead ignorance or that I thought we'd truly just talk. Not with the way my heart pounded exactly as it had way back then. Not with the way I studiously avoided looking at his lips, at his face, and how I intently gazed at the stick shift between the front seats.

But rather than remain safely out of view outside the car, he closed my door, crossed to the passenger side, then climbed in beside me, careful to duck to keep from being decapitated by the seat belt strap angling down from the back seat roof to the front passenger seat. I didn't even scoot away from him, although there's not much room in the back of a Mustang. Basically, sardines have more elbow room.

"There now. Tell me all about it."

Okay, I admit it. My mistake was turning my head to look at him and my gaze immediately landed on his lips. They'd been so soft, so tender against mine and I wondered if they were always so gentle. Since I was caught up in memories of the night he'd kissed me, I didn't respond.

Davin said, "Tell me what's wrong."

I forcibly turned my head away from him and it wasn't easily accomplished. The little voice from earlier started yakking about my being a total dweeb and telling me to get my mind out of the gutter and back onto the topic at hand. Oh, yeah. My week. My job. "I was hoping to be promoted to chef, but they hired someone else and he's awful."

At least I managed to speak, even if it probably made little sense to him.

"Your boss is out of his mind. If anyone should be chef, it's you." He patted his shoulder next to mine, and I laid my head on it.

My mom would probably make snarky comments about being anti-women's lib, but I have to admit, the act of laying my head on his big strong shoulder made me feel cared for and girlish and like my burdens weren't quite so insurmountable.

His body heat relaxed me and for the first time in days, I let down my guard. I may have actually leaned in as he put his arm around me. I craved another of his kisses, so I leaned closer and kissed him.

He tenderly kissed me back, then laid a trail of fire down my face and chin until he reached that special spot on my neck that does things to my brain, like totally shutting it down. It also does things to other parts of my body and I melted into his arms.

It's kind of embarrassing to admit that one heated kiss to that specific location turns off my inhibitions and turns me into a wild woman. But then he kissed me there again and I went into pure and total thought shutdown. It was all about what I felt. How good Davin made me feel, how sweet he was, and . . . Oh.

My. Gawd. What great lips he had.

And his hands . . .

Then he laid one of the best kisses on me that I've ever experienced. Toe-curling, heat-inducing, total seduction.

At some point, I vaguely recall coming up for air and noticing it was dark out, but then his lips claimed mine again. The next thing I knew, I'd pinned him horizontally to the seat, having removed his T-shirt earlier, when he said something about seat belt clips digging into his back.

Hard, yet yielding. He sat up straighter and pulled me toward him. "That's better."

I arched my back when his thumb brushed my nipple. After that, we pretty much got carried away, clinging to each other like teenagers in the throes of hormonal overload, with arms, legs, buttons, and bra straps flying. His body was incredible and I couldn't stop myself from exploring it. Until . . . my leg got tangled in the seat belt strap while I was trying to get closer, meaningfully closer, by straddling Davin. I abruptly broke off our kiss, trying to free myself. "Help. I'm stuck."

Davin thrusted and I moaned, even though I couldn't get free from the stupid strap. I bit my lip and managed to rasp out, "Davin, you have to move your leg. I'm trapped."

"You're trapped? I can't move my leg," he said, thrusting again, but this time I realized he was trying to move his foot.

When I leaned away from him and against the back of the passenger seat, I saw the problem. One of his legs was lying across the console between the front seats, but his other foot was totally wedged between the passenger seat and the door. As I worked my shin out of the seat belt strap, I realized how very much I like defenseless men . . . and this time he was the one who moaned.

ை ை ை

"I've become an exhibitionist," I wailed into my cell phone as I entered the grocery store and grabbed a shopping cart. I was a total basket case. I'd just had M.B.S.—mind-blowing sex—in a frigging parking lot! I'd lost my mind, my marbles, and any vestige of common sense. Did I mention I was wailing?

"Tell me more," said Connie.

"I'm at the grocery store. Do you have time to talk?" I teetered directly to the pharmacy department, passing a little girl who took one look at me and ran for her mother. I probably looked as crazy as I felt and the store's fluorescent lighting only served to make me feel dizzy.

"Do I have time?" asked Connie. "Time? What with your exhibitionist crack, I'll make time."

After checking to make sure no one was watching, not even the little girl I'd scared, I started grabbing every brand of pregnancy test kit I could find. I whispered, "I just had M.B.S. in the back seat of a car."

"How interesting, but how does that make you an exhibitionist?"

"It was in the parking lot in front of the dry cleaners."

Connie cracked up. "At least it's dark."

"Stop laughing. This is serious."

"Why is that?"

Again I checked to be certain there were no other nearby customers. "It broke."

"What broke?"

"His . . . um . . . protection. What brand of pregnancy test is best?"

"Jill! Aren't you on the pill?"

I froze. "Shit."

"You're not?"

"Of course I am." I began emptying the kits from my cart. After the breakup with the Asshole P, I'd gone off the pill, only to start up again in preparation for my salesman auditions. "I forgot."

"You forgot to take your pills?"

"No, I've been taking them. Religiously. When I saw his protection broke, I forgot I was on them."

"It must have been good sex."

"That's an understatement."

"So, was it fun?"

"Yes. No."

"Make up your mind."

I sighed. "It was just a huge mistake."

"I thought you were looking forward to auditioning salesmen."

"That's why it was a mistake. He isn't a salesman."

Connie drew in an audibly large breath, then screamed, "It can't be. You didn't! Ohmigawd! You had sex with Davin Wesley!"

I held the phone away from my ear until she stopped hooting and hollering. "You finished yet? How did you know it was Davin?"

"Like you ever stop whining about him? Admit it. You're hot for the teacher! So tell me, did Mr. Fix-It fix you?"

"It was menopause, remember? Hot flashes, et cetera?"

"Menopause doesn't make you get it off in the back seat of a teacher's car."

"I hate you." I snapped my cell phone closed and stuck it in my bag. It was easier to hang up on Connie than to admit my attraction to Mr.-Absolutely-Totally-Wrong-for-Me. College tuition? On a teacher's salary, he could barely afford Stephen's art supplies. Davin didn't even have a frequent flyer card!

I'd gotten out of his car and into mine so quickly, Davin's head was still spinning as I peeled out of the parking lot. Now he probably believed we had a *real* relationship.

Which we didn't.

It was just a hot flash. Or another symptom of menopause. Or maybe even lust. But it was just one of those things, the kind of thing that would never, ever happen again.

Ever.

No matter how mind-blowing it was, and no matter that I couldn't rid myself of the idea of wanting to do it with him again when we had more room to maneuver. But that wouldn't happen again.

Ever.

It, *he,* was not in my plans.

Even though my life had completely and absolutely spiraled out of control, there was time to get it back on track.

I still had a date with Salesman Number Three.

CHAPTER FIFTEEN

Dear Jill,

My father once told me, "It's just as easy to fall in love with a rich man as it is to fall in love with a poor man."

Boy, was he right!

My first two marriages were a total bust. The first lasted only six weeks. The second lasted just over eight months.

I've been married to my third husband for twenty-five years. I finally got smart. I married money.

Now money doesn't solve all problems, obviously, but it makes problems more surmountable. Trust me, I know. If you're not in love now, why not check out *Fortune* magazine's article on the "Forty Richest Under 40 Bachelors in America"?

That's a great place to start.

And keep this in mind, "Money makes the heart grow fonder!"

Hope you find my survey answers helpful in your quest.

Very truly,

Cassandra Ervine

P.S. The wealthy men I've met seem to prefer blondes!

When I arrived home three nights later, I still didn't feel any less depressed. Even though it was a Saturday and I had a couple of days off, I couldn't stop thinking about my job. Chef Breck was starting work at La Papillon on Tuesday.

I had to shake it off, though, because tonight was date night with Salesman Number Three. Maybe if I gave myself a pedicure I'd feel more enthusiastic? After collecting the mail, I entered my front door, ready to pamper myself.

Guess who was sitting on my sofa? You got it.

My unwanted sperm donor. He and Stephen were watching TV, drinking sodas, and chatting. He sat watching my TV, drinking my soda, and chatting with my son.

So why did my heart beat so fast and give a quick little flutter? A rivulet of perspiration beaded on my forehead, the room was kinda warm, and I hoped like crazy I wasn't about to experience another hormonal meltdown. "Hi, guys."

"Hi, Jill," said Davin.

"Hi, Mom." Stephen clicked off the TV. "How'd your day go?"

"Yucky. How about yours?"

"Okay."

I wiggled the mail in my hand. "You got some mail from one of those art schools you applied to."

"Tres bien."

I handed him the envelope, and he quickly ripped it open.

"Awesome!"

"What?" I asked.

"Did you get in?" asked Davin, shooting me a smile that spoke of happy concern, yet at the same time telegraphed a message about hot sweaty nights spent making love. How did he do that?

"I've been accepted!" Stephen bounded up out of his chair and danced around the living room.

"That's wonderful," I said, but thought the opposite. This was the art school whose tuition was over thirty-five thousand dollars per year, not including living costs. How on God's green earth would I find a way to pay for it? "Isn't this awfully soon? You didn't apply that long ago."

"I think that's what it says." Stephen handed the letter to Davin.

Davin read the letter, then nodded at me and said to a very happy Stephen, "Congratulations. I told you you had the talent."

Stephen grinned. "Yeah, but you're prejudiced."

"I am, a little, but your talent is obvious to everyone."

Stephen looked intently at Davin. "Do I have time to go see Tom before dinner? I can't wait to tell him."

"Sure," Davin said, then paused and glanced my way, the sinful undercurrent still zapping between us.

"If it's okay with your mother, that is."

I wondered when either of them would remember who the parent was around here.

"That's fine," I replied. It would give me time to cook something before my date with Salesman Number Three, the guy who might be the man of my dreams, not the featured player in my night sweats. Maybe I'd prepare mac and cheese to celebrate Stephen's acceptance? Although I didn't at all feel like celebrating. I wanted to mourn. I had to bite my tongue to keep from asking Stephen why he couldn't attend a local college.

With a swift wave, Stephen darted out the front door and I realized he'd soon be darting off to college. I didn't want to think about what it would be like to come home to an empty apartment and only cooking for one, if I bothered to cook at all.

I sniffed the air. Was that the aroma of cooking food? Or had the odor simply clung to my hair? "I hope you didn't make dinner again?"

"Sure did." Davin patted the sofa beside him. "I'm hoping to talk about the other day."

I didn't want to talk about what had happened between us, ever, ever, ever. But I was a mature adult, or at least I passed for one. Mature adults deal with the consequences of their own actions. I owed it to Davin to be honest with him. I merely didn't want to do it right that minute. "We do need to talk, but this isn't a good time."

"What about the broken condom? What if you're . . ."

He trailed off, but I knew what he meant, especially since he was staring at my stomach. "I'm not pregnant."

"How can you be sure?"

"The pill."

"We should talk anyway."

"Maybe we can do it tomorrow or next week?" I would not look at his lips—or his hands. I glanced down at Stephen's discarded letter, hiding from Davin behind my curtain of hair. "I'm sorry you went to the trouble of making dinner, because I have plans tonight."

"What kind of plans?"

"The kind of plans that involve eating somewhere else and genial dinner conversation."

"With your girlfriends? I'd like to meet them."

I shook my head, the hair parting enough so I could see his face. "I'm not meeting them tonight."

He seemed dumbfounded for a moment. "You've got a date?"

"Give yourself a gold star." I was being bitchy, but dammit, I had every right to feel bitchy. Men sow their oats all over the place, but it's always the women who have to deal with the consequences of oat overflow, even if it's only being on the Pill.

Davin rose from the sofa and took a step toward

me. "I was thinking that you and I—"

"Don't even consider it," I interrupted, and held up my hand to keep him back. "Don't put *you* and *me* into the same sentence. It's not going to happen."

"The other night—"

"Was just one of those things."

"You're wrong."

"Davin, I made lov—" I cut myself off and started over. "We had sex the other night because of my raging hormones induced by premenopause and lust. It was a one night stand."

He shook his head. "You're not the type for one night stands. You're the kind of woman a man brings home to meet his mother."

I yanked the remaining hair out of my eyes. "Wasn't it only a couple of weeks ago that you were accusing me of being a party girl?"

"You sound like some men I know, but I never said you were a party girl." His voice was calm as he added, "For what it's worth, you're wrong about it being just one of *those* things."

"I doubt it. We're great when it comes to sex, but we are not a fit when it comes to what we want in life."

"You fit me just fine."

I threw my arms upward in frustration.

"What do you want in life that's so different from me?" he asked.

I was not in the mood to talk about this. If I wasn't

so certain about the kind of man who'd mesh with my lifestyle, who'd suit my needs, I'd . . . I didn't want to go there. "Look, Davin, you're a great guy. A perfect guy—just not for me."

"What if I'm right? What if we'd be good together?"

It was time to take another tack. I breathed deeply. "You're too young to know whether or not we'd be good together. That's the problem with you. Lack of maturity."

"I may be a few years younger, but I don't lack experience." He came closer and brushed away a strand of hair that had managed to fall back over my left eye. "What if you're wrong?"

I shook his hand away. "I'll have to take the chance."

"I thought we were friends."

Friends? That was a new one—unless friendship is defined by how much the other person annoys you? "I suppose we're friends, but partners in lust seems more apt. Look, Davin, I'd love to stick around and chat, but I have to get ready now."

"Fine. Stephen should be back soon. If you don't mind, I'll stick around and have dinner with him?"

"Stephen would like that." Davin was such a nice guy and handling everything so well, I felt guilty for being so bitchy. "Sorry I'm so grouchy."

"You aren't. You needed to bring what you were feeling out into the open."

I most definitely hadn't brought what I felt out in the open. If I had, I'd probably need to buy stock in whichever pharmaceutical company produces condoms.

What was I feeling?

A mixture of antagonism and desire. And a tiny, minuscule, almost invisible bit of regret. The best thing for both of us, though, was to go our own ways. "Well, thanks for bringing dinner. Next time you're in the mood to cook, check with me ahead of time. Okay?"

"You got it."

That was when I noticed the vase filled with fresh gladiolas sitting on the kitchen counter.

I looked back at Davin and said softly, "You brought me flowers?"

"Yeah." He looked a bit sheepish. "I sort of thought you and I . . ."

He trailed off, and again I knew what he meant.

I shot him a don't-go-there look and, then turned away. As I headed for my bedroom, I thought, *God, he's such a nice guy.*

If only he were a few years older, I might have encouraged him to take up a new hobby—like getting his pilot's license or becoming a cruise ship director. Anything that would pay well and frequently take him out of town.

✃ ✃ ✃

When you're married, you tend to look back on dating with a certain fondness. After you're divorced, you tend to look on dating with a great deal of trepidation.

Sure, I was a tad excited about what might happen between Greg and me. As I entered his hotel, I felt more frantic than perky. There was a slight tremble to my hands and my heart beat much faster than usual. After two truly sucky dates, Stephen's pending desertion, my almost-desperate need for college tuition, and everything going on with the sperm donor, it was difficult to work up any exuberance over the night ahead.

I tried to shake off my mood because Greg seemed like lots of fun. I was experienced enough to know that new dates were rarely personality fits. I was too aware of what could, and most likely would, go wrong.

Greg had suggested meeting at his hotel so I could try out his Purple People Mover. Upon reaching the lobby, I called up to his room on the house phone.

"We're celebrating tonight," he said.

"We are?"

"Yup. Tell you all about it when you get up here. Meet me outside my room so we can practice your People Moving skills in the hallway."

"I'm on my way."

Within minutes, as I exited the elevator on his floor, he came zooming up on his Purple People Mover. "Hey there."

"Hey, yourself," I said with a smile as he circled me.

"Let's go to my room. I've got one of these for you to use."

"I get to ride by myself?"

"Why not? The more, the merrier. I told you, we're celebrating."

We made our way down the hall, with him doing little happy circles with his People Mover. I asked, "Exactly what's got you so excited?"

"I bought my dream house today."

"Cool! Tell me about it." Considering how far away my dream house seemed, I looked forward to hearing about his.

He described the house, and it sounded enormous, then he named a lush Vegas neighborhood that was even more expensive than it was prestigious.

"Wow. People Moving must be a great business."

"It is. In six weeks I'm relocating here to set up a regional sales office. I can't wait."

We reached his room and he quickly handed his People Mover to me, then opened his door and grabbed another to use himself.

His mood was contagious and my worries dissipated as he taught me how to use the People Mover.

Fifteen minutes of instruction later, he said, "I think you're ready to take this thing on the road. You're a fast study."

"That's what all my dates tell me." I waggled my eyebrows and he laughed while pushing the button to call an elevator.

"Where are we going?"

"The hotel has a great all-you-can-eat lobster bar tonight. I tried it on a trip last year and was impressed. Since we're celebrating, I hope that sounds okay to you?"

"It sounds better than okay. I love lobster."

As we scooted through the mezzanine, through banks of slot machines and flashing lights, people stopped and watched us. Greg waved at gawkers and I soon felt confident enough to use only one hand now and then, so I could join him in the waving. My Purple People Mover was lots of fun.

We reached the restaurant before long, where I learned Greg had made prior arrangements for them to safely stow our People Movers and seat us at a nice table looking out on the strip.

"This is very nice." I noted the romantic lighting and inviting atmosphere.

"Would you prefer to dine *beneath* the table?"

"Very funny. Trust me that was *all* Connie's idea of amusement."

"I'm relieved to hear that, but wanted to make the offer, just in case." When he smiled, I noticed tiny laugh lines near his eyes, which seemed sort of endearing and made me like him even more. There's something extremely appealing about a man who laughs often.

The waiter came up, took our orders, then served a

perfectly chilled white wine I hadn't tried before. It was crisp and delicious and would go perfectly with lobster.

Greg chatted about traveling, and I watched how animated he was when talking about new experiences and unusual places he'd visited. It didn't hurt that he was really cute, too, with lively blue-green eyes and a quick smile.

By the time I'd eaten an unconscionable amount of lobster, I was feeling very friendly toward Greg. He made me feel as if I was interesting, with the way he drew out my thoughts on various subjects. With the approving gleam in his eyes, he made me feel very attractive, too.

I smiled at him.

"Your mount awaits, my sweet," he said, pointing toward our People Movers. He'd already taken care of the bill, and I'd silently rejoiced that for once I didn't have to pay.

"I think you're ready for a spin around the Strip. What do you say?"

"Maybe we should walk off some of that lobster."

"This'll be more fun."

"You're right," I agreed.

We left the restaurant on our mounts, and headed for the great outdoors, namely the very busy Las Vegas Strip.

It was as brightly lit as midday, with an almost-full moon that could still be discerned over all the lights.

Although I couldn't make out any stars, it was gorgeous.

As we zoomed along, tourists gawked, pointed, and some even stopped us to ask about our Purple People Movers. Greg handed out business cards and told them to call for information since we were on a date.

"You sure know how to treat a girl." I made a little loop around him.

"Do you say that to all your men?" he quipped.

"Only ones who treat me to lobster and Purple People Movers."

We stopped in front of the fountain at the Bellagio and watched part of the water show, but Greg caught me yawning.

"Are you tired?"

"A little. How about you?"

"Me, too. Let's head back now. I've got a bottle of wine in my room and we can toast my new house."

I nodded, pleasure playing about my lips. It sounded about perfect. Everything had gone so well I could barely keep the idea of "auditioning" him out of my thoughts. My first two dates with salesmen hadn't progressed far enough to get to the audition stage, but everything was different with Greg.

Spending time with a mature man, *a grown-up*, who shared my interests was a novelty. Better yet, he was well-traveled and didn't seem inclined to stop traveling any time soon. He made me feel smart, desirable, and best of all, he made me laugh.

Besides, during my loop around him, I'd checked out his derriere. It was A-1 prime, UPS-brown-shorts quality.

We made quick work of returning to the hotel and it didn't take long to reach his room. He opened his door and clicked on the light. "I'll take care of these." He motioned to our People Movers. "Have a seat."

He had a small suite, furnished with a seating area in addition to the bed area. I sat down on the sofa and tossed off my shoes as he plugged the People Movers into a power supply.

"That was lots of fun. I bet you'll sell several to people who stopped us tonight."

He went to the small refrigerator and pulled out a bottle of wine. "I hope you're right. It'll help pay for my new house."

You gotta adore a man who has a dream house. I wondered if it was very different from mine. The picture was in my handbag and I considered showing it to him.

He handed me a glass of wine, Riesling, and I patted the cushion beside me on the sofa so he'd take a seat. We held up our glasses and clinked them. "To your new house. May you happily live there for years to come."

"Thanks," he said.

I took a sip of wine. It was very good and a vintage I was fond of. Greg had very good taste, but did *he* taste good?

Figuring there was no time like the present to find out, I leaned forward and kissed him lightly on the lips. He not only tasted good, like lobster and wine, but he smelled good, too, like musk and some woodsy outdoor aroma. Nice.

"What was that for?" he asked.

"A very nice evening with a very nice man."

He smiled, took my wineglass, and placed it on the coffee table in front of us. Then he leaned in and kissed me.

It was pretty good in terms of first kisses. I deliberately avoided the comparison to Davin's kisses and concentrated on other first kisses. Not bad.

Greg placed an arm around me and pulled me closer, then we did some serious necking.

I'd like to take this moment to say that I was very much enjoying myself and feeling pretty good about how things were progressing. When he took my hand and pulled me toward the bed, I willingly went along.

Everything was great—and I liked the way he kissed the side of my throat—until it came to undressing.

I should have known something was up when he promised mood music and pulled a tape player from his suitcase.

While it was a little odd, I figured it was good that he hadn't had the tape player sitting out, as if expecting that we'd *need* mood music.

The first song was Ravel's "Bolero." While

unoriginal, it wasn't an awful choice. He came close and kissed me a little more, then removed my shirt and bra. That was when he began peeling off his shirt.

And the music changed, almost on cue, to "The Stripper." It blared as he did a striptease with his shirt.

Again, a bit odd for a first date, but since I'd only been with three men, ever, my ex-husband, my ex-boyfriend, and the sperm donor, I didn't have a lot of experience with these things. Maybe it was not *that* weird.

"I think you've practiced," I said, wanting to ease my tension.

He gazed at me through hooded eyes and camped up his dance routine by jiggling a bit more.

His wriggling and shimmying was definitely amusing. His hand lowered to his belt buckle, and he snapped it out in one quick flash. As his hand hovered over his zipper, he turned away from me.

I sat up, biting my lip to keep from giggling nervously, and waiting for a nice view of studly male butt, while he slowly inched down his slacks. Although his derriere was prime, it would have been more prime if he had kept it a few inches farther from my face.

I leaned back, but still got a better view than I could ever have imagined.

I blinked. I blinked again. He wasn't wearing underwear?

Or was he?

I scrunched my eyes almost closed while he

continued gyrating around the bed, with his pants around his ankles. He mooned me as he bent to remove them. Then he spun around to face me.

I schooled myself not to look shocked, expecting some sign of his arousal. Instead what I saw was . . . chiffon?

And sequins?

I did a double take as he did a thrust, a wriggle, another thrust to the last notes of the melody.

Another song started, and he started gyrating. Badda-Boom. Badda-Boom. Badda-Boom.

He turned around and wiggled that UPS butt at me again, and I was ready to swear off men.

Shocked? No shit. I was floored.

When I finally got my jaw off the mattress, and the bed covers pulled up to my chin, my voice squeaked, "Is that a g-string?"

"You like?" He did a pirouette that had my eyes bugging out. Sure enough, Greg wore a woman's g-string—and he must have been wearing it beneath his pants all night!

He wiggled his hips to the left, then to the right, then to the left again.

Gag. Gag. Gag.

My first impulse was to flee, then I decided I didn't require a second impulse. "I'm sorry, Greg, but this isn't my kind of thing."

"I can take it off," he offered.

I shook my head. "Did I mention that my first husband is now a woman? I've already been there, done that, on the sexual ambiguity thang."

"I'm not the least ambiguous about my sexuality." He just stood there, beside the bed, looking ridiculous in the tiny bit of fabric festooned in bling-bling.

"I'm sure you're not ambiguous. I'm simply not ready for . . . this." I pulled my shirt back on. "I'm sorry. No can do."

"Maybe we went too fast?" He grabbed his pants and pulled them on.

"It wouldn't have made a difference." He'd been lots of fun, until we'd reached the gag-me stage, but there was no way I'd go out with him again. Ever. Ever. Ever. "I should go now."

I walked over to the sofa and stepped into my shoes, then grabbed my handbag and stuffed my bra inside, not wanting to take the time to put it back on. I wanted to get the hell out of there. With my hand on the door, I said, "Thank you for dinner and an *interesting* evening."

"Thank you, too. Sure you don't want to stay and have more wine?"

"Nah. I'm going to head out."

And so much for Salesman Number Three. I'd bombed out with every salesman I'd met. I knew not to expect much when I arrived for the date. Something inevitably had to go wrong. I just hadn't expected anything *this* wrong.

Maybe I wasn't ready for dating?

Maybe you have to be a certain kind of woman to find a good salesman?

I'd like to blame it on Connie since she introduced me to Greg, but I hadn't suspected anything.

All I knew for certain was that I'd had it with my Salesman a.k.a. Tuition Plan. I'd find some other way to send Stephen to school, no matter how high the tuition, no matter how much debt I had to rack up.

Anything would be better than the dates I'd been putting myself through.

CHAPTER SIXTEEN

Dear Jill,

I'm returning your survey unanswered. Sadly, my Leonard passed away last month. After fifty years of togetherness, I miss having him by my side. I'm sorry. I can't complete your survey.

I hope you'll find a man like Leonard. The right man enriches your life in ways you can't imagine. Don't let my heartbreak over losing him discourage you.

There is loss in life. There is heartache so unbearable you'll think you don't have the strength to endure. But there is love and tenderness. There are wonderful moments and delicious laughter. You'll learn that they more than compensate.

Don't settle for anything less.

Sincerely,

Mrs. Leonard Norton

I like to think I'm a patient person.

I like to think I'm an understanding human being.

I learned I'm neither of those things when it comes to Control Freaks from Hades, a.k.a. Chef Breck.

There's something about having someone standing beside you, breathing down your neck, watching each and every movement you make that makes you feel— oh, I don't know—postal?

At the very least, I was feeling pretty livid because that's exactly what Chef Breck had been doing to me since the moment I'd arrived at La Papillon at five o'clock that morning.

Until then, I'd thought Davin Wesley was the quintessential control freak. Wrong.

Over the past four hours, I learned that Davin Wesley was a gentle pussycat with leadership qualities whereas Breck was a manic dictator with domination issues.

"Why are you standing so close?" I asked. Breck's exhalations made the hair on the back of my neck writhe like inhabitants of Dante's *Inferno*.

"So I can see what you're doing."

"Can't you do that from two steps back? You're making me nervous."

"You're making me nervous with the way you're measuring ingredients."

"What's wrong with the way I'm measuring?" My

hands shook. The gravel-like tone of my voice sounded a little like a werewolf in an old movie, but it didn't
deter the Phantom of the Breck.

"You're going to spill some of the ingredients."

"No, I'm not."

"Some will leak over. Perhaps you should stand
over the sink?"

"There's no room for me to work at the sink." I
gestured toward the salad prep going on at the sink.
Since I was measuring flour, not some toxic chemical, it
wasn't that big a deal.

But evidently it was to Breck. "And what will you
do when it spills?"

"I won't spill any." Nerves got the better of me and
my hands shook harder. A trace amount of flour drift-
ed from the top of the measuring container.

"Look. You're spilling already!" He leaned forward and flicked at the microscopic amount of flour on
the stainless steel counter below where I was working.
"And who do you expect to clean up your mess?"

I should have realized where he was going with this,
because he seemed to have some fixation with cleanli-
ness. Only an hour ago, he'd given the entire kitchen
staff a lecture on garbage.

That's right. Trash.

No garbage was to go into the waste containers (I
kid you not, that's what he called the trash cans), until
it had been thoroughly washed and rinsed. He even

demonstrated by washing—with gusto, mind you—an empty lettuce bag, prior to folding it neatly, like a napkin, and placing it properly in the waste container.

So, I wasn't surprised when he pulled his *personal* bottle of antiseptic spray cleaner from his back pocket and began to hose down my work area, regardless of the fact that the flour could have been blown away by his exhalations if I'd leaned out of the way.

"Attention, staff." He held up his spray bottle. "This is the cleanser of choice." He glanced at me. "You'll see to it that enough is ordered so that each member of the staff will have a bottle."

I nodded. What else could I do? Kurt had warned me that Breck was a control freak. I'd thought that meant he ran a tight kitchen. Ha. Kurt had also suggested that I watch my back around the controlling chef, but with the way Breck watched my front, that didn't seem necessary. He wasn't a control freak; he was a control perv.

Breck continued hovering over my every movement until all the lunch banquets had been served up. That was when he transferred his attention, at least momentarily, to one of the cooks—who'd probably arrange for INS to find him and ship him home for vacation soon, if Breck kept it up.

It was my chance. Escape. I felt as if I was breaking out of jail when I snuck out of the kitchen for a little break.

I needed to make a phone call to check on my skillet.

With my cell phone in hand, I headed to the restroom and locked the door behind me. Thank goodness Breck couldn't monitor my bathroom behavior.

I called Goodwill and asked for Meg.

"Oh, you're in luck," Meg said. "The lady who bought your skillet was in just this morning."

"She was?"

"Yes. She gave me her phone number so you could call her. I told her that you needed to talk with her."

"Okay. Thanks very much for your help." I wrote down the woman's name, Penny Cullen, and phone number on a Post-it pad I'd stored in the restroom for emergency suicide notes.

"Penny is such a sweet old dear," the saleswoman continued. "She seemed thrilled to be getting a call from you. I don't think she has much family. She comes into our store a lot. I think she's lonely."

I should have paid more attention to what Meg was saying. Instead, I was thinking about getting my skillet back.

So what if my son was deserting me? So what if I had no clue how to pay his tuition? So what if I'd totally blown it in the Salesman Sweepstakes and even Davin Wesley had been avoiding me since Saturday? My skillet was about to return home where it belonged.

I dialed Penny Cullen's number.

"Hello?" Penny's voice sounded elderly, but very sweet.

"Mrs. Cullen? This is Jill Morgan Storm."

"Ohh, you're the young woman Meg said would call."

"Yes, ma'am. She said you'd bought my skillet."

"Yes, indeed. It's so perfect. You know, dear, it would have taken me months to season one up so perfectly."

She took a breath, so I jumped in with, "I know—"

But she cut me off. "I can cook anything in my new skillet. Why I made up a mess of cornbread just this morning. You're a very good girl to donate it to Goodwill."

"I didn't exactly—"

Again she broke in. "Good Samaritans. There's a special place in heaven for them. At church last weekend, Mr. Wainwright, he's our minister, did a sermon on exactly that subject. You know what he said?"

I started to answer, but realized it was a rhetorical question when she kept talking. At this rate, I would have to subscribe to a different cell phone calling plan.

As she chatted on, I didn't pay much attention, thinking I'd be able to get back to my skillet after she ran out of steam. It didn't take long to amass a pile of toilet paper origami.

Then Mrs. Cullen said something about a fire and I had no clue what she meant. I exclaimed, "What fire?"

Mrs. Cullen stopped her monologue to ask, "Didn't

Meg tell you?"

"No." Had my skillet been damaged in a fire?

"It was just awful. Losing everything that way is so difficult."

"Who had a fire?"

"You didn't see it on the news? An electrical wiring fault. It's a good thing I spent that day volunteering at the hospital, because if I'd been home . . ."

"You had a fire?"

"That's what I was saying, dear, when you interrupted."

"I'm so sorry to hear about the loss of your home."

"Meg has been very kind. She lets me know ahead of time when a new shipment is coming in, so I can replace the things I've lost, you see. I've furnished my new place with items that are so like my old ones, you almost can't tell."

"That's terrific."

"I was just thrilled when I saw your skillet in the store. I don't have any pictures of her anymore, but looking at that skillet made my mother, God rest her soul, come to mind, almost like she was standing right here, teaching me how to cook like she did when I was a girl. Her skillet was exactly like yours."

What could I say? What could I do? I wouldn't be able to face myself in the mirror if I asked for her to return it. "I'm glad you were able to give my skillet a good home. Do you need anything else? The fire and all."

"No, honey. I'm just as happy as a lark."

Penny Cullen was a much braver woman than me. She'd made a full life for herself, without a husband, without a family, but with friends who truly cared about her.

After hanging up, I realized I had a lot of thinking to do. So what if I had to replace my skillet? I could buy a new one exactly like my old one, and eventually I'd get it seasoned just right. It might take a while, but if Penny Cullen could replace her whole household, I could replace one pan.

Someone began pounding on the restroom door. Big E called out, "Jill, Breck wants you."

"Go away."

"He's timing how long you've been gone. Come now!"

"All right. I'll be right there." Argh.

I had to get back to Breck purgatory to handle prep for the dinner banquets, but after work I determined I'd go buy myself a new skillet.

ひ ひ ひ

Target was crowded when I arrived and there were only a few red carts left in the corral. I snagged one and threaded my way through the aisles to Housewares.

Let me tell ya, Target has a huge selection of pots and pans made up of almost every imaginable material.

Calphalon, T-Fal, Teflon, ceramic. Unfortunately, this made it more difficult to find a cast-iron skillet.

Shiny new pots gleamed from the racks where they were hanging. Brightly colored enamel pans glittered in the overhead lighting.

There were hundreds of pans and at first I didn't think they carried cast iron. I persevered until I found a few on a lower shelf.

The skillet only came as part of a three-piece set, but the price was extremely reasonable. I headed for the checkout.

While I would have much preferred my old skillet, this one would do. I knew exactly how to season it and make it nearly as perfect as the other. All I required was a little time.

My universe was crumbling beneath my feet. Preparing my new skillet was something I *could* control. Heck, if I wanted to, I could really live it up and season all three.

CHAPTER SEVENTEEN

Survey Comments:

Face it, men lie. They don't always need a good reason to lie. They just do it.

Assume the worst when it comes to your man. It's the added ingredient for making a marriage happy.

It's up to us women to keep our guys on the straight and narrow. If you tell him you'll be verifying anything he tells you, then he'll be on his guard. It's possible it'll keep him honest. If it doesn't, at least his lies will be doozies and good for a few laughs.

Gloria Gable

Mad Chef Breck didn't improve with familiarity. Between his hovering and timing my potty breaks, I was forced to find another place to escape. It kept me from carrying out my fantasy about stuffing him in Fang.

By accident, I lucked out in finding the perfect answer.

"Where are you going?" Breck asked as I slunk toward the kitchen exit.

"Oh." Since my intended destination was Mandy's office, I pointed upward with my thumb. "Upstairs."

The look of annoyance on his face disappeared and was replaced by a more studious expression. He nodded, as if he knew what my mission was.

It became my favorite excuse whenever I needed to escape his far too frequent attentions. Like, three times a day.

Since he'd just overseen how I quartered chickens, it was time to go while the getting was good. I quickly made my way to Mandy's office. When I arrived, she didn't look too busy to be tempted to stop what she was doing and instead chat with me. "How are you today?"

"Okay. Hiding from the Mad Chef?" She looked up from her computer monitor. She'd been in the process of keying in information from a stack of forms sitting on the desk beside her keyboard. Definitely not too busy to chat and escape boring detail work.

"Sorta."   I slumped into one of the chairs in front of her desk.

Mandy slid a newspaper across the desk toward me. "Your parents are in today's paper. I saved it for you."

"Cool! Fiftieth anniversary photos?"

"They turned out very nice."

I snorted as I lifted the paper. "For prison photos?"

"Actually, the warden's son-in-law did a very good job."

I glanced at the photo and had to agree. My folks looked happy, in love, and ready to go at it for another fifty years.

"And speaking of your mother . . ."

Mandy trailed off and I looked up from the write-up on my parents. Speaking of the she-devil, my mother waltzed into Mandy's office.

"Hello, dears," said Mom, blowing air kisses at each of us, as she breezed to the chair beside me.

I shot Mandy a you-should-have-warned-me look, but said, "What a pleasant surprise, Mom. What brings you here?"

"Didn't Mandy tell you?"

"I was getting ready to." Mandy grimaced.

As usual, my mother was beautifully dressed and flawlessly made up. I looked her up. I looked her down. This was a woman who could only be up to no good.

I shot Mandy another look.   This one said,

you-really-should-have-warned-me-because-I-need-more-coffee-or-tequila-would-be-even-better.

Mom brushed an imaginary crumb from her flawless Chanel slacks. "I'm here to plan our anniversary party. What else would bring me here?"

Like matchmaking wasn't scheduled in her PDA? Since she'd been in frequent contact with Mandy, maybe she'd transferred her matchmaking to her? In my dreams.

My brow furrowed as I realized what she *had* said. "Anniversary party? Dad's in prison. You can't have an anniversary party."

"I don't see why not. We're celebrating, even if he's unable to attend."

Mandy broke in, probably sensing enough mother/daughter tension that it could be cut with a meat cleaver. "We've almost finalized her menu."

"How nice," I said to Mandy then turned to my mother. "Are you nuts?"

"What a fine way to speak to your mother," said my mother, who always referred to herself in the third person when she wanted to make me feel guilty.

It didn't work.

She asked, "Are you on your period?"

Why is it that if I'm the least bit contentious, someone asks if I'm on my period? Why can't they just assume that whatever makes you bitchy might not have anything whatsoever to do with hormones and might have something to do with the person asking the question?

Mom always goes on the offensive when her reasoning is on shaky ground. I asked, "Is an anniversary party appropriate, given the circumstances?"

"Circumstances be . . . damned." Mom seemed pleased with her choice of words. She doesn't usually curse in front of her children.

She angled her head and looked at me consideringly. Seconds later she brightened. "I see what's bothering you. Don't worry, Jill. You don't need a date."

Like a date was on my mind at all? "That's reassuring."

"I've asked all my friends to bring along their single sons. You'll have a splendid opportunity to view the available selection."

"You what?!"

I was all set to spring out of my chair and call the men in white coats to drag Mom off, but that was the moment when Mr. Nagasaki's assistant tapped at the open door, thus saving my mother from certain institutionalization. "Jill?"

"Yes?" I asked, wondering why she'd addressed me rather than Mandy.

"Mr. Nagasaki wants to see you in his office, Jill." The assistant glanced at my mother then turned and fled back down the hall. My mother can have that effect on people.

Mandy grimaced as I stood and grimaced back at her.

"Guess I'd better go see what he wants." I turned my attention back to my mother. "We're going to talk more about the invitations, Mom." She might believe she'd escaped my wrath regarding her friends' sons, but I wasn't about to let her get away with it.

"I'll look forward to it." She smiled and I could have sworn that smile hinted at evil machinations. She added, "Mandy explained that with your employee discount I can afford more, so we'll finalize the appetizers before I dash off to a fund-raiser."

"Talk with you later," I said to Mandy, then mouthed, "Sorry" over my mother's head.

My steps to Mr. Nagasaki's office were slow, as if I were walking through thick mud. Being called to his office did not look good.

What did he want? Since he'd hired Breck, I hadn't expected to see Nagasaki until the staff holiday party, where we'd take turns bowing at each other.

Unfortunately, I arrived before coming to a conclusion about what was going on. The assistant showed me directly into Nagasaki's office. For once, he remained seated at his desk, making those Japanese hieroglyphs on a pad in front of him.

He didn't acknowledge me right away. I stood awkwardly, watching him. It took a moment for him to finish before he stood and greeted me with a bow. I bowed back.

He gestured toward a chair. I took a seat, bowing first.

He didn't say anything at all for several minutes.

When his staring got to me, I asked, "You wanted to see me?"

He nodded and looked me over.

It was fairly early in the day, so I wasn't wearing as many menu items as usual. He couldn't be concerned over the stains on my uniform. And my hair, while not perfect, didn't yet resemble a bird's nest.

He was totally silent.

I asked, "Is there something I can help you with?"

"I believe so."

Now we were getting somewhere. Not.

He leaned back in his chair, his eyes hooded. "Perhaps you can explain to me how the rumor that you and I have a personal relationship got started? My wife would be very disappointed to hear such a rumor."

"A personal relationship? As in . . ."

He nodded again.

Ohmigawd. People thought we were having an affair? Surely not. I must have misunderstood. There was the language, or at least accent, difference. Seconds ticked by before I asked, "As in we're an, um, item?" I crossed my fingers for luck as I awaited his reply.

He didn't keep me waiting long. "Precisely."

My thoughts whirled like the contents of a blender.

How could there be rumors about us at all? And more importantly, why was I the last to hear of them? I thought I was the chairperson of the gossip mill at this hotel. "This is the first I've heard of any rumors. Who told you this gossip?"

"That does not matter. What is important is that you and I each do whatever is necessary to dispel such a patent untruth."

Yeah, like I'd be glad for such a rumor? I can't imagine it doing my reputation any good. "I whole-heartedly agree."

"I do not wish to see my wife disappointed."

"Neither do I." I'd only met her once and she was extremely sweet, charming, and, I suspected, deadly when it came to protecting her family and her man. She was decidedly not someone whom I'd like to disappoint.

"You're certain you know nothing of how the rumor got started?"

"Positive. This is the first I've heard of it."

He shuffled some of the papers around on his desk.

"Don't you think that calling me to your office like this might add fuel to the gossip?"

"Point taken." He lifted a sheet of paper and scanned it. "According to sources, you have been spending considerable time in the administrative offices. Is this correct?"

I gulped. "Kind of."

"Where have you been?"

"Consulting with the catering manager, Mandy."

"Three to four times daily?"

I cleared my throat. I couldn't exactly tell him that I was hiding from his new chef, could I? Additionally, I didn't want to get Mandy into any hot water. "Sometimes it's necessary."

"I've also been informed that you have been taking prolonged personal breaks."

Now, that had to come from Breck. Who else would call potty runs "personal breaks"? "Can you define *prolonged*?"

"Over five minutes in length?"

"The majority of the kitchen staff is male. Being female, I require a bit more time."

He nodded and consulted his notes again. "It's also been reported that you've been visiting the guest and ballroom areas quite frequently."

"I have?"

"You were seen at the Classical Cookware, Future Home Builders, and Tool Depot conventions."

I should have expected someone would notice how I'd been attempting to scope out salesmen. But all of that was pre-Breck. "I had to check on the catering. Sometimes that's necessary, you know."

He nodded. The silence grew so loud I could hear the seconds tick on his fancy wristwatch. At last he said, "I previously promised that you'd always have a job at La Papillon. Do not make me regret that promise, Ms. Storm."

My words gushed out, "I won't. I'll do whatever I can to dispel rumors of a personal relationship with you."

"When Chef Breck asked about bringing over the sous chef from his previous kitchen, I informed him that he would find you an exceptionally talented individual. When I make a recommendation like that, I expect to be found correct. Do we understand each other?"

"Completely." He was saying that either I get my act together or I was outta there. Breck was smearing my reputation so he could bring in the guy he wanted. Great. Just great.

"Thank you." He stood and gave a quick bow, obviously dismissing me.

My life obviously hadn't tanked enough. Although he hadn't said so directly, if I wanted to keep my job I needed to do some serious sucking up to Breck. Gag.

I bowed to Mr. Nagasaki and headed back to the kitchen. While I waited for the elevator to arrive, I had a sudden notion.

Basically, Nagasaki had told Breck he couldn't replace me. Six members of my kitchen staff had quit in as many days, and Breck had seamlessly replaced them with employees from his last kitchen. If he wanted to replace me with his old sous chef, perhaps Breck had decided to make my life at La Papillon a living hell?

He'd done a marvelous job of it.

Kurt warned me to watch my back around the Mad Chef. Perhaps he wasn't the control freak he'd appeared to be. Perhaps he was extremely devious. The more I thought over his recent activities, the more convinced I became.

He'd set me up.

And it pissed me off.

What if the incident with the flour, the spray cleansers, the way he'd told me I was heating the ovens incorrectly, the proper manner of disposing of waste materials, the whole nine yards, were all an act?

He wanted to make me outraged enough to leave.

It wasn't going to happen.

I wasn't going to let Breck to do it to me. I'd buckle down. I'd not only tolerate his micromanagement, I'd welcome it—maybe even return it!

With a new attitude, I straightened my uniform and entered the kitchen. The man might be devious, but he didn't know who he was dealing with.

ဢ ဢ ဢ

The problem with outscheming someone is coming up with a better scheme of your own. I'd planned to start with staying later and arriving earlier than Breck.

I failed to take into account the second shift, the members of which had arrived and were giving me dirty looks because I was in their way.

Biting back an urge to stick my tongue out at them all, I checked my watch. It was already a quarter hour later than I generally left and Breck showed no sign of budging, no matter how many dirty looks he received.

He kept watching me, as if he knew what I was up to.

If he was going to spy on me and run telling tales to Nagasaki, two could play that game. Although half the kitchen staff had been replaced by his stoolies, there were still enough loyal staffers in place to cover my ass and monitor his. Turnabout is fair spying?

I wasn't convinced I wanted to go that route, but it wouldn't hurt to keep tabs on him and burn the late night oil.

I checked my watch again. I was late meeting Connie. We have standing arrangements to rendezvous weekly at the gym. With a sigh of defeat, I grabbed my stuff and headed out.

When I entered the gym, the day's stress slid off me like butter off freshly baked bread. It didn't take long to change into my gym shorts and reach the rowing machines where Connie and I always met. We row slowly and chat a bit, before getting down to the serious business of shaping and toning.

Connie sat on a rowing machine, but she wasn't doing any rowing. She was just sitting there with her chin in her hands.

"I'm sorry I'm late."

She looked up and smiled. "I only got here a few minutes ago."

I took a swig from my water bottle and sat on the machine next to her. "What's up?"

I rowed.

She rowed.

She made a little kitten noise. "Not too much. I booked an entire family on a European cruise today."

"That's great."

I rowed.

She rowed.

"I received a query about rates from a restaurant company looking to do a corporate retreat. That'll be lucrative."

"Awesome."

I rowed.

She rowed.

"And I kicked Mike out yesterday."

"What?" I stopped mid-row. "You did this yesterday and haven't mentioned it until now? What happened?"

"That's why I didn't tell you until now. It's a long and stupid story."

I rowed.

She didn't.

"I like long and stupid stories."

"Well, yesterday started out pretty okay." Connie shrugged and began rowing again. "Not good, but decent anyway. Mike had a second interview scheduled at the electronics store. I had a hair appointment at Murzo."

So far, Connie hadn't said anything that would lead her to kick Mike out, but it was interesting that she had a hair appointment at Murzo. It's the latest trendy hair salon and happened to be located at the mall. I'd have to ask her what she thought sometime when we weren't discussing more important things, like evicting Mike's no-good ass. "Go on."

She rowed.

I rowed.

"I said I'd drive us to the mall. We agreed to meet at the food court following each of our appointments."

I nodded.

Connie rowed.

"What happened next?"

"I got to Murzo's only to find out that I got the date wrong. My appointment is for next week."

"What did you do next?"

I rowed.

Connie took a sip from her water bottle.

"I wasn't sure what time Mike's interview was, although I knew it was soon, so I walked to the electronics store. I didn't see him. I thought he might be in back interviewing."

I rowed.

She rowed half a stroke and then stopped. "So I decided I'd do a little window shopping and maybe I'd see Mike. If he wasn't interviewing yet, maybe I'd run into him at the food court or around somewhere. Or maybe he'd finish his interview and run into me. So I dawdled, looking in the windows of every shop as I passed."

She rowed.

I rowed.

"Did you find him?"

"Oh, yeah. I was dawdling, right?" She did a couple more strokes, at last coming to a halt. "I looked in the window of the video arcade. And there he was. He had a huge cupful of game tokens and was starting to play some big video game machine. I stood there watching, kind of frozen in place. You know?"

I nodded.

She continued, "He had an interview, but he didn't seem to be worrying about the time. He seemed to be settling down for a long session at Halo or whatever."

"That's odd."

"What was odder, Jill, was all of the employees knew him by name. But they were all kids. They would have been about ten years old back when Mike left town."

"Strange."

"I started to go in and let him know my appointment was canceled, but something stopped me. Maybe it was those kids, maybe it was his cup of tokens, maybe it was . . . I don't know, but it felt off. Like something was wrong."

"I can see how it would."

"I walked back toward the hair salon, thinking maybe I could see if another stylist had an opening. Maybe it would be better not to know what Mike was up to."

She rowed.

I rowed.

"Then I realized I couldn't bury my head in the sand. I had to know."

"Did you confront him?"

"I went to the electronics store and asked for the manager. The manager was a woman." Connie's breathing became labored from the exercise. "It was a little awkward at first. I finally leveled with her. Said I needed to know, for romantic reasons, if she had any employment interviews scheduled for today."

Connie took another sip of water and both of us gave up all pretense of rowing.

"The manager understood about man troubles and said she didn't have any job openings, much less any interviews scheduled. I was stunned. I thought Mike had only misled me about the second interview. I never considered the idea he'd lied about everything. I asked if he'd applied recently. She said his name wasn't familiar and pulled out her applications file. He hadn't put in an application. He's been lying about everything. Applying. The first interview. The second."

"That's awful."

She rowed.

I rowed.

She rowed harder.

I rowed harder.

We both stopped.

"All along, he planned to mooch off me. He conned me into believing he'd changed. The only change is his lies are better."

"Is that when you confronted him?"

"No. I started thinking. About Mike. About myself. Some lonely part of me wants to have someone, anyone, even if he's a total liar and thief, rather than be alone. My daughter's gone. I don't have a significant other. I don't even own a pet."

"You've got me and Susan and MaryEllen."

"Why do you think I'm not a basket case?" Connie smiled. "You're my family. We may not live in the same household, but in every way, you're there for me. I don't need more than what I have already. You guys and my friends at work. A fantastic career that allows me to travel. I certainly don't need a lying asshole like Mike messing up my life."

"What about sex?"

"From now on, it's strictly recreational."

She rowed.

I rowed.

"Why is it women feel they aren't complete without a man?" Connie asked. "Who carved that message into our heads? On what mountain has it been written? Dammit, I may have an empty nest, but it's *my* empty nest. I don't have to share it to make my life more complete. I'm already complete. I'm enough."

As Connie talked, I realized what she was saying also applied to me. Had my mom's propaganda about finding a man been absorbed into my psyche when I wasn't looking?

Connie stopped rowing and picked up the rest of her story. "I went home, packed Mike's belongings into his backpack, then went back to the game arcade. Mike was still there, playing his stupid game. He didn't notice me when I stuck a five-dollar bill into the token converter. Then I waited for him at the food court and ate every carbohydrate I could find. By the time he arrived, I'd finished a triple dip cone."

Since we'd both been rationing our carbs, this was significant. "What did Mike say?"

Connie snorted. "What could he say? He took a seat, said my hair looked great, then told me he thought he'd gotten the job but wouldn't know till next week."

"What a freaking liar."

"You said it. I asked what he thought of the store manager. The bastard referred to the manager as a male."

She rowed.

I rowed.

"So you told him not to come back?" I asked.

"I said that was very interesting since I'd met the manager and *she* was very nice and very informative. You should have seen his face. Do I know how to pick 'em, or what?" Connie grinned and shook her head.

She was taking the whole Mike matter better than I would have. Better than I dreamed she could have. "I'm awed by the way you handled him."

"It gets better. I pushed the cup of game tokens I'd purchased across the table at him and said he'd need a few more tokens to get him through the afternoon. I lifted his backpack from the chair beside me and handed it to him."

"Did he try to come up with another excuse?"

"Probably. I wasn't listening. It only took me nineteen years, but I finally saw him for what he was. I told him not to call me ever again."

She rowed.

I rowed.

"I'm so proud of you, Connie. I was worried about what would happen if Mike left again."

"You know what's ironic?"

I shook my head.

"Mike's always done the leaving in all of his relationships. He freaked out when I told him to get lost.

He just looked at his backpack like he didn't recognize it, as if it were a foreign object. When I walked away, he yelled, 'You can't kick me out, I'm leaving you!' I didn't turn around. I didn't stop. I shot him the finger and went on."

"That's priceless. I wish I could have seen Mike's expression."

"For the first time in his life, he didn't have the right words to say to change my mind."

"And look at you! Mike didn't have the power to hurt you!"

"Oh, I cried a little as I packed his backpack, but only because of the fantasy. It pissed me off that a fantasy could have that kind of hold over me. Never again."

And where did that leave me? Clinging to a fantasy about traveling salesmen, college tuition, and a week of incredibly hot sex.

CHAPTER EIGHTEEN

Dear Mr. Stephen Storm:

Have you talked with people about their college years? Even though everyone's college experiences are different, there are common themes in their stories. They talk about how excited they were, how much fun they had, and the discoveries they made about themselves.

To help you commemorate college, one of the most important times in your life, enclosed you will find an Official Certificate of Acceptance. We think you will want to save it for a lifetime.

We're excited about your joining our community of artists and look forward to a rewarding collaboration.

Sincerely,

Collette O' Brien

Dean, School of Art

Some days the best thing to do is go back to bed. I was having a day when the best thing to do is hide beneath the covers.

I'd learned about rumors circulating that Nagasaki and I not only bowed to each other, we were doing it with each other. I'd learned that the Mad Chef wanted me outta my job and was scheming to get rid of me.

And there was the empty nest issue.

The topper came when I checked my cell phone for messages after finishing up at the gym.

The message was from Davin, who had called from my house. Since I hadn't heard from him in days, I listened with interest.

"Jill, you asked me to warn you ahead of time when I'm bringing dinner. I'm ordering Chinese. See you later. Bye."

What a tool. I finally hear from him and he's not asking if I want dinner, he's already ordering it. What if I didn't feel like Chinese? What if I had plans?

I actually *had* plans—for introspection. I needed to think about what Connie said and that whole self-awareness shtick. I needed time to figure out what was going on in the jambalaya of my life.

I needed time to think, not someone to annoy me.

And Davin Wesley never failed to annoy.

Hiding under my bed was sounding better and better.

By the time I arrived home, I'd worked up an attitude. I took one look at Davin and held up my hand to silence him. "Don't talk to me yet." I made a beeline to my bedroom, dumped my junk on my bed, then sailed into the bathroom for a quick shower.

Only after pulling on a pair of jeans and a comfy T-shirt did I make an appearance in the living room. "S'up?"

"Better now?" asked Davin, sidestepping my question.

"Much. Is dinner here yet?"

"It should be in about ten minutes."

Did I mention an attitude? I was in a *mood*. I looked at him lounging on *my* sofa, in *my* living room, after spending time with *my* son, and it irked me. "In the interests of being very clear, when I asked you to warn me about dinner, I *meant* that you should ask if it was a good time. Not announce impending food deliveries."

He stood up in reaction to the sting in my tone. "Normally I would have, but we need to talk."

"I thought I also made it clear I didn't want to talk—at least not about us. Obviously we're having communication problems." I took Davin's hand in mine. "We do not need to talk about our relationship because we don't have one."

He opened his mouth to speak, but I talked over him.

"Yes, I know I said we are friends." I petted his hand. "We don't have to talk about our friendship, do we?"

Again he started to speak and again I interrupted.

"Friendship means never having to talk about your relationship."

Davin lightly placed the forefinger from his free hand over my lips and whispered, "Shh." With his other hand he gave my palm a gentle squeeze. "Are you finished?"

"For now."

"Good. Because we seriously need to talk."

This time he interrupted me when I opened my mouth to speak.

"Can you please be quiet long enough to listen?"

I dropped his hand and sighed. "Fine."

"We need to talk about Stephen."

"Is something wrong with him?" I made a move in the direction of his bedroom. I could bear all the career and romantic turmoil but if something happened to my kid . . . "Where is he?"

"He's in his room." Davin put his arm around my back and guided me to take a seat on the sofa. "He's not sick, if that's what you're thinking."

"So what is it?"

Davin settled next to me and spread his arm behind me on the back of the sofa. "Stephen has been forging artwork."

"I know."

"Copying the masters."

"Yes."

"Don't you have a problem with this?"

I shrugged. "Isn't it part of learning how to paint?"

"It is *if* you're not trying to pass the art off as the master's original work."

Stephen had created a number of paintings, similar to the ones painted by various artists. "He's trying to pass off his paintings as having been painted by famous artists?"

"I think so."

"Why would he do that?"

"For as long as there have been successful artists, there have been forgers trying to capitalize on their fame."

"Stephen's doing it for the money? For college tuition?" I asked hopefully, not that I wanted my kid to commit crimes for college, but I could understand that motivation.

"No and no." Davin looked apologetic. "It's more likely because of the challenge—because he can. Or wants to know if he can. It's pretty typical of teenage boys."

"Forging artwork?"

"That's not what I mean." He patted my shoulder. "They test things, the status quo. It leads some kids to computer hacking or writing viruses. They do it because they can. To see if they can get away with it."

"Oh." My son the forger. Not something I wanted to brag about in my yearly Christmas letter.

"Some boys have a talent with computers. Stephen has a gift for artwork."

"I'll make him give the money back." My chest ached and my heart slowed. "He won't be arrested, will he?"

"Not unless he actually tries to sell something. I don't think he's done that yet. I checked his paintings and none seem to be missing."

"That's a relief." My heart started beating again. He wouldn't have to share a jail cell with Dad. "Are you sure he's planning to try?"

"I wasn't sure until this afternoon. What first got my attention was when he started using materials from the correct time periods, like the old canvases he was collecting and the lead-based paint."

Stephen's use of lead-based paints *had* seemed unusual. I felt like slapping my forehead. I knew he and Tom had been up to *something*. Duh. "What happened today to make you sure?"

"Today the paintings were signed."

"He always signs his paintings."

"Correction. Until today he'd always signed with his *own* name." Davin grinned. "You have to hand to the kid. He did a great copy of Van Gogh's signature."

"I'm going to hand it to him, all right. Right on his butt."

"Surely that won't solve anything?"

"Of course not." The man who thought I was a candidate for Worst Mother of the Year had just conclusively proved that I was even worse at mothering than I thought. To top it off, judging by his serious expression, he thought me capable of beating my child. "So what do I do? What can I do?"

"He needs to understand the consequences of what he's doing," said Davin as the doorbell rang.

Our dinner had arrived.

I automatically got out plates and flatware while worrying over what could have happened if Davin hadn't noticed the signatures.

Davin brought the sacks of food into the kitchen.

"I can't tell you how much I appreciate your noticing what Stephen's been up to. I hate to think what would have happened if you hadn't been there for him . . . for us. Thank you."

"You're welcome. Whether we're in a relationship or not, I care about both of you."

"Thanks. I suppose my next step is to talk to him." I reached for tumblers from the cupboard.

"Do you want me to talk with him, too?" asked Davin, opening one of the bags and sniffing the aroma of Moo Goo Gai Pan. "Or would you rather I leave?"

"Would you mind staying? He likes you a lot and respects your opinion."

Davin stood beside me, pulling boxes of fried rice

out of the bag. "No matter what he's done, he's a good kid."

"I think so, too. Let's talk to him over dinner. It'll come up more casually that way." When I grabbed the stack of plates, Davin grabbed the food, and we walked into the dining room.

"Casual is good," he said. "You ready?"

I nodded and took a seat. My voice squeaked, "Ready."

"I'll call him." Davin stepped into the hallway and said, "Stephen, dinner is here." He then rejoined me and sat down at the table.

"So, how was school today?" I asked Davin, struggling to sound normal. My voice seemed to be an octave higher than usual.

"Good. We've been working on adjectives this week and the kids have been doing very well."

As Davin spoke, Stephen came in and settled into his seat.

Davin continued, "I was just telling your mom what a great group of students I've got this year."

I looked at Stephen more closely. Was he now sporting green streaks along with the neon blue spikes in his hair? This probably wasn't the moment to ask, but I wished the lighting was better. "How was your day, Stephen?"

"*Bien.*"

We passed around the Chinese food containers.

Once we began eating, Davin's gaze met mine over the Sweet and Sour Shrimp. I think he wanted me to bring up the subject of art forgery. I couldn't come up with a way to approach it. Since he seemed to be in such a hurry, he could do it. I crammed my mouth full of egg roll and shot him an innocent look.

Davin shook his head, then cleared his throat. "During my break today, I had an interesting discussion with the art teacher."

Stephen looked up from his plate. "Mrs. Donovan?"

"Yes. She's been doing research for her Ph.D. thesis on art forgery."

Stephen lowered his head and took a quick bite of General Tso's Chicken. He'd obviously learned the art of conversation avoidance from a master, namely *moi*.

"How interesting." I shot Stephen the Look. The Look I learned from my mother. The one she learned from hers. The Look all children wish to avoid.

"Mrs. Donovan said even though there are huge legal penalties for art forgery, people keep doing it."

Stephen kept his gaze lowered.

"I was surprised," continued Davin. "What amazed me was how many kids evidently try it, despite the fact that when they're caught they face years of prison."

Stephen tossed down his fork and it clattered on the table. "You're talking about me, aren't you?"

"Where'd you get that idea?" Davin asked.

"Never mind." Stephen picked up an egg roll and bit into it. A minute later he said, "The kids forging artwork are minors. They don't go to jail."

"Technically, they're minors. These days, most kids your age are tried and sentenced as adults."

Stephen looked at Davin, then looked at me, then jumped from his chair. "What is this, an intervention?"

"You got it," I said. "You're just lucky I didn't invite your grandmother. By this point she'd be chasing you around the apartment with turpentine."

"Like, she'd be worse than you?"

"Like, she is." I lowered my fork to my plate.

"Like, she doesn't spend all her time chasing traveling salesmen. At least she'd be chasing *me*."

I cringed. Stephen had a good point, one that hurt like hell. Had I been ignoring him, funneling my attention to chasing salesmen, rather than giving him the attention—and supervision—he needed?

My excuse had been that if I found the right salesman, the college tuition issue would be resolved. Was I being selfish?

"Sit down, Stephen." Davin's tone was not to be argued with.

Stephen took his seat.

I was majorly impressed. How had Davin done that? If I'd told Stephen to sit down, he would have cursed at me in French.

"Here's what you're going to do. You're going to paint over the signatures on your artwork and replace them with your own. You sign them. They're good." Davin's voice was calm and quiet, but even I heard the steel in his tone. "Claim the work as your own."

"Why should I?" asked Stephen.

"Because we told you to," I piped up.

"You're a gifted and talented artist," Davin said, "and you're entering them in the art show coming up."

"There's the little matter of entrance fees." Stephen smirked, as if he had the last word.

Davin pulled his checkbook from his rear pocket. Talk about coming prepared.

But Stephen is my kid. I don't let other people pay when it's my obligation. "Put your checkbook away. Stephen, you have birthday money saved up. You'll pay half and I'll pay the other half."

Davin glanced back at Stephen. "How much?"

"Twenty-five dollars per entry."

"You've got six paintings." Davin turned back to me. "Since it was my idea, how about thirds? Fifty dollars from each of us."

"Yeah, *Maman*. It was his idea."

I knew Stephen was thinking about the twenty-five dollars he wouldn't have to pay, but it was sweet of Davin to offer. He'd feel bad if I didn't let him participate. I smiled at him. "Okay, but next time dinner is on me."

By the time I returned to the dining room with my checkbook, Stephen and Davin were chatting comfortably. Stephen looked almost relieved. Maybe he hadn't *really* wanted to be a forger?

Their topic of discussion was my mom's anniversary party, which reminded me that I needed an escort or she'd spend the entire evening attempting to fix me up with someone unsuitable. It was an anniversary party. Since my mom would necessarily be attending stag, I'd feel embarrassed to do the same. I needed someone hot. I needed someone charming. And if I couldn't have that, at the least I needed someone presentable.

I eyed Davin, who was a lot more than merely presentable. He was the answer to my dilemma. But would he agree to come, especially after I'd been so rude to him earlier? I cleared my throat. "So, Davin . . ."

My voice squeaked, so I tried again. "Since you seem to be into the whole rescue thing tonight, want to help me?

"My hobby is rescuing damsels in distress. What's wrong?"

"Nothing's wrong. I need an escort for Mom's anniversary party. I was hoping you'd come with Stephen and me."

He didn't say anything right away, so I quickly said, "Never mind. Stupid idea. Besides, you probably don't dance."

"Oh," his voice deepened, "I dance." He looked at Stephen's hopeful face, then glanced back at me. "How formal is it?"

"I can get you a discount on tux rental."

"I have one of my own." He shook his head at Stephen, then cocked a half smile at me. "I can't believe I'm saying this, but I'd love to come."

"You're a true knight in shining armor. Thank you!"

"It's all in a day's work, ma'am. Now where did I leave my white horse?" He rose from his chair and turned to Stephen. "Come on. I'll help *you* paint over the signatures."

While I did the dishes, wondering exactly what I'd gotten myself into, they went off to remove the evidence.

Which brings me back to where I started when I arrived home. My job was in jeopardy. My new boss was spying on me and starting rumors about me. My Salesman a.k.a. Tuition plan was down the tubes. And now my parenting skills were below the baboon level.

On my birthday, I'd made out a list of my life to date. Little had I known then, but it was optimistic compared to now.

1. A failed marriage. (That was the least of my worries.)

2. My recent breakup. (Screw the Asshole Professor and the sports car he rode in on. My skillet was hopelessly lost to me.)

3. $1,000 in savings and nearly $2,000 in checking.

(Now it was more like $500 in savings thanks to the new outfits I bought for my salesman dates.)

4. A wonderful son. (He's still wonderful, but was he an inmate-in-the-making? He also still needed a fortune in tuition, a fortune I was even farther away from coughing up.)

5. My job as sous chef. (What a laugh. I'd be lucky to be employed at all by month's end. And I'd found making three thousand identical Southwestern chicken breasts repetitive?)

6. Fabulous friends. (Thank God, I still had them. But that was about all I had left.)

Self-awareness is scary and something I don't recommend you try at home. Connie's mention of an empty nest made me feel uncomfortable. Stephen's barb had hit home. Did I have separation anxiety? Were my attempts at finding a salesman simply methods to avoid facing my upcoming reality?

Was I afraid of being alone?

My life had gone from sucky, sucky, sucky to miserable, miserable, miserable, and now it had reached down-the-toilet, down-the-toilet, down-the-toilet.

I placed the last plate in the dishwasher, set it to run, and then wandered back into the dining room.

The stack of surveys piled on top of my desk snagged my attention. Why had I thought anything like a survey could change my life for the better? I'd totally crashed and burned with the traveling salesmen, and if I valued my job, I'd stop hunting for one.

Gainful employment is mandatory to support my lifestyle, such as it is. I opted for my job.

I grabbed the survey responses and jammed them into the file drawer at the bottom of my desk, then literally and figuratively wiped my hands.

I was forty flipping years old, about to face an empty nest, and was envious of the parenting skills of the-man-who-most-annoyed-me—and he wasn't even a parent.

C'est la vie, non?

CHAPTER NINETEEN

SURVEY COMMENTS:

Honey, what you want to look for in a man is an ability to support you in the style in which you wish to be supported. He needs to be good with kids and know when to obey you and when to stay out of your hair.

Men want sex. Men look at car parts and think sex. They look at a basketball and think sex. A man wants sex with the most attractive woman who'll agree to it. He wants sex with the woman other men want to have sex with. He wants to be seen with you, this desirable woman, by his side because other men will respect him more.

So here's what you need to do. Once you find Mr. Right, you want him to believe you're incredibly desirable to other men and *not* easily available. Then you let him know he's the exception! After he's wrapped around your little finger, don't push him to commit. Instead, make sure he's aware that if he doesn't commit, some other man will be happy to take his place. He'll spend the rest of his life looking after you and trying to please you.

That, my dear, is how to achieve marital satisfaction.

Annie Potter

Shopping exemplifies female bonding at its best. Doing it in person, rather than via cell phone, is even better. If you want to become closer to another woman, go shopping with her. Somewhere between Housewares and Couture, you'll find yourself sharing Most Embarrassing Moments. Talk about bonding!

There's one exception to this rule. Never shop with an eight-months'-pregnant woman. Trust me.

The mere act of window-shopping with a very pregnant woman is a subtle form of torture. While I'd like to say this isn't true of my dear friend, Susan, I'd prefer Chinese Water Torture or announcing my age over the intercom at the Thomas Mack Sports Arena.

"This is like being set loose in a candy factory and not being allowed to sample." Susan fingered the slinky fabric of a cocktail dress with skinny spaghetti straps and the kind of clingy material that only fashion models or prepubescent girls can wear.

I cringed. I felt for her. We were at the mall, looking for outfits to wear to Mom's anniversary party. But couldn't Susan have considered what would happen to her waistline before starting her I-want-another-kid campaign? "I'm sure we'll find something in the maternity department."

Susan snorted. "Yeah, right. When was the last time you shopped in a maternity department?"

It was a rhetorical question and I was smart enough to keep my mouth closed. There's something about being eight months' pregnant, especially considering the swelling, the inability to see your feet, and the feeling that you might explode at any moment that tends to make a woman . . . uncomfortable. This discomfort comes out as, shall we say, a certain bitchiness? Bottom line, I didn't want Susan to go off on me.

At eight months' pregnant, she was a ticking bitchiness time bomb.

When we reached the maternity department, the offerings weren't exactly appropriate for a fancy fiftieth anniversary party held in a ballroom. "I see what you mean."

Susan sighed. "I'm going to have to wear a potato sack."

"No. We'll find something. We'll be creative and come up with something perfect."

"How do pregnant movie stars do it? At the Oscars and the Emmys, they wear gorgeous designer gowns. Where do *they* shop?"

"Hell if I know. Maybe if you bought that full-length black skirt"—I pointed to a faux satin skirt—"we could find a beaded top to wear with it in the Couture department?"

"That might work."

"If we can find the right top, you'll be able to wear it A.B." We'd long ago established that A.B. stands for After Baby.

A short while later we stood side by side, admiring

ourselves in floor-to-ceiling mirrors.

"I want to gag," said Susan.

"Aren't you past morning sickness?"

"It's not morning sickness. I'm as big as Caesar's Palace. Just look at us." She indicated our reflections in the mirror. "The Beauty and the Roman Coliseum."

She had a point, but I wasn't about to agree with her. If I pissed her off, she might sit on me. "You look gorgeous. Not a day over seven months' pregnant."

"You're a size six, the same size I was before my hubby impregnated and inflated me." She eyed my image. "You have to buy that dress. It's awesome."

The dress was a cobwebby silver, not a color I considered my best until I pulled the silk confection over my head. I extended my arm, revealing the price tag dangling beneath the sleeve seam. "Hold all compliments until you check the price. If it's over $200, the color makes me look sallow. Got it?"

Susan nodded and looked at the tag. Her eyes got big and her mouth shriveled into a dried-up apricot. "You know, that blue dress you tried on really brought out the green in your eyes."

"I was afraid of that." The blue dress was acceptable, but even more acceptable was that its price was well within my budget. I could even afford to buy matching shoes and handbag, if I wanted to. "So how much is this one?"

Susan gulped. "You don't want to know. You like

the blue dress better."

"The blue dress it is, then. It'll be perfect for Mom's party."

"Are you bringing a date?"

"Kind of."

"What does that mean?"

"It means I'm bringing an escort, but it's *not* a date."

"O . . . kay. Who's the lucky guy?"

"Davin Wesley."

"I'm having trouble keeping all your men straight. Is he the one who stiffed you for dinner?"

"Davin is *not* one of my men. He's Stephen's ex-teacher."

Susan's mouth formed an *O* but she didn't say anything, which basically meant she had a lot to say but was holding out on me.

"What?"

"Nothing."

"Spill."

Susan cleared her throat. "You really think I can wear this beaded top A.B.?"

"Yes, I really think so, but don't change the subject. What do you have to say about Wesley?"

"From what Connie said—"

I cut Susan off. "Connie blabbed, didn't she? I told her to keep the teenage back seat sex to herself. It was just a momentary lapse on my part. Lust. One night stand."

"What teenage back seat sex?"

Shit. Evidently Connie hadn't blabbed. I flipped my hand in the air. "It's nothing. Meaningless."

"Correct me if I'm wrong, but I can count your sexual partners on one hand. You don't have meaningless sex."

"I could if I wanted to." I started to object more strenuously, mainly because I so desperately wanted my sexual escapade with Wesley to *be* meaningless, but then I clamped my lips shut. Susan was right. I don't have meaningless sex. And if that was the case, what did sex with Wesley mean? "I don't want to talk about this."

I didn't even want to think about it. I'd been picturing back seats a little too often.

"Let me get this straight," said Susan. "You had meaningless sex with a guy who's not a salesman and now he's your escort, but not your date, to your parents' fiftieth wedding anniversary party? And you don't want to talk about it? I think you need a good therapist."

"Who needs a therapist when I've got friends like you guys?"

Susan considered that for a moment. "Did you tell MaryEllen, too? Am I the last to know?"

I shook my head. "Just Connie and now you."

"Davin Wesley probably knows."

Shit. "You don't think he told anyone, do you?"

"Why do you care, if it was meaningless?"

"Maybe it wasn't meaningless."

Susan looked at me in surprise. "Oh. My. God. You have a thing for Stephen's teacher!"

"Shh! Everyone will hear you."

"You're not denying it."

"I'm not confirming it, either. Just keep your voice down."

"What happened to your Salesman Plan?"

"Nothing happened to it. I haven't met the right salesman." I wasn't about to admit that I'd given up on it, mainly because I wasn't about to admit to her or *myself* that there was anything between Davin Wesley and me.

Wesley was totally wrong for me, even if I wasn't going to look for more salesmen. He doesn't travel. He's as poor as I am. He's a control freak. Worst of all, he expects me to talk to him. There's nothing wrong with wanting a mature guy who is gone a lot, gives me lots of space, and doesn't expect anything more than periodic sexual gymnastics while handing me his paychecks.

I expected her to argue with me some more, but she was silent. I looked at her image in the mirror and she had gone totally pale.

"What's wrong?"

"Contractions. Braxton Hicks."

"False labor? Are you sure?"

"I'm sure. Just give me a minute."

There was a chair near the mirrors, so I led her over

to it. "I've got a bottle of water in the dressing room. I'll be right back."

I dashed to the changing room, grabbed the bottle of water, and then ran out to Susan.

She'd regained a little of her color and a saleswoman was chatting with her. I unscrewed the cap on the water bottle and held it out to her. She took a sip.

"I think I got overheated from trying on clothes. I'm better now."

"You sure?"

"Yes. I just need to sit for a few minutes. Why don't you go put the blue dress back on?"

"Nah. I'll change clothes. I don't need to try it on again."

The saleswoman reassured me she'd stay with Susan until I came back out, so I agreed. A few minutes later I was wearing my own jeans and carrying the affordable blue dress, having left the silver evening gown in the changing room.

Susan looked like herself again. "Are you buying the blue one or do you want to try on some other dresses?"

"I'm getting this one." The saleswoman took it from me, saying she'd take it to the register.

"What about you?" I asked. "Are you getting that outfit or is it too hot?"

"I think I overdid it a little today." She looked toward the mirrors. "I doubt I'll find anything that'll make me look like a size six and this seems practical."

Once Susan had changed and we paid for our dresses, I was still worried about her as we made our way to the Animal. "Are you doing okay? Want me to take you to the hospital, or maybe we should call your doctor?"

"I'm perfectly fine." Susan peeked into my bag. "I really like this blue formal on you."

"The more I think about it, the more I like it and my budget loves it."

We reached my car and I opened Susan's door. As she lumbered in, she said, "That reminds me, have you been to the student loan Web site I told you about?"

"Not yet." I made my way to the driver's door, andthen got inside. "The idea of repaying the loans seems scary. But I need to do something since Stephen isn't likely to qualify for a scholarship."

"You never know. You need to fill out the forms because he might even qualify for a grant."

Like they're anxious to give grants and scholarships to low-scoring art students who speak French?

ↄ ↄ ↄ

I love tuxedos. They transform the men wearing them. The right tuxedo can take a beer-swilling couch potato and turn him into a man of industry. The right tuxedo can take a construction worker and give him an air of sophistication. The right tuxedo can take a third-grade teacher and turn him into a total hottie. If the clothes make the man, then the tuxedo made a sex symbol out of Wesley. Wow.

At least that's the first idea that struck me as I ogled him. Davin was attired in a gorgeous black tux with a snappy blue cummerbund. (He'd called to ask my dress color so he could coordinate with me.)

He must have liked my dress, too, because he emitted a low whistle. "You look beautiful."

"Thanks. Come on in." I held the door open for him. "Stephen's almost ready, but I think he's having problems with his tie."

"This is for you." Davin handed me a florist's box.

"I told you this isn't a date. You didn't have to do this." I opened the box and found a wrist corsage made of white roses with blue ribbons. He didn't have to do it, but it sure was nice of him. "It's lovely."

"Glad you like it. I'll go help Stephen with his tie."

"Thanks." I slipped the corsage on my wrist as Davin tapped on Stephen's door.

"Need a little help?"

"I think I need a lot of help," said Stephen, pulling open his door, then coming out into the hall. "Every time I clip the ends together, it falls apart."

"Tuxedo ties are difficult." I watched down the hall as Davin took the tie from Stephen, made an adjustment on the neck, then handed it back to him. "Try it now."

Stephen slipped it on and Davin snapped the ends together. This time it didn't droop open.

"All set?" Davin returned to the living room, with Stephen following behind.

"You look very handsome tonight, Stephen." How could my toddler grow into a poised young man so quickly?

"Thanks, Mom."

"Being in the presence of all this male beauty has made my mouth go dry," I said, wiping a little moisture from my brow. "Let me grab a sip of water before we leave."

I headed to the kitchen and noticed the mail that had come for Stephen. "Stephen, there's a letter for you on the kitchen bar."

I grabbed a quick drink of water, with lots of ice cubes, hoping it would cool my libido. Down, libido, down. Even if I was willing to repeat our back seat gymnastics, which of course I wasn't, I sure didn't want to dwell on the idea in front of my kid, no matter how much he'd grown.

The cool water did the trick and I felt in control again. I joined the menfolk in the living room. "I'm ready now."

Stephen was just folding his letter and sticking it in his pocket. "*Tres bien*."

Davin, at his most gallant, opened the door for us.

"Your pumpkin awaits."

"*Sacre bleu*," cried Stephen. "We're not going in the Animal, are we?"

"We're taking my car," replied Davin, who turned and gave me a significant lift of one eyebrow.

I knew what he was thinking about. Heat crept up my neck to my face, which had to be as red as an overripe beefsteak tomato. The last time I was seated in his Mustang, it had been the scene of our sexual hijinks. Now I had to ride in it with my son and in a formal gown.

I kept my lips sealed tightly, hoping I'd get through the drive with the few shreds of my dignity remaining.

That was when Stephen looked at me. "Why are you blushing, Mom?"

"I'm not blushing."

Davin grinned. "I'd say you are."

"Must be a hot flash." I fanned my face.

Stephen kept his eye on me. "Must be really hot."

Oh, it was. But I wasn't thinking about menopause.

છ્ય છ્ય છ્ય

Entering my workplace as a guest, rather than an employee, was a pleasurable experience. The Grand Ballroom at La Papillon had been elegantly decorated, from tasteful flower arrangements, to the lace and teal table coverings. When I glanced over the buffet offerings, my heart swelled with pride. It looked mouthwatering.

Stephen headed toward a group of teens near the punch, while Davin and I scoped out the ballroom. As we passed by, I waved at the cook who had meat-serving duties, then Davin and I looked for my mother.

"Oh, there you are, Jill." Mom looked fabulous in a beautiful white lace gown. It had a dipping neckline and reminded me of Southern belles, magnolias, and the Old South. "There are so many men, dear, who are dying to meet you," she said, all the while eyeing my escort.

"Mom, I'd like you to meet Davin Wesley. He was Stephen's third-grade teacher."

"What a pleasure to meet you." As they shook hands, my mom looked at me in confusion.

I knew what she was thinking, and I didn't put her out of her misery. She was thinking that she had told me I didn't need a date. Hah. It didn't matter how many of her friends' sons littered the ballroom, I wasn't going to mingle with any of them. Without a doubt, there would be something unsuitable about each one. Guaranteed. Which is why I brought Davin.

"Let me introduce you to Wilhelmina's son, Victor. He's a successful architect."

"Um, Mom? You don't need to introduce me to any men. Davin's my date."

I had forgotten Davin's grating personality. He

piped up, "I thought I was merely your *escort*."

I stepped on his instep with the pointy heel of my shoe. "Don't be ridiculous. Of course you're my date."

I rather enjoyed the pained expression on his face as I turned back to Mom.

"But what about all these men?"

"You can introduce them to Mandy or Connie. Are either of them here yet?"

Mom frowned. "They're both here and both have dates. What am I going to do with all these men?"

"They're adults. If they get bored, they can leave."

Mom smiled. "Of course you're right." Her attention was distracted. "Oh, look. There's Harvey and his wife, Jean. I'd better go greet them."

Mom dashed off to do her social thing, stranding me with Davin.

"I thought you said I was just your escort."

"That's exactly right."

"So why did you tell your mother I'm your date?"

"Because otherwise she'd insist on introducing me to every single man in the room, no matter how ineligible."

"In that case, if you need to use me further, I'll be over by the punch bowl with Stephen." Davin walked off. I frowned. Maybe he stalked off? I decided that at the very least it was a pouty walk.

I hadn't intended to hurt his feelings. Unfortunately for my conscience, he was dead-on about me using him. That's what I'd blatantly done, all because I didn't want to admit, even to myself, that I did want his company. Being with him made me feel more alive, more interesting, and most definitely more sexy.

I considered following him, but thought better of it. He wasn't happy with me, deservedly so, and could use some cooling-off time before I approached him again.

A cloud of discontent settled over me as I searched for Connie and Mandy, wondering who they'd each brought. I stumbled into Mandy first. Literally stumbled.

"Oops, sorry. Didn't mean to . . ." I trailed off when I saw the woman whose foot I'd stepped on. "Hey, Mandy!"

"Great party," she said.

I glanced beside her to check out her date.

Up until now, I haven't mentioned the fact that I'm not an only child.

Yes, I have a brother, Gerry, although now he goes by Gerald.

I don't mention him because he's a total weasel, in the fullest sense of the word: *weasel-est*. He's also dry and very, very boring and only wants to talk computer-speak. If you had a brother like him, you wouldn't admit it, either.

I looked back at Mandy and pointed at Gerald. "You're not here with *him*?!"

Mandy nodded happily. "You didn't tell me your

brother writes software. In fact, you didn't tell me you had a brother at all."

I couldn't believe it. How had she met my brother? Then it dawned on me. "Did my mother introduce you?"

Again, Mandy nodded happily. She looked at my brother with the look of a woman who was completely infatuated. I wanted to barf.

"I'm going to kill her," I muttered. I'd warned Mom not to introduce Weasel-Breath to any of my friends. Ever.

"Nice to see you, Sis," he said.

"You, too," I replied. "How's work? Written any good computer viruses lately?"

"I've told you, I don't write them." He smiled at Mandy. "I write the code that kills them."

Mandy gazed at him with a look mixed of awe and adoration. Gag. Gag. Gag.

Just then, my son and the-teacher-who-annoyed-me strolled up. Stephen said, "Hey, Uncle Gerald."

Davin pulled me aside and whispered, "You have a sibling?"

"Don't mind Gerald. He's the family dweeb."

"Have any others I don't know about?"

"Just the one too many."

"That's a relief."

"Are you still mad at me?" I asked.

"Why should I be mad at you?"

"Because I'm a jerk."

"I've come to expect that from you," Davin said. "It's one of your most admirable personality traits."

I snorted. "I want you to know, I didn't mean to use you. I wasn't sure what I wanted."

"Do you know now?"

"Sorta." I wasn't ready to admit I wanted to spend time with him or that my discontentment had lifted when he'd joined us. I wasn't at all ready for that.

So, of course, he asked, "And what you want *is*?"

I glanced around the room, searching for something safe I could say. A few couples were dancing on the parquet dance floor in front of a small orchestra playing a mix of songs. Right now they were playing a slow dance. "I want to dance."

He looked at the dance floor and raised a lone eyebrow.

"I want to dance *with you*."

"That can be arranged." He took my hand and led me to the dance floor. My heart thudded in anticipation over the chance to be embraced by him, the opportunity to be in his arms again. He didn't disappoint as he swung me into his embrace.

Tucking my head in the cradle formed by his arm and chest, I relaxed for the first time that evening. The music was perfect, as was the lighting. The dance floor was smooth and even, and a little voice inside my head said the man was nearly perfect, too. I couldn't allow myself to be too swept away. Some light conversation was called for. "I'm very impressed by how well you dance."

I was pleased by the way my words came out sounding fairly normal rather than as breathless as I felt.

"Do you have any idea of how many middle school dances I have chaperoned?" he asked.

"You teach elementary school."

"I taught middle school before switching to third grade."

This was news. I'd always pictured him surrounded by nine-year-olds. "So how many middle school dances have you chaperoned?"

"I lost count at sixty-five. Middle school dances give me hives. However, I did perfect my Lindy."

"You're only thirty-five. That dance was out before you were born."

"Shows what you know." He stopped, made a few moves, then pulled me back into his arms for a slow dance.

I had to admit, he did the Lindy very well. We were dancing along and I was enjoying the legitimate excuse for snuggling in public thanks to the music, when someone tapped Davin on the shoulder.

"May I cut in?"

The voice sounded familiar and I glanced up. Dad?!?

"Dad," I cried. "What are you doing out of prison?"

CHAPTER TWENTY

Dear Friends,
It's our fiftieth wedding anniversary!
Please join the celebration!
Zelda and William Morgan

8:00 p.m.

Grand Ballroom
La Papillon Hotel and Casino
Black Tie

Dad enfolded me into his arms for the rest of the slow dance. He didn't answer my question, so I asked again, "What are you doing here?"

"You think I'd miss your mother's and my anniversary party?"

"You're supposed to be in the state pen." I couldn't believe he was acting as if nothing was wrong. "You know, the place with orange suits, not black tuxedos."

He laughed and led me in a swift dance move. After a quick dip, he said, "I think they played this song at our wedding reception. I wish you could have seen your mother. She was so beautiful. I thought I'd won every jackpot. Still do."

"Mom *is* beautiful." She's also interfering and oblivious to the real world, but I suppose Dad was feeling romantic and didn't much want to deal with reality—like SWAT teams and dragnets to cart him back to prison. "Dad, I'm worried. I've got my cell phone. Let's call your attorney. I'm sure he can help get you out of this fix."

"Jill, this is one fix I don't need my attorney to get me out of."

He probably didn't need an attorney. He probably needed a team of them. I wondered if Gloria Allred was available.

Just then, the orchestra leader called for my dad to come to the podium. Dad released me, saying, "It's time to dance with your mom."

Reluctant to allow him to walk away, I said, "As soon as you're done, we have to talk."

"I promise to explain everything then," he said, pulling a long, narrow jewelry case out of his inside front pocket. He flashed a white toothy grin. Amazing. Prison dentists now did teeth bleaching?

"I've got the perfect gift for your mother." He flipped the jewelry box open and I stopped breathing. An ornate diamond necklace twinkled at me.

Dad snapped the case shut and headed for the podium before I got my breath back. Oh. My. God. No wonder he didn't want to call his lawyer. This would be way over his head. The man specialized in white-collar crime, not prison escape followed by jewelry heist.

I joined my friends at the edge of the dance floor and watched Dad present the case to Mom. The necklace took her breath away, too, judging by the way she gasped. She smiled sweetly up at his grinning face. After tonight, they were going to lock him up for much longer than his original sentence.

In a matter of minutes, Dad had draped the necklace around her neck and swept her out on the dance floor for their celebratory dance.

All of the party guests hovered around the edges of the dance floor and started applauding at the sight of my parents dancing.

Are you the type who gets choked up over AT&T commercials, the smell of babies, and anything remotely sentimental? I am. It's not any wonder, then, that I had tears in my eyes as I watched my parents dance.

Yes, I was worried about Dad being hauled off to jail for the rest of his natural life, but there was something very sweet and heart-warming about the way my folks gazed into each others' eyes as they swayed to the music. No matter how odd my parents are, they have a love that will last a lifetime.

Susan stepped closer to me and asked, "Do you think your dad escaped from prison?"

"I hope not."

Connie suggested, "Maybe they gave him some kind of get-out-of-jail-free-for-the-night pass? For good behavior?"

Davin commented, "I don't think prison works that way."

"I'm afraid you're right." I nervously chewed my lip. "But look at them. Look at the glow on my mother's face."

"Are you sure that's not a reflection of the chandeliers in the diamond necklace she's wearing?"

"Do you think my dad escaped, then robbed a jewelry store?"

"Jailbreak and Tiffany's jewel theft, news at eleven," quipped Connie.

My stomach began churning as if the ballroom was on a cruise ship during a monsoon. Stealing wasn't in

Dad's character, I assured myself. He's more of a "mess with the accounting methods" type, a white-collar criminal. But I was anxious. He'd been hanging out with the wrong elements in the state pen. There was no telling what new skills he'd learned. Lock picking, jewelry heisting, grand larceny. The sky's the limit.

"As soon as they finish dancing, I'll tell him he has to go back. Right away." I didn't like the way my voice came out sounding like Minnie Mouse.

"Maybe there's some other explanation," said Davin. He gave my hand a reassuring squeeze. Then not so reassuringly, he added, "He needs to contact his attorney and arrange to turn himself in."

"Whoa," said Connie. "Look over there."

I glanced in the direction in which she pointed and observed a man in a black suit. Not that the room wasn't filled with men in black, but this man stood out from the run-of-the-mill high-society riffraff. Maybe it was his starched white shirt, maybe it was the way he seemed focused on all the party guests, maybe it was the way he was watching everyone and everything so intently. I turned back to Connie. "Do you mean that guy?"

"That guy, as you so casually put it, is law enforcement. I could swear he's Secret Service, but that's not likely. See the earpiece he's wearing?"

Sure enough, the man was wearing an earpiece. "Maybe it's a hearing aid or an iPod?"

Connie shook her head. "It's part of his surveillance kit. Trust me, I know."

Susan added, "I see three more of them. Over by the door."

Sure enough, all three men looked as rigidly observant as the first man. I noticed several hotel security men milling about in the hallway outside the door. Gradually, the men spread throughout the ballroom and began working their way, like spokes on a wheel, to the center. My dad. Shit.

"It may be too late for your dad to turn himself in," said Davin.

My forehead broke out in perspiration. What a lousy time for a hot flash. "He's got to turn himself in. Otherwise they'll probably throw away the key." I had to do something. But what? First, I needed to make Dad aware of what was going on. I headed across the dance floor, resisting an urge to run for the nearest deep freeze to cool off and tapped on Mom's shoulder.

Her eyes were dreamy as she looked at me, then her expression changed to confusion. "What?"

"I'm cutting in." I grabbed Dad's arm and swung him around the dance floor, closer to the exit. My chest felt hot, beads of moisture formed on my upper lip, even my fingertips were burning up. If I could convince him to go now, then I could head for the closest ice sculpture. "You've got to get out of here, Dad. I'll lead you over to the door."

"You're not supposed to cut in on a celebration dance, Jill. I thought your mother and I taught you better manners."

"Manners be damned." That was when the hot flash hit its peak. Nuclear reactions had nothing on this puppy. Although Dad's situation was of paramount importance, visions of ice buckets danced in my head and I struggled against the impulse to disrobe. "If you value your freedom, Dad, you'll get out of here now. The police have arrived. Go. Now."

Just then, the first agent had made his way to the podium and said something to the orchestra leader, who then said on the mike, "Mr. Morgan, you're wanted."

He was wanted, all right. Probably by law enforcement in all fifty states. "Run for it!" I cried.

"Trust me. It's fine." Dad stepped away and walked to the podium.

I dropped my arms and just stood there, my heart breaking. At least he was willing to face the music like a man, like the good example he'd always given me about living up to your responsibilities. But I still wished he'd run for it.

When he stepped up to the podium, several agents came up, began talking with Dad, then led him to the exit. Rather than slap handcuffs on him, more agents and hotel security joined him just outside the doorway.

He was surrounded by the agents as he made his way back into the room, approached the orchestra leader, and borrowed a microphone.

Maybe the police were going to let him say good-bye before hauling him off?

"Thank you to our friends for coming to help us celebrate fifty years of marital bliss," said Dad. "Waiter, please serve the champagne now. We've got some toasting to do."

That was when I noticed that numerous waiters had been waiting for this cue. Their arms were filled with trays of champagne glasses. I grabbed two flutes off the nearest waiter and downed them then grabbed a third. The waiter offered me his entire tray of champagne, but I waved him away and turned back to my father. The cool beverage staved off the worst of the hot flash.

Dad was waiting patiently for all the guests to be provided with champagne then raised his glass.

"To my wonderful wife, Zelda." His voice broke as he said her name. "She's kept every one of her wedding vows, including sticking with me through the bad times. You're the best woman who ever lived."

Everyone drank to my mother, who came forward to join him. Dad then turned and looked at the contingent of law enforcement officers. "Governor Richards. Can you please come up?"

Connie exclaimed, "I knew they were Secret Service. He's running for president!"

The governor waved at everyone as if he was at a political fund-raiser as he joined Dad and Mom at the podium.

"I wouldn't be here tonight," said my father, "if it weren't for Governor Richards. Thank you, Dick, for the pardon. A million thanks."

Dad hugged the governor, who seemed a little surprised at first, but recovered quickly and returned Dad's hug. "My pleasure. Everyone who knows you knows you wouldn't do anything criminal."

He'd been pardoned? What a relief. No tear gas, no SWAT teams, no high-speed car chases. Why couldn't Dad have told me earlier and put me out of my misery?

"Did you know about the pardon?" asked Connie.

I cleared my throat. "Uh, sure. Knew it all along."

"Yeah, right. Not," said Susan. "How does your father know Governor Richards?"

I was only slightly embarrassed at being caught in my little white lie. "They were fraternity brothers during what Dad describes as their wild university years."

"I find it difficult to believe either of them had wild university years," said Davin, pulling me aside.

"Who do you think invented streaking?"

"Isn't your dad a little old to have invented it?"

"It had to start someplace." I shrugged. "It took the nation twenty years to catch on."

I could tell he was looking at both my dad and our governor in a whole new light. He said, "Does the press know about this?"

"No. And you're not going to tell them, either."

"Spoilsport."

"Deep throat," I whispered.

He gave me a funny look. "Isn't that supposed to be the other way around?"

I slapped his shoulder. "You are *such* a baby. I was talking about Watergate."

"I knew what you were talking about, but I was thinking about the movie."

"Get your mind out of the gutter."

"Don't need a gutter." He leaned even closer and whispered in my ear, "It's still stuck in my back seat. I'm thinking about having it preserved in bronze."

I blushed. I did not need the reminder. I didn't want to talk about it. I didn't want to think about it. So of course whenever my mind was at rest, it was *all* I could think about.

That was when Connie piped up. "I seem to have lost my date."

"Hey, that's right!" I glanced around and there weren't any unattached men within our general area. "Mom mentioned you brought someone. Who is he?"

"Here he is now," she said, pointing behind me.

I turned to look. Since I knew she hadn't brought Harrison Ford to my mom's party, her date had to be Salesman Number Two, Aiden Campbell. I half-expected the band to strike up the theme to *Raiders of the Lost Ark*.

"You're dating Aiden?" I looked at her as if she'd lost all sense. She didn't appear to be crazy or drugged. Her eyes twinkled with good-natured charm.

"Can you believe it?"

"But he wants kids!"

"What makes you think I don't?" she whispered as Aiden arrived and kissed her cheek.

Whoa. Connie wants more kids? I was dumbfounded, but it wasn't completely irrational. Just because I didn't want another child didn't mean my friends felt the same way. Just look at Susan.

Speaking of which, I eyed her stomach. Something seemed to have changed with it since we'd shopped. Maybe the baby had dropped?

I glanced back at Connie and Aiden. "Hi, Aiden. How are you doing?"

"Great. How about you?"

After the basic pleasantries and introductions all around, I asked, "How did you two meet?"

"He came into the travel agency one day. Can you believe it? It wasn't until I asked him to come with me tonight that I learned you two knew each other."

"Talk about a small world." First my brother and now Aiden. The world was getting so small, it was almost creepy, but not enough so that the theme from *The Twilight Zone* played in my head. Nah. It was Disney's "It's a Small World."

Davin chipped in, "How do you know Aiden?"

"We met at work. Aiden was in charge of a sales convention."

"We met in La Papillon's Cocoon Ballroom," Aiden said, making a putting swing.

I fought a desire to roll my eyes. Not seeing a need to mention our one extremely uncomfortable date, I added, "He's with Classical Cookware."

"He owns Classical Cookware," corrected Connie.

This was news to me.

That was when Stephen wandered up with my dad, who gave us a three-way hug. "Congratulations on fifty wonderful years, Dad," I said. "And on your pardon!"

"I'm truly blessed." Dad hugged me and Stephen again. "The best wife a man could have, two great kids, and a wonderful grandson."

He stepped back. "Now that I'm out of prison, Stephen, I can handle your college expenses."

I hadn't thought of that! A wave of relief washed through me as Stephen pulled the letter he'd received earlier from his pocket.

"There's no need, Grampa. I'm going to Paris instead."

"What?" Stephen had never mentioned Paris before.

"Look at this." He handed me the letter he'd received before we left home. It was from a large art institute in France, but thankfully, the letter had been written in English. I quickly scanned it. "*The* Frederieco Mandovi wants you to study under him?"

I was floored. Fredericco Mandovi was, according to Stephen, the most famous *living* artist in the world. My mouth must have been gaping like a dry-docked mackerel. "How did this happen?"

"He saw my exhibits at the spring art show." Stephen's grin was contagious.

"But this? This is an offer for him to mentor you?"

"All expenses paid by the institute. Can you believe it? *Moi.* I get to study under Mandovi!"

"I can believe it," said Davin. "I've been telling you all along that you're immensely talented."

"But what about college?" I asked.

"The institute is fully accredited. It's more like a conservatory, but anything I do through them will count toward an art degree later if I want." It didn't seem possible, but Stephen's grin grew larger. "Mandovi has only mentored three students and *all of them* are big names already. You know what this means, *Maman*?"

"Tell me."

"It means I'm going to be successful artist." His chest puffed out and he stood taller somehow. My *liebling*, my cherry on top of the whipped cream of my life.

"If—," said Davin.

"If I do the work and put in the time," finished Stephen.

"I'm really proud of you." My son. The famous artist! And no need to go broke in pursuit of college tuition. This new development was almost too good to comprehend.

"What a night," said my dad. "My cup is running over with pride for you, Stephen."

Did I mention that my dad tends to speak in platitudes? I love him anyway, and the stockholders of his corporation used to love him for it, too, but sometimes I felt as if I were in one of those AT&T commercials I mentioned earlier. I caught myself checking for TV cameras, but all I observed in my peripheral vision was the latest crop of Las Vegas's social elite mixed with Secret Servicemen guarding Governor Richards.

It was a glamorous group. Tuxedos, evening gowns, diamonds, rubies, and pearls—all of which were most likely the real thing rather than paste. My mother really knows how to throw a party.

"Oh, dear God!" screamed Susan. The musicians stopped playing and all heads turned to stare. "My water just broke!"

CHAPTER
TWENTY-ONE

WHITE-COLLAR FELON RELEASED BY PRESIDENTIAL CANDIDATE GOVERNOR DICK RICHARDS

A.P. Las Vegas, NV—It was announced today that Governor Dixon "Dick" Richards pardoned ex-NewMark CEO William Morgan in a surprise action this afternoon. Richards's office gave no comment, but anonymous sources stated that Morgan had been a victim of a nation on a witch hunt following the recent financial scandals. "William Morgan is as honest as the day is long," said NewMark's CFO, Archibald Acuff. "Sending him to prison was an injustice, not just to Morgan and his family, but to every NewMark investor. I'm only surprised Governor Richards didn't pardon Morgan sooner."

Susan had come to the anniversary party with Connie and Aiden because her husband refused to attend. The man swears he's allergic to tuxedo fabric.

We soon determined that Davin had parked in my employee slot and it was the closest vehicle. It would take less time for him to get his car than waiting for Aiden's SUV to be brought around by the valet.

You have to hand it to hotel Security and several of the Secret Servicemen. When they realized it was an emergency, they went into action, personally escorting us to the curbside pickup area, where we waited for Davin to bring around his car.

One of the agents even notified the hospital to await our arrival. A few minutes later, Connie and Aiden joined us while the valet scurried to get their car.

"We're coming, too."

"The more the merrier," said Susan between gasps. "Can you call Tom and tell him to meet me there?"

"You got it." Connie flipped out her cell phone and began punching numbers as Davin drove up.

Within seconds, we were on our way with a police escort to the hospital. I always wanted to have a police escort, but with Susan having labor pains, it wasn't as enjoyable as I'd hoped.

I gave the seat belt an evil eye. There I was, in the back seat of Davin's Mustang, and between timing Susan's contractions, I couldn't help reliving what it had been like making love with Davin. The experience had been satisfyingly mind-blowing, despite the cramped quarters.

Susan started panting again. "This one's a zinger."

Davin said, "We're at the hospital now."

By the time I got Susan settled in at the hospital emergency room, she was more than halfway to full dilation. While she waited for transfer to a birthing room, I went out to the waiting room to give Davin, Connie, and Aiden an update and to see if Susan's husband had arrived yet.

Connie spotted me first. "How's she doing?"

"She's fine. The doctor said she's coming right along, and he's having her moved to a birthing room."

"But isn't the baby early?" Connie asked.

"He didn't seem concerned about that. They did an ultrasound earlier this week. The baby is healthy and less than two weeks early."

Connie chewed her upper lip. "I thought Susan wasn't due for another month."

"The doctor said it's not an exact science." I looked up and saw my mother, father, and son entering the waiting room.

"What are you guys doing here?" I asked.

"It only seems right since she went into labor at our anniversary party," said Dad.

"I feel responsible," Mom added.

"I didn't have a ride home," groused Stephen as he took a seat beside Davin.

Oops.

MaryEllen wandered into the room. "I've been trying to reach Tom, but I'm not getting an answer."

"Did you reach him, Connie?" I asked.

"I left a message on his home voice mail to get his butt down here. Maybe he's on his way?"

"Do you have his cell phone number?" Susan had been asking for him and would be upset that we hadn't reached him—especially since he was her Lamaze coach.

"I've been calling both numbers every ten minutes," said MaryEllen.

"Okay. Please, keep trying."

She nodded and I turned to go back to Susan. Connie grabbed my arm. "I'm coming with you."

"Me, too," said my mother. "A girl wants her mother at times like this."

I stopped in my tracks. "You're *not* her mother."

"I'm the next best thing since her own mother passed away. You'll see. Susan needs me."

I didn't have time to argue with her because I was afraid they would move Susan before I returned.

When Connie, my mother, and I approached the room where Susan was dilating, we heard a loud voice, which sounded amazingly like Susan, cry out, "Let me get my hands on the dickhead who did this to me!"

It was probably a good thing we hadn't found her husband, I thought, upon learning the threats were coming from Susan. My mother rushed in and began soothing her. Mom had been right. Susan needed someone to mother her and she immediately responded to my mom's attentions by calming down.

Mom began brushing Susan's hair and Susan smiled at Connie and me. "Do either of you know Lamaze?"

"It's how I delivered Rachel," said Connie.

"Not me," I said. "I had an epidural."

The hospital staff came in to wheel Susan to the birthing room. Within a few minutes, she was comfortably relocated, Connie had figured out how to turn one of the chairs into a bed, and my mother sat beside Susan, holding her hand.

I wanted to help, but didn't know what to do. "Do you need anything?"

"Maybe you could ask the nurse for some juice?" Susan turned and began questioning my mother about her own two births, which was extremely ironic since Mom had been knocked out cold for both Weasel-Breath's and my deliveries.

I nodded and headed to the nurses's station. "Can you please have someone bring juice to my friend's room?" I asked, pointing to the room.

"Will do." She went back to the chart she was making entries in. I hoped she wouldn't forget, but decided to see if Tom had arrived yet. When I went out to the waiting room, it had become extremely crowded.

In addition to my father, Davin, Stephen, Aiden, MaryEllen, and MaryEllen's husband, more of my parent's party guests had arrived, including Governor Richards and his Secret Service entourage. What was this, a birthing party? Maybe someone should tell them there wouldn't be appetizers. But then I realized there was a vending machine that was being raided by two men in tuxedos and a woman in sequins. Guess not.

When I saw Mandy come in with my brother, I about-faced and went back to Susan's room. An interchange with my brother wasn't actually on my to-do list on the best of days. If he spoke to me now, *he* might need a nurse. I stroked Susan's shoulder reassuringly and updated her on the latest news about not reaching Tom.

Her face was pale and she'd broken out into a sweat. "If I get my hands on Tom," she yelled, "he'll never do this to anyone again!"

Tom would never believe how lucky he was that we couldn't reach him. "MaryEllen is still trying to reach him."

"Lucky son of a bitch," muttered Connie. Susan was squeezing her hand so hard that Connie's hand had turned an interesting shade of scarlet.

About that time, we heard footsteps approaching and I assumed it was the doctor coming to check on Susan's progress because of all the screaming, which was a good thing, because a strong labor pain hit Susan at the same instant.

"Ohhhh," she moaned while my mom patted her free hand and Connie ordered her to breathe.

Susan began panting as Aiden entered the room.

"What are you doing here?" I snapped. He didn't even know Susan. "Giving birth is *not* a spectator sport."

"I told the nurse my girlfriend was back here and she assumed I meant delivering, not"—he looked at Connie, who was busy breathing with Susan—"not hyperventilating."

"What do you want?" I didn't mean to be rude, but his presence was superfluous. "We're kind of busy."

"MaryEllen reached Susan's husband. He was at a movie and had turned off his cell. He's on his way."

"That's very good news."

"No, it isn't," said my mother.

"Why not?"

"The baby is coming *now*."

I opened my mouth to ask how she knew, but Connie yelled, "Go get the doctor!"

"QXMRSEHEIFPWEHFLSM," screeched Susan.

Aiden and I tore out of the birthing room and down to the nurses's station. "We need the doctor," I said.

"What's the problem?" the nurse asked in a bored tone. "The juice will be delivered soon."

"The only problem," I said, "is the baby is coming *now* and the doctor isn't here. Get him."

I turned to go back as Aiden added, to the nurse, "Stat."

He laughed as he joined me en route back to the room. "I've always wanted to say that."

"You did it well. You might have missed your calling."

"Where's the doctor?" asked Connie as we entered.

"The nurse is getting him now."

"He'd better come fast. The baby is crowning."

And so it was that my dear friend Susan had her second child at that moment. The infant was lovingly caught by me when I realized what was happening and I dove head first, like a baseman stealing second, to catch the infant.

His tiny mouth crunched up in a silent wail, but all I had eyes for was his darling, sweet face.

Babies.

Gotta love 'em.

CHAPTER TWENTY-TWO

Dear Miss Storm,

I'm replying to your unseemly inquiry into the marriage of my sister. Sister and her husband are on an anniversary cruise and I am pet- sitting her poodle, Dizzy.

Her mail has piled up and I, quite innocently I might add, went through it simply in case there was an overdue bill, when I came across your letter. Since she is away and unable to answer your missive in the next few days, I have decided to give you the benefit of my years. Although I have never been a Nosey Parker, nor do I give advice, I believe the information I am sharing will be *most* helpful in your case.

My dear, your desperate attempt to find a suitable mate will not do and will likely be deleterious to your health and well being. I am speaking from the Authority of Someone who has assiduously avoided such circumstances.

Naturally, Sister, who was a gently bred woman, has put a brave face on her fifty-odd years of marriage. As a diplomat, her husband is frequently away from home. However, I regret to say one could not help but observe Sister's precarious state of health when her husband returns from his travels.

I cannot tell you the countless times I have popped over to visit Sister, only to find her slovenly man in various states of undress in *broad daylight*, with poor Sister still in bed, with, her husband informs me, one of her severe headaches.

Imagine my distress when I realized Sister has suffered bouts of severe headaches over the years, always directly linked to her husband's homecomings. Why, in one instance, I insisted upon checking on her, only to find her in bed, sans nightclothes, red faced, perspiring, and breathing heavily! Despite my protestations that she see a physician at once, Sister insisted she would be back to her normal good health the following day, when, I might add, her husband was scheduled to leave again.

One can see why an Objective Observer would recommend against pursuing matrimony. I pray you will rethink your inclination to seek out a mate.

Most sincerely,

Miss Eiulah Perry

First, let me say, babies rock!

There's something about cradling a brand-new life in your arms that makes you think about the past, the future, and even the present.

The armful of future potential I held made me wonder about where he'd be heading. What kind of person would he be? Would he be happy? Was I holding a future astronaut or president?

It may seem like a no-brainer to you, but it occurred to me that anything is possible, not just for the baby, but for me, too.

Even at forty flipping years old, I could start over. I, too, could be or do anything if I wanted it enough and worked hard enough—like Stephen dreamed of being an artist and now his dream would soon become reality.

What did I dream of for me?

I dreamed of being a chef, in charge of my own kitchen. I dreamed of my house with the picket fence. I dreamed of finding a man who wouldn't make me whole, because I dreamed of being whole on my own, but a man who would add substance to my life.

Susan's newborn baby's blue eyes reflected back a world of promise. I knew anything could, and probably would happen. That's the exhilarating thing about the future.

"He's so beautiful," I whispered, not wanting to disturb him since he was sleeping so innocently and peacefully.

It didn't matter if someday he'd have blue and green spiked hair, as long as he'd be happy and find a life of fulfillment.

None of society's rules matter once life is boiled down to the simplest measure. Will this child be happy?

I eyed Susan who was drowsily watching her new child. Her husband was curled up on the chair/bed, snoring softly, and her gaze would seek him out periodically.

Susan looked happy, complete, and absolutely exhausted.

My mother, however, was in her element. She appeared to be as perfectly dressed as when she'd arrived at her party. Not even a strand of her hair was out of place. My blue dress was crumpled and stained; her white dress was pristine. How the hell did she do it?

I stifled a yawn. It had been a long night.

Connie and Aiden left soon after the baby arrived. Mom's guests and the security detail departed after viewing the baby through the nursery window, but my dad, Davin, and Stephen were still there.

Sleep was the main thing on my mind as I placed the infant in Susan's outstretched arms.

"Why don't you both go get some rest?" Susan whispered.

"That's an excellent idea," Mom said briskly. "You've got my phone numbers in case you need anything. Don't hesitate to call."

"Thanks."

We took turns kissing Susan and the baby good-bye, then headed to the waiting room.

"I don't suppose you'd like to give me another grandbaby," said my mother as we strolled through the hospital corridors.

"Absolutely not."

She sighed. "I was afraid so. Maybe Gerald and Mandy—"

"I doubt the world is ready for Weasel-Breath's progeny. That reminds me. I thought I told you never to introduce him to any of my friends?"

"I couldn't resist. I adore Mandy and Gerald is exactly her type."

She had me there. Mandy loves geeks. But my brother? "I don't think he's *any* woman's type."

"Aren't you a little *mature* for the sibling rivalry routine? It was cute when you were six, but it's getting old. Gerald is a wonderful son, just as you are a wonderful daughter."

I opened my mouth to insult my brother, but then I closed it again. Hadn't I just been thinking about starting over? My relationship with Gerald was a good place to begin. He wasn't a bad guy for a techno-nerd. Mandy could do much worse.

"You're right, Mom. I hope they get married and have dozens of grandchildren for you to dote on."

"I know you find my attempts to introduce you to a good man annoying, Jill. You have been so sad and had such a rough time of it since Daniel became Stormy. You deserve happiness. Is it wrong of me to want more for you?"

"I wouldn't want you to be any other way, Mom." We hugged as we reached the entrance to the waiting area then went through the door. "But I've found a good man on my own."

She raised her eyebrows, which was quite a feat considering the amount of Botox in said brows. "Really?"

"Maybe." I glanced into the waiting room and I know my expression softened. "I think so."

I felt wiser, like I'd turned some corner, as I eyed Davin and Stephen. They were both asleep and Stephen's head was leaning against Davin's shoulder in a gesture of total trust.

As Dad hugged Mom and led her to the exit, Mom turned back, gestured toward Davin, and gave me a thumbs-up sign. I stood and savored the moment.

Outside the glass doors the first golden streaks of morning dawn glittered the sky. Like Susan's baby and me, the world was starting a new day.

I took a seat on the other side of Davin and leaned my head on his shoulder, too. He stirred and placed a gentle kiss on the top of my head. "Beautiful baby."

"He is."

"Ready to go home?"

I nodded.

He pointed to a nearby table. "Got you some coffee."

"You're a genius." I picked up the paper cup and took a sip of the warm coffee. "Perfect."

He softly roused Stephen and the three of us gathered our belongings. As we headed through the exit doors, the sun made its full appearance.

න න න

When we got back to the apartment, Stephen wearily toddled off to bed.

"I should be heading out," Davin said. His tuxedo was wrinkled, and he'd removed the cummerbund and tie, but otherwise he looked as handsome as the night before.

Although I should have been exhausted, I was wired with adrenaline from the night's activities. Holding Susan's baby had woken me up fully and it would be hours before I could sleep.

During the past twelve hours, I'd undergone an internal shift. I wanted Davin to stay so I could talk it over with him. "Why don't you take a shower and I'll scramble us some eggs first?"

"You sure?"

"Stay. I'll get you a towel."

He leaned in and gave me a tender kiss and I eagerly returned it. It had been a long night, but his kiss filled me with anticipation. With a soft stroke on my arm, he stepped back and headed to the bathroom.

Once he was settled, I quickly went into my bed-room and changed out of my dress. I pulled on my COOKS DO IT T-shirt and shorts, then entered the kitchen.

It didn't take long to whip the eggs. I pulled out the skillet I'd been trying to season and grimaced.

I didn't want this skillet. I didn't want my life to go on as it had in the past. I needed a new skillet, a totally different type to take into my life of the future. Where anything was possible. Where I could do anything if I wanted it badly enough.

Goodwill wasn't open yet, so I put the skillet aside. I pulled out a microwave-safe bowl and dumped the eggs in, along with some cheese. I nuked them and they were just coming out of the microwave when Davin wandered into the kitchen and gave me another kiss. It robbed me of breath and I didn't want it to ever end. But like all good things, it did.

Nuzzling my cheek, he said, "Good morning."

He'd put his tuxedo pants and shirt back on, but had rolled up his shirtsleeves and several buttons on his shirt were left undone. With just enough beard stubble to give him a rakish look, he looked more appetizing than the jam, and I have to say it looked and smelled delicious.

"I need to grab something from my car," he said.

"Okay." I wasn't sure what he had in the car, but

maybe he had some spare clothes? While he was gone, I poured orange juice, made some toast, and brought it all into the dining room. I checked on Stephen, but he slept the sleep of innocents, with a huge grin on his face. Most likely dreaming about Paris.

Davin returned from his car, carrying some papers in a file folder. "Breakfast smells great."

We took seats and Davin placed the folder on the table beside him.

Baby delivering makes you hungry, I realized as I finished off my eggs.

Davin slathered a slice of toast with jam and said, "I figured out how to convince you that I'm the right guy for you."

"How will you do that?" I asked, thinking he'd probably make some snarky comment about my cooking.

"With this." He slid the folder across the table to me, then handed me a pencil from my pencil jar on my desk . . . and my new reading glasses.

I slipped the glasses on the tip of my nose, even though I suspected they made me look like a grandmother and opened the folder. "The Stanway Mental Maturity Test? This is going to convince me? You've got to be kidding."

"I'm serious." He pulled another paper from the folder. "I already took it and this is my score."

I read the score and it meant nothing to me. "And what does this prove?" He'd totally lost me.

"I'm more mature than you. Take the test and see. You'll come in younger than me."

"So what if I do? You'll still *be* younger than me."

"Only five years. If you're worrying about your boobs drooping, I promise not to notice. Take the test."

"Even if you're right, and you're more mature than me, that still doesn't mean you're the right guy for me."

"I'll be a third of the way there."

"What about travel?"

"I found a long-lost cousin who lives in Albuquerque. I plan to visit him frequently."

"What about children? I don't want any more."

"And you think I do? I've been substitute parent for hundreds of kids during the past fifteen years. The last thing I want is one of my own for me to screw up. Look, Jill, I think you're setting up roadblocks to keep us from being together. You're afraid to become involved with *anyone* for fear of being hurt again. Stormy really did a number on you."

Was he right?

"It's safer to focus on an imaginary perfect man. I gotta tell you, perfect men don't exist. Neither do perfect women or perfect relationships. Life doesn't work that way. Love doesn't work that way."

I gulped. My heart was pounding and I felt all my defenses come up. But I'd promised myself that today I'd start over. A new life. A new outlook. A new me.

And a definite maybe for Davin. He was a good guy, a great father figure to Stephen, a wonderful role model to his students. He understood me better than I did myself, and did I mention the M.B.S.? "If I take the test and I come up more mature than you?"

"Then I walk away and promise not to darken your door again. Unless you want me to. But . . ."

"But what?"

"If I'm more mature, then you have to move in with me."

"That's crazy. Where would we live?"

"My house, of course."

"You don't have a house."

"Of course I do. It's a *great* house." He took another bite of toast. "There's a zillion things you don't know about me. Think of all the fun you'll have learning about them. Think of the fun you'll have reading my diary."

"You keep a diary?"

"If you move in I will."

"That sounds like a threat."

"It's a promise. Take the test."

I checked the time. It was nearly eight o'clock, the hour the Goodwill store opened, and it had been on the back of my mind since I'd held the baby. "I've got to run an errand first, but when I get back I'll take the test."

"What do you have to do?"

I jumped from my chair and started toward the

bathroom and a shower, but called to him, "Buy a new skillet. Do the dishes or something because it won't take me long. Whatever you do, don't leave!"

Forty-five minutes later, the salesclerk Meg and I stood looking at the Goodwill skillet offerings. At first I didn't see anything I wanted, but then a gleam of stainless steel and copper caught my eye. It was perfect!

The skillet was a little tarnished, like me, but it was great quality. "I'll take it."

It didn't take long for Meg to accept my donation of the partially seasoned skillet and ring up my new one.

As I climbed into the Animal, thrilled with my purchase, my cell phone rang.

"Hello?"

"Jill, it's Aiden."

Why would he be calling me? Maybe it was something about Susan? "What's up?"

"I have a business proposition for you. Can we meet?"

"Now?" I asked.

"Any time will do, but now would be convenient for me if it is for you. I want to talk with you about a job."

"What kind of job?"

"I know of an opening for a chef."

"Cool! Meet me at my apartment . . . in half an

hour?"

"Sounds good. Connie says she's coming, too."

Since my job had totally gone down the tubes, I was excited. I didn't think Connie would want to come, too, if she didn't think the chef position would work for me.

"Hey," I greeted Davin as I entered my apartment, skillet in hand. "Look what I bought."

I showed it to him and he was suitably impressed. Stephen wandered out of his bedroom and I quickly made some eggs for him, in my new skillet. My supposition was right. The skillet was perfect. Stephen took a seat in the dining room.

"Are you ready to take the maturity test, Jill?" asked Davin.

"What test?" asked Stephen.

"I'm trying to convince your mother that I'm her Mr. Right. The test will help prove my case."

"Don't be a tool, *Maman*." Stephen rolled his eyes. "I asked him to marry us back in third grade."

"You didn't?!"

"He did." Davin grinned. "I wasn't sure about the marrying you part, but I was interested. When the school year was ending I tried to hint about you needing some help and, as usual for me, it didn't come out right. You thought I was putting you down. And you were still reeling over Stormy leaving. It wasn't the right time, but I think it is now."

"He's your Mr. Right," added Stephen.

"Well, he can't prove it to me now. Connie and Aiden are on their way over." I checked the clock. "They'll be here in about ten minutes. Aiden's heard of a chef job!"

"*Tres bien*," said Stephen. He scooped up some eggs and took a bite.

It dawned on me that all his French phrases would be helpful since my baby would soon be living in France. He seemed to know where he was going and how he was going to get there on an instinctive level that I didn't have myself. I ruffled his spikes.

The doorbell rang. I leaped to answer the door and Davin followed.

Connie and Aiden came in with gigantic grins on their faces. I offered them eggs, but they declined.

"We ate already," said Connie, tucking a leg under her as she took a seat on the living room sofa. Aiden sat beside her and didn't once look in a mirror or take a pretend golf putt.

Davin took a seat on the chair, and I perched on the arm.

Stephen came out of the dining room and greeted everyone. "Hi and bye. I'm off to Tom's, Mom. Be back around four."

"Have fun."

As soon as Stephen left, Aiden scooted forward. "I've decided to create a new position at Classical

Cookware. We have a small fleet—three jets. We need a chef to create a limited menu for them."

"A plane chef?"

"There's more to the job than that. We'll be doing weekly demos with lots of press coverage. The chef will create interesting meals . . . using Classical Cookware, of course, to promote our new line of Chefware."

"Oh, that sounds like fun." I was almost hopping up and down. I'd *kill* for a job like this. But . . . Aiden hadn't offered it to me. What if he only wanted me to recommend names of qualified chefs? "Are you looking for someone well-known?"

"I'm looking for someone exactly like you. You, in fact. I want you to be the Classical Cookware chef. I've seen you in action twice, once with Chef Radkin and again at the hospital. You've got the talent and the brains to handle a job that requires quick thinking like this one. It won't pay that much to start, only—" Then he named a sum that was nearly double what I was making at La Papillon, making me question if this was legit or I was suffering from sleep deprivation after the night's chaos.

I surreptitiously pinched myself. It hurt. This was real!

Aiden asked, "Can you start in two weeks?"

By the time they'd pulled me from the ceiling and left me alone with Davin, I was beside myself with glee. "I can't believe it. Just today I decided to start over and everything is falling into place. A new skillet. A fantastic new job!"

"You could add a new boyfriend to that list if you'd sit down and take the test. Unless you want a nap first?"

"I'm not tired."

"Take the test, and then we'll decide how soon you and Stephen can move in with me."

"You're awfully confident," I said, but I did as he asked.

After I completed the test, Davin quickly scored it. Imagine my surprise—not—when my score came back with the mental maturity of a thirteen-year-old girl.

I cheated a little. So sue me.

"You know you're never going to live this down."

I looked up and we gazed into each other's eyes, trading smiles with one another. Then Davin's pupils darkened, sending me back in time to when he'd taken my breath away in his Mustang.

But now we had the apartment to ourselves and there was nothing to prevent us from making love again, this time in comfort and privacy. With that thought in mind, I opened my mouth to suggest it, but Davin shook his head.

"What?"

"Don't you need to freshen up?"

I felt pretty darn fresh already and didn't immediately understand what he meant, unless he wanted me to change clothes?

"Powder your nose," he said, with a twist of his head toward the bathroom.

Reaching up, I touched my nose, but I didn't feel anything unusual except for the reading glasses. I removed them. "Do I have a smudge?"

He shook his head. "You are just no good at taking a hint."

He rose, grabbed my hand, and led me down the hallway to the bathroom. "Look inside."

Yipes. I couldn't help wondering if I looked totally awful. I entered the bathroom and turned to the mirror, my face already cringing as I prepared for the worst.

But I didn't see my reflection. The entire surface of the mirror over the sink was covered with Post-it notes. I spun back to him. "What's this?"

He gave a shooing motion with his hands. "You're supposed to read them."

Smiling, I turned back and started at the top left, removing each Post-it as I read.

"I."

"Love."

"You."

"You do?" I asked.

Davin stepped forward and kissed my neck from behind. "Absolutely. I love everything about you."

The warm emotion I'd kept bottled up inside me came rushing to my heart, almost like the sensation of a hot flash, but, oh, so much better.

Worlds better.

Leaning back against his strong chest, I turned and kissed his rough chin. "I love you, too. I've been trying hard to fight it."

"I know. It's okay, because you're with me now." He tenderly stroked my upper arms and shoulders with his calloused hands, the sensation sending trails of warmth throughout my body.

Could life get any more wonderful?

"Now," he ordered. "Keep reading."

I bit my lip, holding back a happy tear and then reached forward to grab another Post-it.

"How do I love thee? Let me count the ways," the next note said, quoting Elizabeth Barrett Browning.

Each succeeding Post-it was numbered and I realized there were over a hundred of them covering the mirror.

1. I love the way it's so easy to tell what you're thinking and feeling. You wear your heart for everyone to see.

2. I love the way you scrunch up your nose when you're happy.

3. Even though you've been hurt before, I love the way you drum up the courage to try again and again.

4. I love the way you feel in my arms.

5. I love it when you laugh. Your happy gurgle does something to my insides.

6. I love the way you have of making me laugh.

7. I love the way you never give up, even when life is stacked against you.

8. I love the way you love your son.

9. I love your crazy logic.

10. I love making love with you.

That was when I stopped reading and attacked the poor man. He didn't know what hit him.

I kissed him once, twice, three times. "I love making love with you, too. It's all I can seem to think about anymore."

He glanced heavenward. "Thank you." Then, he attacked me right back.

And let me tell you, it was absolutely mind-blowing.

EPILOGUE

How Do I Love Thee? (Sonnet 43)
by Elizabeth Barrett Browning

How do I love thee? Let me count the ways.
I love thee to the depth and breadth and height
My soul can reach, when feeling out of sight
For the ends of being and ideal grace.
I love thee to the level of every day's
Most quiet need, by sun and candle-light.
I love thee freely, as men strive for right.
I love thee purely, as they turn from praise.
I love thee with the passion put to use
In my old griefs, and with my childhood's faith.
I love thee with a love I seemed to lose
With my lost saints. I love thee with the breath,
Smiles, tears, of all my life; and, if God choose,
I shall but love thee better after death.

Three weeks off and one week of incredibly sizzling sex.

Be careful what you ask for, because that's exactly what I got. During our seven months of blissful cohabitation, we'd even squeezed in a little hot sex during my three weeks away from home, on occasional weekends, and especially when school was out and Davin traveled with me.

Thursday nights are always pizza nights and I was eager to get home. Stephen was flying to Paris the day after next and this would be our last family evening for a long while, since we were having dinner with my folks the following night.

Stephen and I had settled into Davin's house as if we'd lived there all our lives. It was a very comfortable three-bedroom home with a tiny lawn of very green grass that Davin enjoyed tending.

You wouldn't believe how great our relationship is or how perfect our living arrangements are. Because my new job requires extensive travel, I didn't have to worry about leaving Stephen while he finished out his senior year, since he got home from school around the same time as Davin.

Davin truly is a homebody, but I hadn't realized how much I would look forward to coming home to a guy like him. Or how much I wanted to come home to him specifically.

When I pulled into the driveway, my temple

furrowed. Something was different. I grinned when I saw what it was. What a sweetie!

My favorite hottie had added a small section of white picket fence in front of the walkway.

I pulled my wallet from my handbag and dragged out the photo of my dream house. There was the same green lawn and the same picket fence. They were smaller, but I couldn't love them more if we'd been transported to Kentucky. I'd only shown the photo to Davin once and I was touched that he remembered. Talk about a keeper!

I returned my wallet to my bag and my cell phone rang. "Hello?"

"We need to discuss your wedding plans," said my mother.

Some things never change. I'd forgotten to check caller ID.

"Who said I'm getting married? Why don't you bug Gerald and Mandy?"

"Mandy said they're eloping."

Wise woman.

Just then, Davin came out of the house to greet me.

"Your mother?" he asked, pointing at my cell phone, and I nodded.

He leaned through my open car window and took it from me. "Hi, Mom."

I heard her say something to him, but couldn't make out the words.

"I'm working on her. I've got some survey responses to show her tonight."

You know, maybe life isn't like a box of Tampax. Perhaps it's more like a Goodwill store. There are useless items all over the place, but you never know when you'll uncover a treasure.

A special excerpt of *In Stereo Where Available* by
Becky Anderson

IN STEREO
WHERE
AVAILABLE

CHAPTER ONE

Oh be-yootiful, for spacious skies,
For amber waves of guh-rain . . .

    I took a few kernels from the bowl of popcorn and slowly put them in my mouth, crunching delicately, my gaze fixed on the TV. The blonde with the microphone gestured soulfully to the smirking crowd, wet-eyed, the bronzing powder a little too heavy around her cleavage. Her strappy high heels glittered. The shoes were important. Your legs are only as good as your shoes. I glanced at my cell phone beside me on the sofa, checking once again to be sure I'd turned it on. The name across the bottom of my TV screen was "Grace Kassner."

For purple mountain ma-hajesties
Above the fuh-ruited plain!

The note went flat and I quickly turned down the volume. Camera angles shifted; the judges winced, their pens tapping against the table. I hit the "mute" button and picked up my cell phone. Less than two minutes later, it rang.

"Hi, Madison."

"Phoebe." I could hear her sobbing, muted, as though she were pressing a tissue against her mouth. "I got eliminated."

"I know. You were *great*, though. Those judges don't know anything."

"The one guy said I sounded like a seventh-grader doing karaoke at a sleepover party."

"That guy says stuff like that to everyone. *I* heard you, Maddie. You sounded wonderful. And the crowd loved you."

"Did they really?"

"They did. If they went by crowd response, you'd definitely have made it. That's just one little show, it's nothing. You're just paying your dues. You'll have your chance yet, and then you'll be able to say you earned it."

She sniffled. "You think?"

"Absolutely. Anyway, can you see the other girls?"

"No. I'm backstage."

"Well, I'm watching it right now, and the girl who's up there is a cow. She's wearing this scarf shirt, totally trashy, and *flats*, Maddie. Flats." I was speaking her language, for her sake. I didn't like cutting people down, but Madison needed this. "Those judges are going to be so sorry they eliminated you. I can't even turn the sound on. She sounds like those dolls that sing when you go through the 'It's a Small World' ride at Disney World."

Madison laughed in relief. "Thanks. Look, Mom's trying to call through. I'll be back in town tomorrow, okay? I'll call you then."

"Okay. Love you."

"Love you, too."

I set my cell phone down and sighed. Madison's little white dog, Pepper, was sitting on my lap, nuzzling her nose down into the cushions in search of dropped popcorn. Clicking off the TV, I stared at the stack of uncorrected crayoned math papers in a file folder on my desk. Tomorrow was Friday; they needed to go home in the responsibility folders, along with the handwriting sheets beneath them. I scooted Pepper over and forced myself off the sofa, reaching for the folder from beside the computer. It knocked the mouse, making the aquarium-fish screen saver vanish. And in an instant, there it was. The e-mail.

Dear Phoebe, it began.

Regarding dinner at your parents' place this Saturday, I don't think I'm going to be able to make it. I know you've been looking forward to them meeting me, but to be perfectly honest with you, I feel like it's almost a little deceptive when the fact is, I don't really have time for a serious relationship right now. I've been thinking maybe we ought to cool it a little, just sort of keep it casual. I think you're a great girl, and I don't want to stop seeing you, but I'm not really in a place right now where I can do the whole meet-the-parents thing. Take care.

Bill

"Read between the lines," Madison had said when I had called her the day before, mystified. "He's saying he wants to get rid of the relationship and keep the sex. You ought to dump his sleazy butt straight-out."

"Really?" I'd asked, disappointed. I'd never even actually gotten that far with Bill. I'd hoped there was some kind of miracle thing that Madison would tell me to say, something that would get him over the hump and on toward producing a ring. I was twenty-nine, after all. It was about time.

"Really. I hate to be the bearer of bad news, because I'm your sister and I love you, but that's exactly what he's saying right there. When a man says 'keep it casual,' that only means one thing. Sorry, Fee."

I minimized the window and took the folder of apple-printed math worksheets over to the sofa, curling my legs up beneath me. I'd kicked off the school year with an apple theme—apple stories for reading, apple crafts for art, apple graphs for science. If you cut an apple horizontally, the seeds flared out in a star. You could dry the halves with a napkin and make prints, pressing the smooth white sides into red tempera paint that oozed up around the edges. Three days into the school year and already a parent had written me a note saying I was encouraging devil worship, promoting the use of penta-grams like that. I had written a quick apology at the bottom and sent the note back home. A lot of teaching was about turning the other cheek. That was something I could do. I've always been better at that than my sister. She's the competi-tive twin and I'm the sweet one, so says our mother. It's better to have only one competitive twin. I realized that early in life, and I guess she didn't. I'm also the smart one.

DIARY
OF A CONFESSIONS QUEEN

Confessions writer Amanda Crosby put her life on hold for the last seven years after the disappearance of her husband, Dan.

In writing for True Lies Magazine, guilt-ridden Amy takes on the abilities her fictional characters confess to, like the time she thought she was psychic after researching clairvoyants. With fatalistic acceptance of the craziness in her life, she uses humor to cope.

The home Dan bought for them is about to be foreclosed on, and her only answer is his life insurance policy. There's just enough time to have him declared legally dead and receive the funds to save her home. Her home is safe—that is, until she receives a blackmail note.

Is it possible her missing husband is still alive?

Kathy Carmichael
ISBN#9781605420950
Trade Paperback / Fiction
US $15.95 / CDN $8.95
FEBRUARY 2010
www.kathycarmichael.com

The Rock & Roll Queen of BEDLAM

Leggy, karaoke-singing Allegra Thome spends her days teaching dysfunctional teens and her nights with wealthy new boyfriend, Michael. The rough patch following Allegra's divorce is over, and life is grand. But when Allegra lands in the middle of a drug bust and meets Sloan, a rough-around-the edges DEA agent and, later that day, a throwaway kid from her class disappears, things quickly head south. Sloan, who has the tact of a roadside bomb, is attracted to Allegra and alienates Michael. To make matters worse, nobody seems to care that Allegra's student, Sara Stepanek, is missing.

Add to the mix a rural Washington State town under the spell of a charismatic minister who doesn't hesitate to use secrets of the rich and powerful to keep them in line, even while withholding his own dark past, and Allegra's search for Sara becomes a race against time with dead bodies piling up and her own life in peril. Under the circumstances, it's not surprising things come to a head at the WWJD (What Would Jesus Drink) Winery.

Marilee Brothers
ISBN#9781934755464
Trade Paperback / Suspense
US $15.95 / CDN $17.95
OCTOBER 2009
www.marileebrothers.com

MICHELLE PERRY
PAINT IT BLACK

DEA agent Necie Bramhall thinks she knows a thing or two about revenge. She's devoted her life to bringing down the drug lord father who abandoned her. When she finally captures him, she thinks she'll be able to put her painful past behind her. What she doesn't realize is that she's created a brand new enemy. A deadly enemy.

Maria Barnes is beautiful, ruthless, and driven by a lifelong jealousy of the half-sister she's never known—the daughter their father could never forget. Her hatred for Necie spirals out of control following their father's arrest, and Maria vows to destroy everything Necie holds dear . . . starting with her marriage and her family.

When her daughter is kidnapped, new revelations reveal the man she always perceived as her greatest enemy might be the only one who can save her from her half-sister's wrath. And now her father is behind bars . . .

ISBN#9781933836003
US $7.95 / CDN $9.95
Romantic Suspense
Available Now
www.michelleperry.com